Better Watch Out

Better Watch Out

A Defensemen Romantic Holiday Adventure

NATALIE WALTERS

Praise for Better Watch Out

A woman with broken expectations, a good-hearted man with a cautious edge, a possible criminal out for the wrong woman, and a New York Christmas with ALL the nostalgic wonder? What's not to love, right? Natalie Walters has given us romance, a touch of suspense, and a whole lot of Hallmark Christmas magic in this sweet novel about a healing heart, a delicious hero, and a dangerous mission. By the way, this hero is a perfect Christmas gift to any romance-loving heart! He's huggable (and for Frannie surprisingly kissable). Take a romantic walk with Andrew and Frannie through Christmas in New York, while occasionally running for your life, in Natalie Walters's newest novel, Better Watch Out.

— Pepper Basham, bestselling author of *Authentically, Izzy*

"A high-spirited holiday romance with just enough suspicion and shenanigans to require the presence of a super hot bodyguard? Yes, yes, yes! Do not miss this one!"

— Nicole Deese, Christy Award-Winning Author

"Move over, Santa, because *Better Watch Out* delivers everything on my favorites' list! This story is the perfect blend of witty romance and daring suspense. One moment I'm laughing at the heroine's antics and the next I'm holding my breath at the impending danger. This book truly is wonderfully balanced. Add in the backdrop of Christmastime in New York City, and you've got a stunning story destined to keep you flipping the pages until the satisfying ending."

— Rachel Scott McDaniel, award-winning author of *The Starlet Spy*

Better Watch Out is the Christmas read you need this year! Natalie Walters will have you laughing one minute, swooning the next, and keep you on the edge of your seat! If you only read one Christmas Book this year, make it this one!

— Christen Krumm, author of *On the Golden Cliffs*

Better Watch Out by Natalie Walters

Cover and Interior Design by Emilie Haney of EAH Creative

Also by Natalie Walters

Novella

Caught in the Crosshairs (Targeted Collection)

SNAP Agency Series

Initium (novella)

Lights Out

Fatal Code

Blind Trust

Harbored Secrets Series

Living Lies

Deadly Deceit

Silent Shadows

To my readers, I'd endure the "sea of swirly-twirly gum drops" for you!

Chapter One

Bells! Literal jingle bells rang out as if the city of New York was saying, *"Welcome to your holiday dreams, Francis Frost, where romance sparkles brighter than the lights in Times Square."*

Frannie's shoulder jerked backward, pulling her out of her rom-com daydream to where the wheel of her luggage was caught on the threshold of the baggage claim exit. The bells stopped ringing as the woman wearing a red Salvation Army vest glanced over, her expression full of pity.

Behind her, Frannie heard people telling her to move out of the way. She apologized, smiling at the harried travelers who were sending less-than-understanding looks her way. She yanked her bag free and rolled it out of the way, allowing those she'd blocked to move past her.

"Better watch out, Frannie. New York City isn't Walton." Her mom had said it like a warning, as if it would be enough to keep Frannie from spending the majority of her savings to fly to the Big Apple and surprise her boyfriend, Calvin.

It wasn't.

Frannie's stomach fluttered with excited anticipation as she checked her phone to see how far away her Uber driver was. Two minutes. Perfect. Buttoning the top of her new North Face coat, an early Christmas gift from her mom and Evan, she stepped the rest of the way through the sliding doors, and her breath froze in her lungs.

The frigid air burned the inside of her chest, stinging her eyes and blurring New York's stunning cityscape. Well, if she could actually see it, but from where she stood outside the airport, her focus shifted to the overwhelming number of cars, taxis, and people moving in every direction like ants.

"We're not in Georgia anymore."

When she'd left her apartment in Walton, Georgia, it was a balmy sixty-two. Pulling her scarf and gloves out of her carry-on bag, she felt the icy air cutting straight through her clothes to her bones. Frannie shivered and made a mental note to thank her mom for making her pack the long underwear.

Frannie followed the signs to the rideshare line, feeling her excitement grow with each step. *I am here. In New York City!*

For as long as she could remember, New York City had been the place where dreams came true. When she'd studied immigration in her history class, the images in her textbooks of the people who traveled thousands of miles by boat and then landed at Ellis Island to sign their names as new residents of the United States and begin a new life had stayed with her.

Her lips pulled into a wide smile again, and she couldn't help it. In just a few hours, she might begin her own new life with Calvin.

Mrs. Calvin Prescott. It had a nice ring to it. She was about to fan out her ringless left hand again, imagining the beautiful solitaire that might be on it in a few days, but her Uber arrived. Settling into the back seat, suitcase in the trunk, she pulled out her cell phone and reread her messages with Calvin.

Frannie: Guess what?

Calvin: What?

I'm coming to New York City!

...

I know you said you were going to be there with your family for a few days and worried about making it down to Walton before returning to London but I couldn't wait to see you!

...

And you know how much I've wanted to go to NYC for the holidays ...

Are you surprised?

Very. Um, do you have a place to stay?

It wasn't the response she'd been hoping for but Calvin had never been very demonstrative in his affections—still, the question stung a little. Frannie had been hoping Calvin would invite her to stay in one of the extra bedrooms at his family's home, but the Prescotts were a respectable family and Frannie was sure the unextended invitation had more to do with propriety than anything else.

Frannie: I'm staying at the 1911 in Times Square.

Calvin: I'll meet you there when you get in. 6:30 work?

Perfect!

Perfect. Frannie put her phone away and stared out of the window as the driver pulled into the city. Giant buildings towered above her and hundreds of cars and people filled the streets like every movie and picture of New York City she'd ever seen. Garlands, red bows, ornaments, and thousands of twinkling lights decorated storefronts, windows, and the outside of buildings, making everything feel perfectly magical. Just the right setting for—Frannie shook her head. She couldn't get ahead of herself. But it was so hard not to imagine how this week was going to change everything.

It'd been more than a year since she'd seen Calvin and while the long distance had made it hard to maintain their relationship, she knew once they saw each other again, their feelings would be rekindled, and maybe, just maybe ... a proposal.

Two hours later, Frannie had unpacked her suitcase, hanging the clothes she'd carefully curated for the trip and looked over her bucket list of must-do winter activities here in the city—activities she was sure would bring back the spark they'd been missing lately.

For tonight, she'd chosen a black faux-leather skirt with black tights and black boots that were hiding the pink wool socks she'd slipped on her feet. Her sweater was a cashmere blend, a splurge on her after-school teaching salary, but it was the same color blue as her eyes and kept her warm. Or at least that's how she'd justified the purchase.

Checking her reflection in the mirror, she tousled her blonde waves with her fingers before raising the thermostat for her room again. Grabbing her purse and coat, she made her way down to the lobby, her cheeks aching for a break from all the smiling she was doing.

This is it.

The 1911 lobby was a quaint boutique hotel that had at one time probably appeared sleek and modern with its dark wood, marble, and brass. However, anyone looking close enough would notice the chips, frays, and cracks that indicated a need for long overdue renovations. Frannie wasn't concerned with those things. She chose to admire the age of the hotel and be grateful it was at least clean. And it came with views of bustling Times Square. She would need to thank the mother of one of her students who recommended a discount travel website because there was no way she'd have been able to afford this place otherwise.

Frannie chose an empty seat near the bar where she could see the entrance and ran her tongue over her teeth to make sure there was no lipstick on them. Her fingers trembled with anxious anticipation. She had tried and was failing to keep her expectations in check. Tonight might not be *the night* but her bucket list for the week gave Calvin plenty of opportunities to surprise her.

Patience was a virtue and she'd already made it a year after he left for London to work at his uncle's publishing house. What were a few more hours or days?

When she had transferred from USF to Anderson College in Savannah, Frannie felt like a failure. She barely lasted a year away from home before she returned to the familiarity of Walton. Of course, she heard the small-town whispers about her not making it, but she did her best to ignore them and focus on finishing her creative writing degree, if for no other reason than to prove the gossipers partly wrong.

She met Calvin her junior year when he was working as an intern for the *Savannah Daily* and doing a story on the after-school tutoring program she was starting in Walton. He was funny and kind and exactly the opposite of who everyone thought she'd end up with. Unfortunately, she still had another year until graduation and Calvin had the opportunity to work in London and he had assured her it was the perfect time for them to focus on their futures.

Calvin had been so busy and the time difference had made it difficult to find a free moment that worked for both of them to talk. Their weekly conversations drifted into spare seconds that sometimes stretched several weeks apart before a quick text or email allowed them to catch up.

Brushing a piece of lint off her skirt, Frannie shook the melancholy feeling away. All of that was going to change this week. She just knew it. And in true serendipitous fashion, the hotel doorman opened the door and Calvin strode in, looking like he fit right in with fancy New Yorkers in his tailored suit and dark wool coat.

Frannie stood and the second their eyes met, she felt a zip of something shoot through her, but it wasn't the electrical charge she'd expected. Had to be nerves. She smiled. *It's just nerves.*

She hurried to meet him and wrapped her arms around him, breathing in the familiar scent of his musky cologne. Oh, she'd missed it. The sweatshirt she'd *borrowed* from him and brought to sleep in no longer held the scent but they would fix that this week.

"Francis." She'd missed that too. Hearing him call her by her full name always made her feel more sophisticated than her small-town upbringing warranted. He gave her a quick hug before walking them out of the way of guests entering the hotel. "How was your flight?"

"Good."

"Good." His gaze moved behind him and then back to her. "Um, I'm glad you're here."

"You are?" Frannie started to reach around him for another hug but stopped short when he took a step backward. She met his eyes and realized they weren't as warm as she remembered. His lips flattened, removing any hint of the smile ... wait, had there even been a smile when he saw her? Her aching cheeks told her she'd been smiling but she couldn't remember if he had been and why right now that was suddenly important. "Calvin?"

"We should talk."

The fluttering in Frannie's middle died with a thud that made her knees feel wobbly. "What's wrong?"

Calvin rubbed the back of his neck, looking anywhere but at her.

Frannie took his gloved hand in her bare one and the barrier between their skin was as telling as the look in his eyes when he finally met her gaze.

"I was going to call you when I got back to the States but then you said you were coming to New York, and I thought it would be better to do this in person."

This did not sound like the beginning of a proposal, but her stupid heart was hanging on to the shred of dying hope.

"I found someone in London. She works for CK Publishing and we've been seeing each other for a while. It wasn't serious at first but then I was getting ready to fly back home and I just knew."

No. This isn't happening. Frannie swallowed, forcing the emotion building at the back of her throat to stay put.

"I'm asking her to marry me. Christmas Eve."

Frannie dropped his hand. Why had she still been holding it? Maybe her heart wasn't the only thing desperately clinging to the stupid hope she hadn't been a fool for an entire year.

"I'm sorry. Before I left we talked about the break and I thought you understood what I meant, that we weren't dating." He spoke slowly, as if he was making sure that she understood clearly now. "But I got your text that you were coming to New York and I—"

"Decided to ruin the one place I've wanted to go my whole life and break my heart." She managed to squeak the words over the lump in her throat, but it brought her dangerously close to crying—one thing she didn't want to do in front of a crowd. Why wasn't everyone in a rush to get around her now?

"I didn't want to be a jerk, Francis. I thought it would be better to do this in person."

"Right." She let out a sarcastic snort and shook her head. "Definitely not a jerk move. At. All."

"Francis, I'm sorry. We're just in different places in our lives. You said you never wanted to leave Walton and—"

"I didn't want to move to *London,* Calvin." Her raised voice drew attention. "You said you wanted to come back to New York and I told you I'd move here if it's what you wanted."

"I'm returning to London. It's where Gemma's family is."

Well, goodie for Gemma.

"I'm really sorry if I hurt you or made you believe there was more to us than—"

"Nope." Frannie waved her hand as she started to step backward. "We had a good thing, but like you said, we're in different places in our lives."

"Francis."

"I wish you the best, Calvin."

Turning, Frannie hurried toward the elevators and pulled out her room key, anxious to get away from the man she'd given her hopes and dreams to. This was *not* how romantic holiday movies were supposed to go. Looking over her shoulder, a part of her hoped for that cinematic moment where she'd find Calvin watching her, contemplating whether he'd made the right decision and then realizing he couldn't live without her ... But he was gone.

Just like her dreams for a magical holiday in the city.

Chapter Two

"Don't get dead."

Andrew Bishop glanced up at the newbie, Joseph Caruso, and shook his head. "We don't need a slogan." His attention dropped to his laptop, where he was working on the final notes of the protection detail the Defensemen Agency had been hired for.

"Come on, every good business needs a slogan." Joey grabbed one of the hockey sticks from the bucket in the corner and hit a crumpled piece of paper on the floor, sending it forward a few feet.

"Pitiful." Oskar Garin laughed. "Let me show you what a clapper looks like." He grabbed a piece of paper off his desk and crumpled it in his palm. "First you need a proper biscuit."

"The only biscuit I'm familiar with is the kind you put butter and jam on."

Oskar sent Andrew an exaggerated look of exasperation. "Why did Amanda hire him?"

Amanda Landry was the owner of Defensemen, a private security firm she'd started after her husband, Joel, a NYPD officer, was killed in a sting gone bad. Their son, Deke Landry, was one of the top players in the NHL, if not the best goaltender for the past seven years. Her idea to use former NHL players as personal security detail seemed smart, using their brawn and innate instincts to protect people, but only half of their six-man team was made up of former players.

The other half, like Doug Bowie, were hired for their background in law enforcement. Joey Caruso had come to them from the Secret Service and seemed to enjoy using his lack of hockey-lingo knowledge to agitate Oskar.

"The biscuit"—Oskar held up the crumpled piece of paper before he set it on the ground—"is the puck." Taking the hockey stick from Joey, he lined up and then, with restrained control, swung, hitting the biscuit and sending it flying into the tight space between a desk and filing cabinet.

Oskar took a bow before giving a toothy grin in Joey's direction.

"You know, your smile's not bad when you have all your teeth in."

"I can show you how I lost them." Oskar squared off with Joey, and since he was six inches taller and at least fifty pounds heavier, it would be easy to assume the former center for the NYC Rangers had the advantage. A person wouldn't assume the former Secret Service agent was a fifth-level black belt in hapkido, the Midwest's version of Jackie Chan. "Or would you rather I give you some tips on how to grow that lip lettuce?"

Joey rubbed his fingers over the mustache. "I've only been here a few months and my mustache still haunts your dreams."

"More like fills my nightmares," Oskar teased. "You look like my Uncle Oleg from the seventies."

Joey sighed. "Those were the good years."

"You weren't even born then."

Andrew could see this conversation wasn't going to end any

time soon if he didn't interrupt and he needed their attention focused on the job ahead. "Fellas, you ready to get some work done?"

Putting the hockey sticks away, Joey and Oskar took their seats in the nine-hundred-square-foot office in Midtown. The brownstone building used to be a pharmacy in the forties before being turned into a law office, a campaign office for Richard Nixon, another law office, and then remaining vacant until the husband of a wealthy friend of Amanda Landry purchased it and offered to rent it to her for a nominal rate considering what a space like this could go for in the current market.

"Tomorrow, Valentina Malone is scheduled to land around three in the afternoon. This is two hours before her father, Simon Malone, will land in their private jet. I will pick up Ms. Malone and escort her to the Waldorf."

"And I'll pick up Mr. Malone when he arrives and take him to a meeting before he goes to the hotel to meet with his daughter." Oskar flipped through the folder Andrew had given to him and Joey. "Do you want Joey Rigatoni with me or you?"

"He'll stick with me," Andrew answered, noticing Joey already seemed unfazed by Oskar's nickname for him—or he understood reacting would only egg Oskar on.

Joey looked up from his file. "And why isn't their personal security detail coming?"

"Mr. Malone has only ever traveled with one security officer, who came down with the flu. The officer was familiar with Amanda and recommended our team."

Andrew had done his homework on the Malone family. Simon Malone had been married to Patricia Kline, who was the daughter of a British hedge fund investor who made billions through his company, Kline Capital. Patricia Kline worked for her father and was expected to take over once he retired but she died in a skiing accident in the Alps. When her father passed a few years later, he left his money and the majority shares of his company in the control of Simon who was to manage the very large trust fund and inheritance that was waiting for Valentina when she turned thirty in five years.

"Mr. Malone is in town to finalize a multi-million-dollar investment with Gerald Kline, his wife's uncle." Andrew sat back in his chair. "It's garnered unwanted attention and threats against the family. Our job is to make sure Mr. Malone and his daughter make it back home safe and sound."

"Failure is not an option." Joey sat forward in his chair. "Great slogan."

"Also, a quote from *Apollo 13*." Andrew laughed.

"Days like today make it hard for me to believe you were allowed to protect the President of the United States." Oskar stuck a piece of gum in his mouth and chewed. "Why did you leave the job?"

Joey shifted in his seat, his expression turning serious. "The career wasn't for me."

Oskar frowned in disbelief before he caught Andrew sending him a silent message to drop it. Amanda hadn't given any of them details on why Joey left the Secret Service but assured them he'd be an asset to the team.

"Back to the assignment." Andrew redirected their attention to the itinerary. This shouldn't be too difficult; Ms. Malone is meeting up with some friends and doing holiday shopping. Oskar, you'll be with Mr. Malone during the day. Doug is working out the details with Mac and Brayden for the overnights."

"Got it." Oskar snapped his gum. "Standard protection detail."

"If we do our jobs right, yes," Andrew answered. "This should be eas—"

"Don't say it!" Oskar cut him off. He rolled his chair

backward and grabbed the biscuit sitting on his desk. He kissed one side and flipped it, kissing that side too before putting it back on his desk. He turned it until it was in the exact same position as before. "Bad luck and all that."

Joey coughed to cover his laugh as he eyed Andrew, who was used to Oskar's superstitious ritual. Back when he played in the NHL, he'd had his own fun teasing teammates for their seemingly silly traditions to ensure luck for a winning game. Andrew didn't believe in lucky charms, such as wearing the same nasty underwear for each game, but when he was growing up playing hockey, his mom always made him sit in the car while she prayed before each practice and game. With one eye open, he'd watch his teammates stroll past the car, making faces at him to see if he'd crack. But eyes closed or not, praying with his mom, it seemed she had the magic words because he'd made it through his childhood without the serious injuries some of his friends endured from the sport.

Until he went pro.

The memory seemed to awaken the old injuries and Andrew rolled his shoulder, feeling the pull of mended muscles still tight from multiple surgeries.

"Speaking of doing our jobs." Oskar rose to his feet. "We should probably head out to get ready for the fundraiser."

"I guess this is one reason I can be glad I'm not a famous hockey player." Joey shrugged on his jacket. "Tonight, it'll be me, a Mario's pie, and the Cowboys."

"Yeah, it'll be tough hanging out with beautiful women dressed like sexy reindeer," Oskar teased and then held his hand up like a measuring stick over Joey's head. "Though, the Radio City Rockettes might be a little too much women for you."

"God knew when to stop once He hit perfection, unlike with you. Needed another foot to figure out it was the best He could do."

Andrew laughed at Joey's witty comeback. "He might have you there, Oskar."

Oskar pulled a knit cap over his head. "You can laugh all you want but if you think a night with pizza and football compares to champagne with beautiful women, I'm going to have to talk to Amanda about that cognitive test."

A flicker of something shadowed Joey's features before he pulled his own beanie cap onto his head. "Isn't Deke Landry going to be there?"

"Yeah," Oskar answered.

"Well, then I'd get ready for a night sipping that champagne on a bench while watching *him* with the ladies."

"Har. Har," Oskar deadpanned and looked ready to say more, but Joey was already waving at them on his way out the door. Oskar faced Andrew. "That kid needs to spend some time with me on the ice."

"Reminds you of your little brother, eh?"

"It's infuriating."

Andrew slid his wool coat on. "How's he doing?"

"Good. Mom says his dental practice is practically the sponsor for the Toronto Jays junior hockey league."

"Clever."

Checking the time, Andrew saw he had a little over an hour to get to his apartment, get dressed for the evening, and head to Glasshouse Chelsea. He didn't mind being a little late, slipping in to find his seat and avoid conversation ... or stares. He would have avoided the entire event if Amanda hadn't requested he be there, and since they were raising money to create a fund for injured athletes, Andrew couldn't say no. *Wouldn't.*

The familiar weight of regret filled Andrew's stomach. He'd hoped with each passing year the pinch of guilt would ease but its lingering presence always reminded him why, as Joey said, failure was not an option, even if the job seemed standard.

"You okay?"

"Yeah." Andrew exhaled. "Just thinking about tomorrow's assignment."

Oskar walked Andrew out. "You know I'm not one to botch our assignments with bad luck, but you've got the Malone assignment squared away."

"Do you need to kiss that puck of yours again?"

Oskar laughed. "Nah." He puckered his lips. "I'm saving these kissers for a Rockette and some mistletoe."

Andrew shook his head as Oskar slipped into the crowd of New Yorkers heading for the subway. The icy winter air seeped through his jacket as he locked up the door to the Defensemen Agency. Slipping the keys into his pocket, he buttoned his coat up to his neck, anxious to fight the chill he couldn't decide was from the weather or dressing in a tux to face off with his past failures.

Chapter Three

W*hen I open my eyes, I will be back in my bedroom, waking up to head to New York City and—* The echo of sirens interrupted her wishful thinking, reminding Frannie she *was* in New York City. Dumped. Alone. *And freezing.*

That's it. She hated New York City. Hated winter wonderlands. Hated cold weather.

Stretching her hand out of the cocoon of warmth, she reached for the phone on the bedside table and hit the button for the front desk.

"Front desk, how can I help you?"

"I don't think the heater in my room is working."

"I'm sorry to hear that, Ms. Frost. I'll send someone up immediately."

"Thank you," Frannie grumbled and then felt bad. "I appreciate it."

There was a *click* so she had no idea if her attempt at gratitude was received. She rubbed her eyes and groaned, feeling the clumpy mascara mess. She was surprised she had any left after her all-night sob session. Her stomach ached with a turbulent mix of hunger and sadness as the events from the night before replayed in her mind. Sometime before one in the morning, her tears went from sadness to confusion to anger—at herself. In the montage of her relationship with Calvin, everything was good until he left. They seemed like they were destined for a long, happy life together. Then, he left. Her cheeks burned with embarrassment as she realized she'd been the one pursuing him while he was gone. She'd send the emails and texts, attempt to make calls. Calvin had checked out and somehow she'd stupidly missed all of the signs.

Not to mention her weird reaction when she finally locked eyes with him. Where was the surge of affection or the burst of heat that would melt her into her secondhand Cole Haan boots? Frannie's brow wrinkled. Now that she thought about it, there was ... nothing. It was as if her heart had known but stubbornly decided not to relay that important message to her brain.

Her cell phone rang and she cringed, pressing her head deeper beneath the covers. It was probably her mom checking on her. Her skin tingled with frustration. Her mom had not wanted her to come to New York. Warned her not to chase after Calvin. *"That's not how it's done, Frannie. If he loves you, he'll come get you."*

Well, that was not how it worked in the real world anymore. Maybe back in her mom's day, but not now. Her agitation grew. Frannie was not her mom. And if she was, she wouldn't have let her first husband, Frannie and Ryan's dad, just walk out on them. She would've fought for the relationship.

Stop. A tear slipped from the corner of her eye, trailing down her temple and into her hair. Frannie's mom didn't have a choice. Too young to remember, Frannie relied on what Ryan told her about their father. That it was better he'd left. That they were better off without him.

She wasn't so sure. In his absence, Frannie was left to face the rumors about her mom that small-town gossips dished out quicker than a cholesterol-laden casserole.

Her cell phone rang again.

Ugh. Might as well get this over with. "Hello."

"Do you realize I was about ten seconds from calling your brother to send the FBI looking for you?"

It wasn't her mom but her sister-in-law, Vivian. Feeling a little relieved, Frannie rolled on her side. Sunlight peeked from the edges of the curtain. What time was it? "Why would you do that?"

"Because you called me last night and left an unintelligible message on my phone. And you haven't answered your cell phone since."

Sitting up, Frannie tried to make sense of Vivian's words. "I called you last night?"

"Yes," Vivian said. "You were sobbing. Something about dreams, a bucket list, and a pig named Calvin. I'm taking a guess here that you aren't talking about an actual pig, though it is New York, so ... tell me what's going on."

Frannie dropped her forehead into her free palm and stifled a groan at having to relive last night's events yet again but if there was anyone whom she trusted not to give her the "I told you so" speech, it was Vivian.

Dragging the comforter off the bed, Frannie pulled it to the chair by the window and curled into it as she rehashed the most embarrassing night of her life. The tears didn't come, thankfully, but the anger resurfaced. How had she allowed herself to get so caught up in some wild fantasy?

Just like your mother.

The words still stabbed at her, eliciting the same painful ache that had her wanting to run and hide. Prove they were wrong. She *wasn't* just like her mom.

"Frannie?"

So much for not crying. Frannie swiped at her face with the edge of the sweatshirt she'd thrown on over her pajamas to stay warm.

"Frannie?"

"I'm here." She sniffled. "Are you going to tell me I'm a royal idiot?"

"No, because you're not." Vivian's soft tone was soothing but didn't hint at pity, which Frannie was grateful for. "Sounds to me like Calvin didn't make it clear what his expectations were for your relationship while he was away and likely was keeping you as a plan B, the jerk face."

Frannie rolled her shoulders back, feeling a little empowered by Vivian's support. "He's a total jerk face." Her mood shifted. Man, she was glad her brother didn't mess up with Vivian because it was nice having her as a sister. "So, what do I do now?"

"What do you want to do?"

Emerging from the comforter, Frannie got to her feet and pulled the heavy curtains back, allowing the morning light to fill her room. "I don't know. It's embarrassing. And I practically spent my entire savings to come here."

Frannie recognized a small voice echoing in the background. Her brother and Vivian had adopted their daughter, Jisoo, from Korea and she was the most adorable little girl in the world. Frannie hated that they lived in Washington, D.C., but weekly FaceTime video chats made her feel closer to her niece.

"Why don't you eat a nice breakfast and think about what you want to do? There's nothing to be embarrassed about if you go back home."

Vivian was wrong about that. Walton was not a big town and everyone knew everything about everyone including Frannie and Calvin's relationship. When she decided to fly to New York, it didn't take long for the speculation of a proposal to hit the streets faster than an army of ants on fried chicken at the church picnic.

"I'm sure I can find a bagel shop nearby. Those are supposed to be good here, right?"

Vivian's voice was muffled, talking to Jisoo before she came back to the line. "I've never had one but I'm sure they're great. I hate to rush off but I have to get Jisoo to school and she's lost the only shoe she's willing to wear today. I haven't had enough coffee to deal with another tantrum while Ryan is away."

Frannie felt guilty for laying her boyfriend troubles on Vivian while Ryan was away on assignment. "Have you been able to talk to him?"

"Yeah, he tries to call every night but the time difference isn't helping. No, Jisoo, you cannot wear ballet slippers because it's freezing outside. Hey, I've gotta run but I'll check in with you once I drop her off at school."

"No problem, I know you're busy. Thanks for calling and checking on me. Do you think you can call my mom and maybe let her know I'm fine?" She really wasn't in the mood to explain the whole ordeal one more time.

"I can do that."

"You're the best, Viv."

"Love you, Frannie."

"Love you too."

Frannie ended the call and shivered. Maybe a hot shower and some breakfast would be good. There was a knock on the door and she was grateful to find the hotel maintenance guy there ... until he showed her that the thermostat in her room had been switched to the AC, so no matter how high she raised the temperature it wouldn't kick on. As soon as he pressed the button for heat, the vents roared to life with warm air and she could've hugged the man.

She didn't. Instead, she thanked him and felt her mood lift again. By the time she was finished with an extra-long, extra-hot shower, and dressed, Frannie's heart hurt less. Would going back home be so bad? She could give a quick explanation that she and Calvin realized they were in different places and ... and it wouldn't matter how she explained it. Some might believe her but others were sure to imagine the worst—especially when his engagement announcement was posted all over social media.

Another knock on her door halted her thoughts from taking another dark turn. She checked the peephole. A man in a hotel uniform stood there with a tray in his hand.

Leaving the chain in place, Frannie opened the door.

"Room service, ma'am."

"I didn't order room service."

The hotel employee looked confused. Checked the card on the tray. "You're Ms. Francis Frost?"

"Yes," she answered hesitantly. Ryan had sent Frannie at least three emails warning her that New York wasn't Walton and that she needed to be on her guard. He told her what to watch out for, sent her self-defense videos, and then a week before her trip, a package arrived in the mail—a keychain bottle of pepper spray. She thought it was overkill but packed it anyway.

"Then I have your breakfast." The hotel employee's smile was beginning to look strained. "Courtesy of Mrs. Vivian Frost."

He handed her the note and Frannie's eyes teared up reading it.

I don't know about bagels but crème brulée French toast sounds amazing! Love—V

Frannie unlocked the door and the hotel employee entered and set her breakfast down on the table. When she assured him she was all set, he left and Frannie re-locked the door before doing a little skip to the table. She'd never had room service before and felt like a queen.

She opened the silver lid covering the plate and squealed

with delight. Berries and powdered sugar dusted the giant pieces of French toast, making it look more like a dessert than breakfast. She took the carafe of coffee and poured herself a cup, adding cream and sugar until it was just right. Before taking a bite, she grabbed her cell phone and sent a thank-you text to Vivian.

Then she took a photo of her meal because social media was nothing if not the place to show off how fabulous life was—true or not.

Flipping on the television, she found *Christmas in Connecticut* and settled in to eat. She hadn't realized how hungry she was but forced herself not to scarf it down and instead enjoy every bite. Room service in New York City wasn't on her bucket list but she made a mental note to add it and then cross it off. She wanted to be able to at least mark off one thing.

Her cell phone rang again and she expected it to be Vivian but the name on her screen twisted her insides. *Ryan.* Vivian was not an I-told-you-so person; her brother—was.

"Before you tell me how stupid I am for coming here and spending all of my money I want you to know that I already know that," she spit out as soon as she answered the call.

"Good morning to you too."

"I don't need a lecture."

"I wasn't going to give you one." Ryan's voice echoed and Frannie wondered where he was and what time it was there. As an FBI agent, he traveled for his job but usually kept the details between himself and Vivian. "Are you okay?"

Prepared for an argument, Ryan's affectionate tone nearly caused her tears to come again but crying would only stress him out and that never worked out in her favor.

"I'm sitting in my cozy hotel room"—finally—"enjoying the most delicious breakfast I've ever had in my life—courtesy of your amazing wife—and living the dream."

"Sounds like it." There was a pause and Frannie readied

herself for a fight. "I think you should fly back home. Back to Georgia. You don't need to be in New York by yourself."

She didn't want to be here by herself either, but going home? Even if she came up with a convincing reason why she returned after one day, it wouldn't be enough to silence the rumors.

"Ryan, I can't go back home. Everyone will know and they'll talk and—"

"So what? At least you'll be safe. Do you know how big New York City is?"

"Eighteen million people. You sent me the statistics, remember?"

"Right," he said. "You've never been in a city that big and it can be dangerous for someone traveling alone. I'd feel better if you went back to Georgia."

"I don't want to." She cringed at how juvenile she sounded. "I can stay here, in my room. Order room service and watch Christmas movies."

"Do you know how expensive that is?"

No, she didn't and truthfully, she'd budgeted her trip carefully, choosing two-dollar-sign restaurants she'd found online that had decent reviews. Calvin always covered their meals but she hadn't wanted him to assume she expected him to pay.

"You made a mistake. No one needs to know that."

"Everyone will know that. You know how Walton is. You know what people will say, that I'm like Mom and got dumped just like—"

"I'm not a fan of Calvin but he's nothing like Dad," Ryan cut in. "The right man isn't going to run out on you, Frankie. Calvin wasn't that man and I'd feel a lot better if I didn't have to worry about my baby sister's safety while I'm on this mission."

Frannie grunted. "Well, when you put it that way." Her understanding of what Ryan did was mostly based off television shows and movies. She didn't want to shift his focus away from the job and then something bad happen.

"What if you go to D.C.?"

"What?"

"Go to D.C. I know Vivi and Jisoo would love to have you hang out with them, especially while I'm gone."

The idea of spending the week with her sister-in-law and niece sounded way better than returning home. "What about my ticket? Will it cost a lot to change it?"

"Don't worry about it. I'll take care of everything and send you the details. Now, do me a favor and enjoy your breakfast and movie while I go fight crime."

"We all know you're a glorified paper-pusher," Frannie teased. "But I've heard those paper clips can be deadly."

"It's the staples I have to worry about."

Frannie laughed. "I love you."

"Love you too, Frankie."

"It's Frannie!" But Ryan ended the call, no doubt smiling that he got the last laugh. Nerd.

Chapter Four

"You missed a great afterparty." Brayden Winick leaned his hips against Andrew's desk. "Did you have a hot date last night or something?"

"No date." Andrew had arrived at the fundraising banquet in time to find his seat, eat his meal, take a photo with the Defensemen Agency employees, and then slip out right after the guest speaker, Dan Spencer, got to the stage. He'd hoped he'd be able to sit there and watch his former Bandits teammate inspire donors to give in support of injured players, but the guilt had spoiled the few bites he'd managed to eat. The cashier's check he passed to the treasurer before he left helped ease that guilt. "It was a long day and I needed to get some stuff done for the Malone detail."

"Spending the whole day with a wealthy heiress." Steve "Mac" McAvoy was sitting in Oskar's chair, flipping his lucky puck in the air. "Our jobs really are horrible."

Andrew had come in early to get some paperwork done and found Mac, Brayden, and Doug already there. Mac and Brayden usually worked the graveyard shift if it was required so it wasn't surprising to find them there. Doug's early presence was curious.

Brayden smiled, showing off the space where two teeth were missing. "Yeah, it feels weird not worrying about losing more chiclets."

Andrew ran his tongue over his full set of teeth, grateful he hadn't lost any in the game like so many of his athletic colleagues. Most wore dental flippers, giving them the appearance they still had all of their teeth, but Brayden chose to keep his gaps exposed like it was an honor almost as exciting as holding up the Stanley Cup—which Brayden had for two seasons.

If Brayden's muscular frame didn't intimidate sufficiently, the missing chiclets at least suggested the man was willing to lose his teeth in a battle.

"Andrew?"

Andrew swiveled in his chair and faced Doug Bowie. He was the oldest team member at fifty-six and a former NYPD officer who had worked with Amanda Landry's husband. He was also the most senior man in the agency and mentored them regularly.

"I just got off the phone with Mr. Malone's head of security and he's informed me they received an email notifying Mr. Malone of a possible ransomware attack if he goes through with the deal here in New York."

Andrew frowned. "Is it a valid threat?"

"Mr. Malone's IT and cybersecurity team are working with the local FBI to determine that," Doug said. Mac dropped the puck on Oskar's desk, his attention reflecting the gravity of the update. "But it hasn't deterred Mr. Malone's intentions. Everything is moving forward as scheduled."

Which meant no changes to the safety itinerary Andrew had created for Ms. Malone and her father. "I appreciate the update."

Oskar and Joey walked in and Mac popped out of Oskar's

seat, choosing to lean against the wall as Oskar sent him a dirty look. He moved the puck back in the exact position in which he'd left it the night before. Mac shrugged with a smile that said he wasn't sorry.

Andrew gave them a brief rundown of the new information Doug had shared and confirmed they were to move forward as planned.

"I don't foresee any issues but if the situation changes I don't want you to hesitate to call any of us," Doug said. "We'll adjust whatever we're working on to make sure the Malones are taken care of."

Andrew nodded, appreciating the support. The weight of protecting people, doing his job, was personal to Andrew. Every successful assignment helped make up for his past and Doug was offering the silent message that he wouldn't let Andrew fail again.

Mac and Brayden left to head home from their shift and sleep. Doug returned to his office and Andrew called Simon Malone's head of security to go over the details of the ransomware attack threat and get information about the FBI's involvement. The man could barely talk but it was clear the flu wasn't going to keep him from focusing on the safety of Mr. Malone and his daughter. After their conversation, Andrew was about to double-check the flight schedule when his cell phone rang.

"Hello."

"Hey, Andrew, it's Ryan Frost. How are you, man?"

"Good." Andrew instantly tried to read the tone of Ryan's voice, trying to detect the purpose of the call even as his gut filled with dread. Was Angelo Evola back? "And you?"

"Better if I was back in the States, which is why I'm calling. I have a favor to ask."

Andrew blew out a breath and forced his shoulders to relax.

"A favor? Man, I thought you were about to tell me Evola tunneled his way out of prison."

Ryan released a short chuckle. "Angelo Evola isn't going to find his way out of Attica unless it's in a body bag."

It was a morbid thought but one that left Andrew breathing easier since the bookie was captured. Convinced Andrew threw the final game in the Stanley championship, the man didn't have the money to pay off the bets he owed to the kind of guys that didn't make their living the legal way. Fearing he'd end up swimming with the fishes, Evola threatened to kill Andrew if he didn't pay off what he owed. FBI agent Ryan Frost was involved in the case and saved his life.

"I'm happy to return the favor." Andrew waved away Oskar's gesture offering a coffee refill. "What do you need?"

"My sister is in New York City and the guy she went there to see dumped her last night and now I need to make sure she gets to the airport for her flight."

Andrew frowned. "You want me to take your sister to the airport?" How old was this girl? "When?"

"I booked her on a flight out of LaGuardia for two this afternoon." The line became staticky before Ryan yelled to someone on his end. "Look, I wouldn't ask but she's pretty upset. This is her first time in a big city and I don't want anyone to take advantage of her emotional state."

In this job, Andrew knew the crime statistics for the city and it wasn't absurd to be concerned. If it was his sister, he'd be concerned for her to be out on her own too but the timing couldn't be worse.

"Man, I'd like to but I'm working an assignment that requires my full attention." Andrew looked at the flight itinerary on his computer screen. Ms. Malone was scheduled to arrive at one and he certainly couldn't have some heartbroken woman with him when he picked her up. It wouldn't be professional, especially with the fee Mr. Malone was paying the agency, but telling the man who saved his life from Angelo Evola's bullet didn't feel right. He calculated the time he'd need to be at the airport to do a perimeter check of the private runway before Ms. Malone's flight arrived. "Do you think she'd mind getting to the airport a few hours early?"

"I don't think that'll be a problem." Ryan gave him the name of the hotel where his sister, Frankie, was staying, along with her flight information. "I really appreciate this."

"It's no problem."

Andrew set his cell phone on the desk after he ended the call and ran a hand through his hair. No problem at all.

"Everything good?" Oskar returned with his mug of coffee.

"Yeah, just a little favor for a ..." Andrew sat forward in his chair and stared at his computer screen. "You've got to be kidding me."

Joey walked over. "What is it?"

"Ms. Malone's flight is going to arrive early. The pilot wants to get ahead of the cold front coming in."

Oskar shrugged. "So?"

"I just agreed to pick up a friend's sister and get her to the airport at the same time as Ms. Malone's arrival."

"Can your friend's sister take an Uber?"

Andrew roughed his palm over the scruff on his chin. "I don't know. Her boyfriend dumped her and I guess she's pretty upset. Her brother is the FBI agent who helped me with the Angelo Evola situation." Oskar raised his brows but it was a lot easier to call it a *situation* than the failed attempt on his life. "He seems genuinely worried and I want to help."

"What if I pick her up?"

Andrew shook his head. "I appreciate that, Joey, but I'm sure

Ryan's already told his sister to expect me, so I wouldn't feel right sending you."

"I meant for Ms. Malone."

Oskar smirked. "Joey Rigatoni thinks he's ready to run lead on an assignment."

Joey leaned back in his chair. "I've been here three months now and I used to protect the vice president." He sent a pointed look at Oskar. "I think I can pick up the heiress and get her to the hotel where you"—he pointed his pen at Andrew—"can meet us and take over as planned."

It wasn't a terrible plan, but last-minute changes left room for mistakes. Still ... He checked his watch. They had two hours to work through the details. Andrew met Oskar's expectant look. "What do you think?"

Joey swiveled in his chair. There was an edge of apprehension in his expression that said he expected Oskar to object.

"Vice President's still alive so Joey Rigatoni's got some skills, but ..." The edge of Oskar's lips tipped up. "You still haven't told us why you left the Secret Service."

"It wasn't a good fit," Joey said and Andrew caught the subtle clenching of his jaw that told him it was more than that. "Oskar can go in my place if that makes everyone more comfortable."

"Can't." Oskar held his hands up. "I've got a meeting at the Waldorf with hotel security before Mr. Malone and his daughter arrive."

Which left Andrew with Joey's offer. "I think it'll be fine." He trusted that whatever the reason Joey had left the Secret Service, it had nothing to do with his ability to protect because otherwise Amanda wouldn't have hired him. "You'll pick up Ms. Malone, get her to the hotel, and I'll meet you there."

"Sounds good." Joey tipped his chin and got back to work at his desk.

Andrew stared at the flight itinerary again and prayed nothing else would come up. There was a good chance that if traffic flowed in his favor, he may even get to the Waldorf before Joey showed up with Ms. Malone. So long as nothing else got in his way, everything would be just fine.

Chapter Five

"I'm sorry, you want to what?"

The woman behind the front desk of the hotel did nothing to restrain the amused confusion lifting her brows. Frannie's own pinched together. Her Southern accent wasn't *that* bad.

"Can you recommend a place to buy souvenirs?" Frannie tried again, slowing her speech just enough. "Someplace close?"

"Oh." The hotel employee gestured to the gift shop at Frannie's right. "We have a nice selection of items."

Frannie leaned over the tall counter. "Yes, but aren't they a bit pricey?"

Another female employee walked over. "Everything is pricey in New York."

Annoyance rose in her chest. "Ma'am," Frannie said before her gaze traveled to the gentleman in a crisp suit, polished shoes, and wearing a hotel name tag on his lapel. She met the impatient expression of the first woman and forced a smile. "Do you know of any nearby shops or should I ask your manager for his recommendation?"

The women exchanged a quick look before the first shrugged. "There's a place down the block. It's a little touristy." She worked her gaze over Frannie. "And you might want to leave that cute purse in your room and just take the cash you need."

"Thank you." Frannie squared her shoulders and made her way back to the elevator, determined not to leave New York City without a few souvenirs and, darn it, if that meant facing off with tough New Yorkers, she would do it.

And then politely thank them because her mama raised her right and she wasn't a savage.

Still, the women's attitude and overhearing them laugh about the city eating tourists like her alive as she walked away gnawed at her the whole way back to her room. It wasn't the first time she'd faced stereotyping due to her accent and use of *ma'am* and *sir* but after what had happened with Calvin and her conversation this morning with Ryan, it was like salt to the wound. Those two women knew nothing about her and assumed she wasn't tough enough for New York. She stared at her packed suitcase. Maybe she wasn't. This trip hadn't gone at all like she'd planned and even though spending the week with Vivian and Jisoo in D.C. sounded wonderful, she was still going to face the same questions and rumors when she returned to Walton. Or even worse—the pity.

Nothing was worse than facing off with everyone telling her *I-told-you-so.*

Her cell phone buzzed with a message from American Airlines. Ryan had purchased a ticket to D.C. and adjusted her return flight from there to Georgia.

Another text message pinged from Ryan and Frannie ignored it, setting her phone on the table. She knew her brother was probably confirming she got the information. She should be grateful he'd taken care of it and was letting her avoid heading back home but she couldn't shake the agitation settling over her shoulders.

This city would not eat her alive.

Frannie wasn't some naïve hick from the South. Her eyes moved to her carry-on bag and she saw the bucket list she'd created for her and Calvin. The backs of her eyes burned but she quickly blinked the tears away.

You're just like your mother.

Was she? Was that why Calvin left? His upbringing was very different from hers. His parents were still married, had college degrees, and had been raised in prestigious homes outside of Boston. Calvin's dad was an editor for a major publisher in New York and his mom, from what Frannie had gathered, had never worked a day in her life, spending her days as a socialite and attending the kind of events that landed in the pages of *Vanity Fair*.

Frannie's mom, on the other hand, had worked three jobs at one time just to keep a roof over their heads and food on the table. She was proud of her mom *now*, but back then it was hard facing the cruelty of kids who teased her for no other reason than to deflect attention from their own issues. And now her mom was happily married to Evan—a successful dentist who adored her mom—but that didn't keep Frannie from wanting to prove there wasn't some family legacy of shame hanging over her.

Staring at her cell phone with her flight confirmation on it, she ground her molars. What was she doing? Cutting her trip short because of Calvin? If people were going to gossip about him walking out on her like her father did to her mom, leaving New York wasn't going to stop them.

Frannie might not be able to control the narrative of what people would say about her but she wasn't going to give them the satisfaction of saying she couldn't handle New York without Calvin.

A tickle of excitement and nerves battled for position in her stomach as she pulled out her bucket list. Eyeing it, she bit her lower lip. The activities she'd added to this list were meant for her and Calvin. Romantic moments that could've been social-media worthy. Doubt crept in but she shoved it back. *I am going to check off every single item on this page!* As an independent, single woman. Her eyes dropped to the last item on the list. Okay, maybe not that one ... but everything else.

She grabbed her scarf, coat, and her purse, slinging it crossbody style. A shot of adrenaline coursed through her and she laughed thinking about the fool who might try to rob her. Picking up her phone, she sent Ryan a text, letting him know she changed her mind and would be staying in New York for the remainder of her scheduled trip.

Frannie marched out of her room on a mission and made it one step before crashing forehead-first into the firm chest of a man who apparently never skipped the gym for a Netflix binge on the couch. She craned her neck up, up, up, her wary gaze inching past an impressively thick neck to a sharp jawline softened just barely by the five-o'clock shadow that was seven hours premature. Everything about this man a touch away said imposing and lethal, especially those no-nonsense clear blue eyes trained on her.

Instinctively, she took a step back, only to knock her backside into the closed door to her hotel room. She was trapped between two walls, one made of wood and steel and the other of solid man.

"Oh, sorry." Why was she apologizing? Darn Southern etiquette. She fumbled in her purse for her room key, her fingers finding the pepper spray instead. *Back pocket.* With one hand on the pepper spray, she reached the other into her back pocket and pulled out her key.

"Are you Frankie?"

Frannie jumped. Startled by the deep tenor of his voice and

then by the fact that this stranger knew her name. How many times had Ryan told her about identity theft? Without answering, she let her gaze flash to his eyes before moving over his body. Broad shoulders filled out the black wool coat. His dark jeans, stylish chelsea boots, and lack of hotel name tag heightened the alarm resonating in her chest.

Hitman. Or mafia.

She'd seen a few mobster movies like *The Godfather* and the goons always dressed to impress and this stranger was using his good looks to disarm her, but Ryan had warned her. Keeping her back to the wall so she could keep an eye on the man who had definitely perfected a handsome smolder as he stared back at her, she tried swiping her key card over the lock. The light flashed yellow and then red. *Come on!*

The man shifted, to scratch his nose or pull out a gun, she didn't know, but she didn't waste a second before whipping out the pepper spray. She'd barely pressed the button before the man, in one quick movement, side-stepped, grabbing her arm to redirect the short burst of spray away from them and into the hallway before knocking it from her hand.

"Let go of me!" Frannie tried for volume, hoping to gain the attention of other guests but immediately choked on an inhalation of breath. She hunched forward, coughing, her lungs and eyes burning so much she hardly noticed the man release her arm. She squeezed her eyes closed, but tears slipped down her cheeks as she continued to hack against the pungent spray.

"Why," she wheezed between coughing fits, "are my eyes on fire?"

Her nose began to run and she tried wiping at her eyes except that only made them tear more, but she didn't miss the low rumble of a chuckle. Was the stranger laughing at her? What kind of twisted game of torture was this?

"You need to get away from the fumes."

Fingers skimmed her arm and she jerked backward, hitting her head against the wall. *Great.* Frannie didn't need to be worried about a criminal in New York incapacitating her, she was doing a fine job herself. She strained to open her eyes, unsure if the heat flooding her cheeks was from embarrassment or if her skin was actually on fire. Through a teary gaze she found the stranger covering his nose and mouth, blue eyes squinting at her in something looking very close to an amused glare, if there was such a thing. "Go into your room," he said through clenched teeth.

Was this guy high on eggnog? No way he was getting inside of her hotel room. She tried to see around his large frame but her vision was too blurry. How much line of sight did she need to have to run down a straight hall? Frannie coughed again, trying to clear her lungs so she could at least scream for help.

Giving her eyes one good squeeze, sending the tears flooding past her lashes before she forced her eyelids open, she was ready to make her run for it when the man spoke up again.

"Are you Frankie Frost?" he said through clenched teeth. If he was feeling the effects of the pepper spray, he was fighting hard not to show it. "Are you Ryan's sister?"

Frannie stilled as a new sense of fear filled her. Had something happened to Ryan? "Who are you?"

"Andrew Bishop." He cleared his throat. "Your brother asked me to take you to the airport."

A tiny bit of relief washed over her but Ryan also had warned her that criminals were good at what they did and often used a little bit of knowledge to trick victims into trusting them. Wiping at her eyes, Frannie looked the guy over. "You're an Uber driver?" But his answer, if he gave one, was covered by another burst of coughing as more tears now mixed with a good amount of snot ran down her face. She cringed. "Good grief, when does it stop burning?"

This time there was no mistaking the chuckle and she narrowed her blurry gaze on him. Or at least she tried. It was hard to know given she could barely open her eyes without them flooding with tears.

The man dipped his chin and then squatted to the ground where she'd set her room service tray outside her door. This was her chance to run. She'd seen his quick reflexes, so she'd have to be fast. Glancing over her shoulder, she saw the red exit sign for the stairs.

"Put this over your eyes."

His voice pulled her attention back to him. He extended a soggy napkin dripping with ... was that creamer? She met his blue eyes, a new fear percolating in her chest.

Is he going to waterboard me with creamer?

The corner of his lips lifted but he didn't laugh. "The fat in the creamer should alleviate the burning."

Frannie squinted at the dripping napkin. "How do I know you didn't just pour formaldehyde on there to take me out?"

The man exhaled. "Do you mean chloroform? Formaldehyde is what they use to preserve specimens."

"Exactly what someone would know if they were going to kill me." Why wasn't she running? She should've been down the stairs and in the lobby calling the police. "That you know the difference only confirms my concern. I've seen *Criminal Minds*."

Her vision was clear enough to see him roll his eyes before he patted his chest and coat pockets. "Seems I forgot to bring my spare bottles of chloroform and formaldehyde but the longer you let that pepper spray burn your eyes, the higher the chance of blindness."

"What!" Frannie grabbed for the napkin but her impaired vision placed her fingers on his very firm chest and she might as well have touched fire for as fast as she yanked her hand back.

"I'm kidding. Here, let me help."

Unsure why she trusted the gentleness in his tone, Frannie stood still, holding her breath when he lifted the cloth to her eyes. *Oh, sweet relief*. The cold creamer compress began easing the burning sensation around her eyes.

"Better?" His breath tickled her forehead, reminding her that other than a name and the vague description that Andrew Bishop had a handsome smolder to give the police, she still didn't know who this man was. Carefully taking control of the cloth on her eyes, she felt the pressure of his touch lift. Dabbing a bit more of her face, she removed the cloth and was grateful her vision was clearer.

"Aren't your eyes burning?"

"Yes."

His short answer drew her attention to the red skin around his eyes making the blue stand out. He watched her watching him, and it made her insides squirm.

"I'm sorry about spraying the pepper spray."

"It's fine."

"My brother gave it to me along with a thousand warnings about how to use it against strange men."

"You were very capable."

"I missed your face completely."

"Because I'm capable." The edge of Andrew's lips tipped up before his gaze moved to his watch. "You have five minutes before we need to leave for the airport. Are you packed?"

"I appreciate the whole creamer-in-my-eyes thing but I'm not getting in a car with a stranger."

"You know my name."

She eyed him. "Supposedly."

Andrew lifted a brow and then produced his cell phone again. "I'm a friend of your brother's, you can check the text messages he sent me with your flight information."

Frannie flicked a quick glance at the texts and then curled her lip. "Any low-level hacker can produce that."

His eyes narrowed on her. "I have a business card and my ID." He pulled out his wallet, produced a card, and showed her his New York driver's license. The business card with his name on it said he worked for a personal protection agency called Defensemen.

Personal protection. *Really, Ryan?* Her annoyance with the hotel employees at the front desk returned with equal parts being distributed between them and her brother. She'd made it from the airport to the hotel just fine—why did he think she needed a personal protection agent to get back?

She eyed Andrew Bishop and chose to identify the warm feelings sparking in her chest as agitation. Oh, she'd make this fun.

"I took enough computer classes to learn how to make a fake business card." She pivoted to swipe her card over her door lock and when the light flashed green, disengaging the lock, she twisted the knob, opening the door an inch. "And I hear fake IDs are as easy to find in New York City as a slice of pizza."

She left Andrew Bishop and his confused expression in the hallway as she quickly stepped into her room and closed the door behind her. Her heart pounded against her ribs as the adrenaline of the last few minutes seeped through her bones. So why was she smiling?

Turning, she peeked through the peephole and saw Andrew Bishop still standing in the hallway, typing something on his cell phone.

A second later her phone dinged with a message.

> Ryan: Frannie, Andrew's a friend. I asked him to take you to the airport.

Frannie: How do I know this isn't a trick and you're actually my brother?

Seriously?

You warned me about these kinds of tricks. How do I know he hasn't hacked into your phone pretending to be you?

...

Frannie peeked through the hole again and found Andrew leaning a shoulder against the wall. With his jaw set and that lock of light brown hair falling over his forehead, his muscular profile was very different from Calvin's sits-at-a-desk-all-day physique. And the contrast unnerved her for the way it was warming her insides. Or maybe that was a lingering effect of the pepper spray?

Andrew moved, coming toward the door like he'd read her thoughts—hopefully not all of them! Frannie stepped back, catching her foot on her suitcase, sending her spiraling backward. A scream escaped her lips, and she immediately covered her mouth, praying Andrew hadn't heard—

"Are you okay in there?"

"Fine." Frannie caught a glimpse of her tangled reflection in the wall mirror and rolled her eyes at herself. Pulling herself up to her feet and adjusting her coat and purse and the stray bits of hair that had escaped her braid, she answered, "Just fine."

"I'm supposed to tell you that ... um ... seriously?"

Who was he talking to? Frannie moved to the door and peeked once more through the peephole. Andrew was staring at his phone and shaking his head. His gaze moved up and she jerked her head back.

"Your brother told me to tell you that ... look, I really am here to take you to the airport."

Frannie put the security latch in place and opened the door. "What does Ryan want you to tell me?"

Andrew's blue eyes looked heavy with dread. He looked down at his phone and then back to her. "He wanted me to tell you that in second grade you had a crush on Johnny Castillo and tried to kiss him but Johnny said you had Grinch cooties."

A growl escaped her lips and Andrew's eyes rounded.

As if he expected her not to believe him, he twisted his phone around and, sure enough, there it was. The text sent by her traitorous brother revealing her childhood trauma to a complete stranger.

"Give me one second." Frannie closed the door in Andrew Bishop's face and then sent a message. A minute later she smiled a very Grinch-ish smile to herself before she grabbed a fresh makeup wipe and cleaned the creamer off her face.

She opened the door and found Andrew Bishop still standing there.

"Do you need help with your luggage?"

"I don't." She made sure her door closed and held her breath, carefully avoiding any chemical haze still lingering in the hallway. Then, pretending like Andrew Bishop didn't know about her humiliating crush on Johnny Castillo, she walked around him toward the elevator. "You can let my brother know I won't be needing a ride to the airport."

"I can't do that." Andrew was at her side in two quick strides. "Ryan gave me implicit instructions to make sure you get to the airport and I don't have time to argue with you."

Frannie jabbed her finger on the elevator button, not liking the way his parental tone made her feel like a child. Ryan may not have approved of her trip to New York but he didn't need to send some bodyguard type to look out for her.

"I'm not leaving, but when I do decide to leave, I'll find my way to the airport just fine."

Beneath the scruff covering his jaw, she saw the muscle there flex as if he was grinding his teeth. "Fine."

"Fine."

Frannie entered the elevator, moving to one side as Andrew moved to the other. Neither of them spoke, but the second more guests stepped inside, she took the opportunity to sneak a look at Andrew's reflection in the elevator's brass interior.

Andrew Bishop. The man had the build of an athlete. Football player, maybe? Her fingertips tingled from where they'd met the firmness of his chest, further proving that he was definitely fit. Of course, his job as a personal protector would require that. The mysterious blue eyes, chiseled jawline, and oh-so-casual hairstyle that made a girl want to run her fingers through it just added to the come-hither appeal.

Just exactly who was he protecting? Certainly no one needing to remain anonymous because Andrew Bishop had the kind of looks that were impossible to ignore.

And that smile—*that smile*. Her eyes darted to where his were reflecting back on her. He'd caught her staring. Heat climbed up her spine until she had to loosen her scarf. Thankfully, the elevator doors opened and Frannie made her escape.

Outside of the hotel, the icy air felt good against the embarrassment warming her cheeks. Still, she tucked her scarf into her coat and pulled out her gloves.

"Are you sure I can't take you to the airport? Your brother seemed pretty worried about you."

"I'm fine." Frannie hoped her expression displayed the confidence she wasn't entirely feeling. "My brother forgets I'm a big girl and I know how to take care of myself."

She started walking down the street with no plan as to where she was headed but she didn't want to give Andrew a reason to believe Ryan's overprotective concerns. When she was a good distance away she'd pull out her phone and put in the address to—

Frannie looked to her right, where Andrew was walking with her. "What are you doing?"

"Walking."

She rolled her eyes. "Are you following me? Because I just told you I'm fine and can take care of myself."

Andrew pointed to a parking sign. "My car."

"Oh." Her cheeks burned.

There was a tilt to Andrew's lips, a half-smile. He dipped his hand in his pocket and pulled out the business card. "In case you need anything."

Frannie hesitated for a second but then reached for the card. Just in case. "Thanks. And I'm sorry again about the pepper spray."

Reaching into his pocket again, he pulled out the tiny can of spray. When had he grabbed it? "You didn't use much so there should be enough in case someone else tries to help you."

His lips tilted in a teasing smile that had Frannie considering that a pretend trip to the airport might be fun just to spend a few more minutes with Andrew. She could always catch an Uber back, right?

"Stay safe, Frankie."

"It's Frannie." She dismissed the thoughts immediately. "Only my brother calls me Frankie."

"Frannie." He tipped his chin. "Stay safe, then."

Chapter Six

Total waste of time. Andrew pulled out the keys to the company vehicle, anxious to get back to his actual job and only feeling a little bit bad for not fulfilling his favor to Ryan. But what was he supposed to do? Force his sister to leave? His tear ducts were still tingling from the pepper spray.

He glanced back over his shoulder to Frankie, who was still standing where he'd left her. He smirked, remembering the way her pretty blue eyes narrowed on him as she corrected him. *"It's Frannie."*

From the airline ticket, Andrew knew her full name was Francis but whether it was the cute nickname or maybe Ryan calling her his *little* sister, Andrew's assumption he was picking up some lovelorn and newly brokenhearted teenager had turned out to be completely inaccurate.

The woman standing on the sidewalk, her blonde waves hanging over her shoulders as she focused on the cell phone in her hand, was definitely not what he'd expected. The woman who barreled out of her room with a quick draw on the pepper spray had certainly made a lasting impression. Capable. And beautiful.

Okay, so maybe not a total waste of time.

Screeching tires pulled his focus back to the parking garage, where a car was exiting. Andrew stepped to the side and checked his watch. Maybe he'd have enough time to get to the airport and pick up Ms. Malone himself?

He was halfway to the black Tahoe but he couldn't help one final look back at Frannie. Her attention was still on her phone but she'd tucked her hair behind her ear, allowing him to see the way she was working her lower lip between her teeth. She glanced up and then around before looking back down at her phone in one hand and a piece of paper in the other.

He paused. She was completely oblivious to him watching her and Ryan's concern for her came back to Andrew's mind. *"This is her first time in a big city and I don't want anyone to take advantage of her emotional state."*

Andrew assumed Ryan was being an overprotective brother but watching her standing there looking like a lost tourist ... maybe he could've tried harder to convince her to head to D.C. At the very least, he could offer her directions to wherever she wanted to go—or give her a ride.

That last idea filled him with a funny sensation, which he quickly dismissed before starting back toward her. If she wanted to stay in New York that was up to her and *between* her and Ryan but he wouldn't leave her there unaware of the temptation she was posing to those of the criminal sort.

He was halfway to her when her head popped up and she started walking away from him and down the street. Pausing, he watched her wait at the corner light. *Guess she figured out where she needed to go. Good.*

Except something close to disappointment pinched at his chest and he wasn't sure why. He wasn't really in the mood to be pepper-sprayed again. As he started to turn back around, a man in a black leather coat, hat pulled low on his head, across the street made eye contact for the briefest second before he pivoted and started walking with the crowd toward the intersection.

Andrew's gut pulled taut the same way it did when he was reading an opposing player's movements. The guy stopped at the intersection, his back to Andrew, waiting for the light to turn, the same way Frannie was. Andrew's attention moved back to her just as the light turned.

The pedestrians moved forward, taking her with them as they crossed the street. On the other side, the man moved too and Andrew caught him watching Frannie.

That quick. That's how fast an experienced criminal made their mark. Andrew didn't hesitate, he started at a jog and barely made it across the street before the light turned. Dodging the foot traffic, he wove his way through the crowd, keeping his distance from Frannie while watching the man in the leather jacket. He kept glancing over at her like he was keeping tabs on her movements and Frannie was completely unaware that she was being stalked.

Picking up his pace, Andrew knew he couldn't report the man to the police because he hadn't done anything yet and he would make sure it stayed that way. There was a good chance the man would think twice if he saw Andrew with Frannie and then, at least, Andrew could assure Ryan he'd done his part to protect her. Of course, he was going to make a phone call to Ryan and insist he convince his sister to board that plane. If it wasn't too late.

At the next block, Andrew pulled back just a bit to see what the man's next move was. When he saw him cross the street to the same side as Frannie, Andrew moved in.

"Hey—"

Andrew started to reach for Frannie's elbow but his sudden

appearance at her side or the barely spoken word caused her to jump and in an impressively quick move, she jerked her elbow back, nailing him right in the gut.

Her head spun to the right, her long hair whipping him in the face. "What? Why—"

"Keep walking." He smiled through gritted teeth as pain radiated from his side. Did she hit a kidney?

Of course, the second the direction left his mouth Frannie pulled up short, causing a woman to run into the back of him. She muttered something he hoped Frannie didn't hear as she and several other inconvenienced New Yorkers moved around them.

"What are you doing?"

"I'm helping you get to your destination." His gaze flicked over his shoulder, searching for the man in the leather jacket, but he wasn't there. "Where are you headed?"

Without touching her, Andrew moved in such a way that he guided Frannie toward a mailbox rental place and out of the crowd. He needed to check their surroundings again for the man.

"I don't need your help, I know where I'm going." As if to prove her point, Frannie held up her phone. "You can tell my brother I'm fine."

Sure she was. Andrew scanned the faces around them but couldn't find the man. Maybe his plan had worked. To be sure, Andrew pulled out his cell phone and tapped the app for Uber.

"Where are you going?" he repeated and when her silence answered him, he glanced up to find her piercing blue eyes staring at him. "What?"

"Did you hear me when I said I don't need help?"

"I did." For a split second he contemplated telling her that up until a minute ago she was being shadowed by a man for a purpose Andrew could only guess wasn't good. "But I thought maybe I could help you get there."

Her features softened and Andrew dipped his chin when his

thoughts went to how pretty she was. It wasn't like he'd never seen a beautiful woman before but he wasn't used to them running away from him. Actually, it was the opposite. His time as a professional hockey player introduced him to women who threw themselves at him and his teammates all the time, waiting outside the locker room or scouting the hotels where the team would be staying. He became skilled at dodging the ladies. So, Frannie's open attempt to ditch him only intrigued him more. Which probably wasn't a good thing.

Yep. Good to remember that. Last thing he'd want to do was get on an FBI agent's bad side.

"I'm headed to the West Village," Frannie finally said. "A stroll through the quintessential neighborhood of stately brownstones is magical this time of year."

Andrew lifted a brow. "Is that from a visitor's brochure or something?"

"No. It's one of the stops on my list."

"What list?"

"It doesn't matter." Determination filled her expression. "It's just a couple of miles."

"You're going to walk to the West Village? From here?"

Frannie put her hands on her hips, probably assuming her pose was intimidating when in fact it was adorable. "Yes."

If Andrew hadn't just caught some guy targeting her, he probably would've agreed to let her leave, but as it stood he'd made a promise to Ryan to make sure his sister was safe—the other half of that promise he'd try negotiating inside the back seat of the Uber he'd just requested.

"Is Levain's on your list?"

Frannie frowned. "What?"

"They have the best hot chocolate and chocolate chip cookies in the city." Andrew had no idea if that was true but one of his ex-girlfriends would always take her family there when they came to visit. "If you're going to stroll through the West Side you should have a cup of hot cocoa. Isn't that what they do in ridiculous Christmas movies?"

A flash of pink colored her cheeks and he caught the slight flare in her eyes before whatever battle she was about to engage him in melted away. "Frozen hot chocolate from Serendipity's is already on my list."

Just then a blue Corolla, their Uber, pulled up to the curb.

"Okay, so at least try the cookie." He gestured to the idling car. "Best in the city and my treat."

Frannie hesitated but a serendipitous gust of icy wind barreled over them, causing her hair to whip around her face. She shivered, hunching her shoulders against the harsh cold weather.

"Fine." She stepped past him as he held the door open for her. "But only because I forgot my hat and my ears are freezing."

Inside the warmth of the Corolla's back seat, Andrew checked his phone again to see if Joey had texted him with any updates on his end. Nothing. Hopefully that meant everything on *his* end was going as planned.

Putting his phone away, he noticed Frannie was smushed against the door, putting more space between them than was necessary. Checking his watch again, Andrew released a slow breath. Maybe he could get her a cookie and then get her in an Uber back to her hotel. Then he'd drive to the Waldorf, where he'd exchange places with Joey to get Frannie back to the airport. Ryan would just have to understand.

"So, this, um, list, is it some kind of last wishes from a dying relative?"

"What?"

"Isn't that how it goes in the movies? Some dying relative hands off a list of things they wished they'd done while alive or something? And now you're here trying to do it for them?"

"First, that's a morbid thought." Frannie pulled out the piece of folded paper and carefully flattened the creases as she unfolded it. "Second, this is *my* bucket list. Coming to New York for the holidays was a dream and ..." Her voice grew quiet.

Andrew shifted in his seat, feeling like an absolute tool. Her boyfriend just broke up with her and that list in her hand was probably things she wanted to do with him. His jaw clenched and he forced his palms over the front of his pants to keep them from curling into fists. *Who breaks a woman's heart during the Christmas season?*

It seemed too cruel even for the Grinch, which reminded him of Ryan's text about Johnny Castillo and Andrew scoffed inwardly thinking that kid probably wouldn't have run away from Frannie if he saw her now.

"Anyway, I already paid all of this money to come here and I want to make the most of my time here even if it's not how I imagined it."

His eyes caught on one of the items on her list. *Nutcracker anniversary date.*

Oof. His gaze traced the planes of her face as she stared at her list. He felt bad for her. How many of those items would remain unchecked simply because she'd chosen them to be shared with her ex as a romantic gesture?

"How long were you planning to stay in the city?"

"My return flight was scheduled for Saturday, so five days." Frannie gave a one-shoulder shrug. "But Ryan wanted me to go to D.C. and hang out with my sister-in-law and niece." She shot him a pointed look. "Apparently, he thinks I'm too naïve for the big city."

The image of the man in the leather jacket flashed in Andrew's mind. "He's just concerned like any older brother would be, especially given what he probably sees in his line of work."

Frannie tilted her head. "How do you know my brother?"

"He stopped a bad guy from killing me."

Her eyes grew wide and Andrew hoped it was enough of a shock-and-awe moment that what he said next would carry the weight he needed it to.

"Look, it seems like you and your brother have a whole thing going on between the two of you but I think he really is looking out for your best interests. Maybe flying to hang out with your sister-in-law and niece isn't a bad idea. I've heard there are fun things to do in the D.C. area for the holidays."

"What my brother and I have going between us is him thinking he knows what's best for me and I'm a little tired of planning my life according to his rules. Or any man's, for that matter."

That last part came out under her breath as she turned her attention back to the window as their Uber maneuvered through the heavy city traffic.

Andrew had the sudden urge to find Frannie's ex and punch him right in the chiclets. If he hadn't broken up with her, this whole thing wouldn't be Andrew's problem. As it was, he looked at the time on the driver's radio and saw he was going to be lucky if he got to the Waldorf before Joey and Ms. Malone arrived. He hated how unprofessional this might look to their client.

Okay, new plan. Now that Andrew had safely whisked Frannie away from the man in the leather jacket, he'd get her a cookie and make sure she knew how to order an Uber back to her hotel after her stroll through the West Side. Then he'd call Ryan and let him know the change in plans and let brother and sister fight it out.

Chapter Seven

Chocolate.

Frannie inhaled deeply when she finally stepped into Levain Bakery. If heaven had a scent, it would be chocolate.

"You okay?"

Her eyes flashed open to find Andrew staring at her, his brow quirked in a way that was quickly becoming familiar and, she hated to admit, charming. Well, it would be charming if the rest of his expression didn't look so ... bothered?

It matched the look he'd given her when she told him she was staying in New York City and not going with him to the airport. Of course, that was after she practically pepper-sprayed him in the face. Which, to be fair, was Ryan's fault for not letting her know he was sending some protection agent Chris-Pratt-lookalike to her hotel.

Those lines between Andrew's brows had deepened when the Uber dropped them off in front of the bakery. There was a long line waiting to get into the tiny establishment and Frannie tried to convince Andrew he could leave, that he didn't need to stay there with her, but he refused, mumbling something about safety before reminding her he'd promised to buy her a cookie. Since she'd pretty much budgeted her entire trip down to the penny, she was too embarrassed to admit that buying an almost-five-dollar cookie would leave her with less money to spend on dinner. *McDonald's hamburgers are still a couple of bucks, right?*

"Hello?" Andrew waved a hand in front of her face and she blinked as a rush of heat warmed her cheeks.

"Sorry. Yes." She quickly darted her eyes to the menu. "So, the cookies are good here, huh?"

Andrew turned his lifted brow to the display case, where plates of cookies were spread out behind the glass. There were other pastries but the staff behind the counter were kept busy tucking cookies into little blue paper sleeves for the crowd of customers.

Frannie tugged her scarf loose to relieve some of the heat climbing into her face. When it was their turn to order, she picked a chocolate chip cookie and a cup of Earl Grey. Andrew ordered a black coffee—no cookie. Moving to the side to wait for their order, she pulled out her cell phone and continued the text message conversation she'd been having with Ryan on the ride over.

Ryan: Vivian just asked me if I prefer Superman or Batman underwear. She's never going to let me live this down.

Frannie stifled a giggle and caught Andrew raising a brow in her direction again. He had to know how disarming that look was, right? She smiled shyly and returned to the text, not feeling remorseful at all about telling Vivian that Ryan used to wear his underwear over his jeans, pretending he was a superhero.

I can't believe you told her that.

Frannie: I can't believe you told Star-Lord about Johnny Castillo.

Star-Lord?

Never mind. Why did you send a protection agent to take me to the airport?

He's a good guy. Wanted to make sure you got there safely.

What's the stats on airport abductions?

You'd be surprised.

Not as surprised as Star-Lord was when I nearly pepper-sprayed him.

Why do you keep calling him Star-Lord?

Her eyes slid to the man next to her. On closer inspection, Andrew didn't look exactly like Chris Pratt. For one, Andrew's hair was lighter and matched the close-trimmed beard covering his jaw line. Both had blue eyes. Frannie didn't know how tall Chris Pratt was but Andrew was at least a foot taller than she was, putting her at ... She tilted her chin up—yes. Putting her at that perfect position she and her friends called the kiss-me-now angle.

Andrew twisted to look around and Frannie's eyes darted down to her phone, grateful he hadn't just caught her looking at his lips.

Doesn't matter. Don't be mad but I'm staying here.

She bit her lip, readying herself for the incoming argument.

Why?

A single question and yet her trying to convey how those hotel employees made her feel probably wouldn't be enough of an explanation for her brother.

It's something I need to do. I'm an adult and can stay in New York City for a few days on my own. Her attention cut to Andrew. Without a protection detail.

...

Please.

When Andrew's name was called, they walked to the counter to get their order. Frannie was surprised at the weight of the cookie in her hand. A West Side stroll was going to be necessary after eating this thing.

"Thanks."

"Sure," Andrew said. He looked around. "There's not really a spot in here where you can eat that."

"Yeah, I guess that's why they use these handy-dandy cookie sleeves. Eat and go."

He checked his watch. Again. And each time it made her feel like maybe he really was inconvenienced by the favor her brother had asked of him.

"I appreciate this and I'm sorry about the thing back at the hotel." Frannie skirted around customers entering as they exited the bakery. The cold air stole her breath for a second. "And for the Uber."

Frannie glanced down the street, unsure how far she'd make it on her stroll before calling it quits.

"No problem." But Andrew's gaze roamed the street for

several seconds before he looked down at her. "You have my number, right?"

"Yes." She patted her purse where she'd tucked the card.

Andrew held out his hand. "Can I see your phone?"

"Why?" Instant panic flooded her chest. Did he know she'd been referring to him as Star-Lord to her brother? *Did Ryan tell him to get back at me?* Ugh, it was something he would do.

"I'd like to put my number into your phone. If you need me, it's going to be a lot easier to hit my name than dig my card out of your purse."

It looked like he wanted to say more but instead he waited for her. Frannie unlocked her phone. "What's your number?"

Andrew gave her his number, apparently not bothered by her unwillingness to give him her phone. Adding an "SL" next to his name, Frannie finished putting him in her contacts.

"Which direction are you going?"

Frannie glanced up and down the streets again, unsure of where she was headed. "I don't know. I was thinking of just walking."

"There's a subway this way." Andrew tipped his head to his right. "I'm headed that way and there's brownstones but I can't make any promises about their quintessential magic."

His sardonic tone almost made her smile. Instead, she started in the direction he indicated, convincing herself that knowing where the subway was would be a smart idea since it'd be cheaper than taking an Uber back to her hotel.

Andrew fell in step next to her and she couldn't help but feel better that he was with her. She would never admit it to Ryan, but the city and all of the people were intimidating. Not that she was scared, but it was nice to have someone here that she knew and could call on because there was no way she'd be calling Calvin or his family for help.

Frannie bit into her cookie and groaned with happiness.

"Wow, this is amazing." She took another bite. "Thank you for the recommendation."

"You can thank my ex-girlfriend. She loved that place."

Swallowing her bite, Frannie couldn't explain why that little knowledge nugget about Andrew's ex made her insides twirl.

"If you really want to see something magical, you should make sure to add Dyker Heights to your list."

Frannie looked over at Andrew, noticing, not for the first time that day, that he seemed to be on alert. It was a behavior she'd learned to recognize with Ryan. The scanning, open posture as if his senses were heightened to the possibility of threats, and poised to defend her against the evils of the city.

Was he always like this? Serious? Focused? Granted, the whole smoldering intensity thing he had going on worked well for him. More than once she'd caught women's eyes lingering on him. And she was pretty sure he was aware of it.

Just as he's aware of me perusing him right now. She scrambled to remember what he'd just mentioned. "Dyker Heights?"

Andrew sipped his coffee. "In Brooklyn. The neighborhood goes all out and puts up elaborate displays and thousands of lights. It's crazy."

"And magical?"

He almost gave her a smile before he dropped his cup into the nearest trash bin. He pointed to a sign for the subway. "This will get you back to your hotel. It's a straight shot, but if you feel like braving the cold you could walk a few blocks that direction and you'll end up at Central Park. You're not too far from the Natural History Museum either if that's on your list."

Frannie thought about the list in her purse. A museum didn't emote romance and so she'd left it off. Perhaps she should reevaluate because, after all, she'd already crossed the last item off her list.

"Lincoln Center." Andrew was still naming off tourist attractions but paused when he saw her face. "What's wrong?"

She swallowed and gave a quick shake of her head, not wanting to reveal yet another item she'd need to check off her list. To celebrate her and Calvin's anniversary, she'd bought tickets to see the *Nutcracker* ballet at the Lincoln Center. Her tutoring job paid the bills to live conservatively in Walton, but to afford the two tickets in the center of the theatre she had to save for four months and eat more ramen noodles than she cared to admit.

"Um, nothing." She spotted a bookshop. "I'm just going to stop in there. Thanks for the company and everything."

With a quick wave, she cut in front of a guy walking a dog and opened the door to the little shop, not wanting Andrew to see the tears that had gathered on her lashes. The bookstore welcomed her with the scent of aged dust but at least it was warm. She folded the cookie sleeve over what was left of her treat and darted a quick glance through the storefront window to find Andrew typing a message on his phone.

Probably letting Ryan know he wouldn't be doing any favors for his crazy sister again. It felt rude to walk off the way she did but she didn't know what Ryan had told Andrew and she didn't want to give the guy the impression she was unstable and couldn't take care of herself.

"Ma'am, you can't have food or drinks in here." A tall man in a sweater that looked like a cat had been skinned to make it stood behind a counter. He pointed at her cup of tea and then to the trash can next to her.

Frannie obliged, discarding what was left of her tea, but she tucked the cookie in her purse. "Do you have a restroom?"

The man's shoulders heaved with an exaggerated sigh before he pointed to another sign behind him. "For customers only."

A book was definitely not in her budget but there was a table filled with used children's Christmas books and Frannie found one under ten dollars that would make a cute gift for Jisoo. Satisfied, the clerk pointed to a hallway near the back of the store.

With her new purchase in hand, Frannie walked through the narrow aisles to the dimly lit hallway. The first door she passed was an office, the second, a closet. She saw the sign for the unisex bathroom and had just reached for the knob when she was shoved forward.

"Hey." She started to turn but another shove pushed her against the exposed brick wall before a gloved hand clamped tightly around her face.

"Keep quiet and I won't make this painful." A low voice spoke against the back of her neck, causing her skin to tighten in fear. "Move."

"What?" Her voice was muffled by his hand but her confusion kept her cemented to the ground. Was she being mugged? Inside of a bookstore? "You can have my wallet," she tried again but her attempt to negotiate was silenced by another rough shove toward the emergency exit door.

There was a sign that warned an alarm would sound if the door was opened and, fighting the panic, Frannie prayed the clerk had read enough action hero books to know how to come to her rescue.

Her hopes died when the guy behind her used her body to open the door with another shove and no alarm sounded. They were in the back of an alley and not even twenty feet away to her left was the city street where people and traffic were unaware she was about to be mugged, or assaulted. *Or killed.*

Fight, Frannie. How many times had Ryan warned her that in this exact scenario she needed to fight back? Make noise. Get attention.

Swinging her elbow back, she hit the guy and heard him grunt but his grip on her arm and face tightened until she squealed from the pain. She tried again, twisting until the man's hand slipped from her mouth.

Screaming for help, Frannie twisted as hard as she could, breaking free of the man's hold but losing her balance in the process. She fell backward, landing hard on the ground.

"Help!"

The man growled as he towered over her with a look in his eyes that terrified her.

"Hey!"

On her right, Frannie saw Andrew running toward her. She turned on her hands and knees, anxious to get to him.

"Are you okay?" Andrew's strong hands lifted Frannie off the ground before he tucked her against his chest. "Who was that?"

"No idea." Frannie dared to look over her shoulder. The man was gone. "He came out of nowhere in the bookstore and pushed me out the door."

Andrew turned her so that she was no longer up against his chest as he looked her over. "Are you hurt?"

Frannie removed her gloves, checking the skin on her hands. They were red and sore but fine. Her backside hurt from hitting the ground but that wasn't an area she wanted to discuss with Andrew. "I'm fine, I think."

"I think we should get you back to your hotel."

Frannie started to nod and then stopped. "Shouldn't we go to the police?"

Something close to pity crossed Andrew's face. "We can call them from the hotel and they'll send someone to take a report if you want."

His tone and the crime stats Ryan had sent her made her think the NYPD was unlikely to put much effort into investigating whatever just happened. Nothing was stolen so it wasn't a mugging. She was barely hurt so it wasn't assault.

"I guess I can cross that off my bucket list." Frannie's voice wavered in her attempt for humor and when she glanced into Andrew's hard gaze, she shivered. "Sorry. I've never been almost mugged before."

"You're sure you've never seen that guy before?"

Frannie found his expression unsettling. "No, why?"

A darkness shadowed his eyes as he looked over her shoulder. "Let's get you back to your hotel."

Chapter Eight

"I think you need to reconsider leaving New York." Andrew thanked the doorman holding the door for him and Frannie as they walked into her hotel. "You might be able to catch a flight out tonight."

"Why?" Frannie turned a sharp gaze on him, the look making her blue eyes shine with a spark that further justified his opinion that she had a stubborn streak that burned bright. A fact Ryan hadn't mentioned—or maybe conveniently left out—when he asked his favor.

A favor that was growing more difficult by the second.

They stepped inside the elevator. If he could convince her to take the next flight out of New York, then maybe the guilt from nearly allowing her to get mugged at the bookstore would lessen.

Doubtful. Andrew thought he caught sight of the man in the leather jacket as he was about to head down to the subway but he wasn't sure. He hesitated for a few seconds before circling back to the bookstore in time to hear Frannie's scream.

He stretched his jaw, trying to ease the ache from grinding his molars. He'd let her down. He'd let Ryan down. If this had been a paying job with the agency, he'd certainly be fired. It was bad enough thinking about how he was going to explain this to Ryan. The man saved his life and he couldn't even keep his sister safe for a few hours, much less get her on a plane.

He roughed a hand through his hair and down the back of his neck. "Most people would be scared out of their minds if they were attacked like you were. Aren't you scared about what just happened?"

Frannie tucked a piece of long hair behind her ear. "Oh, I was terrified." The elevator doors opened. "But I'm okay and the guy didn't get anything. Thankfully, you were there."

Andrew couldn't wrap his head around her cavalier attitude. "If I wasn't there, what do you think would've happened?"

"He would've stolen my purse, which would've been embarrassing once he realized the only thing of real value inside was the rest of my cookie and my bucket list." She twisted her lips to the side in an infuriatingly cute way that would charm the socks off any guy. "Now that I think of it, I'd be pretty upset about losing both of those things."

"And your wallet? Credit cards? ID?"

Frannie patted the front of her jacket. "Inner pocket. You know"—she crinkled her nose up at him—"just in case."

Frustration pulled at him. Partly because she didn't seem to be getting it and the other part ... the woman was attractive. There. He'd said it—safely to himself.

At her door, Andrew took in a slow breath. "Frannie, I think you should listen to your brother and fly to D.C. tonight." He avoided looking at his watch. He'd been messaging back and forth with Joey about the delay in his arrival to the hotel and while his colleague assured him all was well, Andrew hated how unprofessional the whole situation was becoming. And even though he wasn't hired to protect Frannie, he'd failed to do what he was trained to do.

He flinched at the way the painful memories flashed to mind.

"I already told you I'm not leaving New York." Frannie swiped her key against the lock and opened her hotel room door. "What happened today was unfortunate but honestly, I'm not surprised."

"You're not surprised?" Andrew's voice came out an octave higher than usual and Frannie gave him a curious look. "You were expecting to be attacked?"

"Well, no, but if you'd seen the crime stats Ryan sent me, the odds were definitely not in my favor."

"All the more reason to take that flight to D.C."

"Look." Frannie turned, standing in the doorway. "I'm really, really thankful you were there when I needed you, but it's over. I'm a little shaken by it, honestly, but I wasn't hurt and I'm not some naïve woman who can't take care of herself."

"I didn't say you were."

His response seemed to take her by surprise. Her blue eyes searched his face as if she was trying to judge if his words were true. "Right, so, I'm not going to let some man ruin my trip."

There was a slight dip to her lips when she said the word *man* and Andrew wondered if she was referring to the thug in the leather jacket or the one who broke her heart. An unexplainable heat radiated in his chest.

"Besides"—Frannie smiled up at him, the wrinkle of her nose making the freckles scattered there scrunch together—"I have to finish my bucket list and thanks to you I can check off my stroll through the West Side."

"And NYC mugging," he grumbled.

Her smile reached her eyes and dang, if Andrew didn't like the way it lit her face. "Right."

Andrew shifted before running a hand down the side of his face. "Are you sure I can't convince you to leave?"

"I know you're concerned." She tilted her head to the side.

"And my brother is, but I really am fine. And honestly, what are the odds of it happening again, right?"

Andrew was never good at math, but the odds of Frannie getting mugged again were pretty slim. And yet, the fact that the man in the leather jacket had followed them—followed her—didn't seem to fit some mathematical equation either. Most criminals liked easy targets. Quick marks. So why had this guy followed her?

He set that question aside as he walked down the hallway toward the Malones' suite at the Waldorf. His job and his focus needed to be on his assignment.

He knocked on the suite's door and was surprised when Doug Bowie opened it.

Andrew's pulse spiked. What was he doing there?

"Everything's fine," Doug said, reading Andrew's concern, but his tone sounded hesitant. Stepping aside, Andrew walked into the suite and saw Joey standing near a window with a million-dollar view of the Empire State Building. "Caruso's done a good job handling her."

Doug was the only one in the agency who insisted on calling Joey by his last name.

"Handling?" Andrew met Joey's eyes and the man looked beat for someone who spent the day in a luxury suite. The ornately decorated room was divided into a sitting area with two couches and some armchairs and a dining area for eight that was empty except for an elaborate bouquet of flowers on the table. The polished-oak doors to the two ensuite bedrooms, the powder room, and a butler's kitchen were closed. "Where's Ms. Malone?"

"Getting her second massage." Joey rolled his eyes. "Because I've stressed her out."

"Ms. Malone's been a bit of a handful." Doug stifled a chuckle. "The young woman isn't used to not getting her way."

"Thanks for the warning." Andrew was used to the type, wealthy individuals living unencumbered thanks to their giant bank accounts. It used to surprise him when clients who had *hired him for protection* balked at the inconvenience of the security measures put in place for their safety. Now, he was used to having to compromise. "I'm sorry I wasn't here earlier but I've worked out the security details around her plans so I should—"

"Actually," Doug cut in. "That's why I'm here."

An uneasy feeling filled Andrew's gut. Was he in trouble for not being here?

Doug and Joey walked toward the long dining table and Andrew followed. Picking up a folded piece of paper, Doug handed it to Andrew.

"This came an hour ago with the flowers."

Andrew opened it and read the contents, his stomach muscles tightening with every word.

> *This is more than a warning.*
> *Your daughter is in danger.*
> *She'll pay with her life.*

Andrew looked away from the note to the bouquet of flowers. "This was sent here?"

"Yes," Doug said. "Caruso received the delivery while Ms. Malone was having her first massage—"

"Because travel stresses her out." Joey's sarcasm thickened his Jersey accent. "Those private jet flights are just awful."

Doug cleared his throat with a look that said to keep it professional. "Mr. Malone has been receiving threats for a few months but they've increased as his plans to invest in Hope

Village went public. He's kept it from his daughter, not wanting to worry her."

"Not enough masseuses in the world."

Andrew bit the inside of his cheek. He'd never seen Joey so worked up and from Doug's furrowed brow, it was clear neither had Doug.

"Mr. Malone feels it's better and safer the less his daughter knows. However, it seems clear that someone is wanting to make sure Mr. Malone knows his daughter is in danger."

Doug nodded. "It does, but I'm not sure it makes sense. Caruso said the pick-up and drive here went smoothly." He looked at Joey. "You said there weren't any obvious tails or suspicious interactions."

"None. I got to the airport early, did a quick check around the private airfield. Ms. Malone landed, I escorted her to our vehicle. Drive into the city was smooth."

There was some noise behind one of the closed doors and Doug lowered his voice. "Who all knows she's here?"

"In New York? Or at the Waldorf?" Andrew asked.

"The flowers were delivered here so let's start there."

Doug's tone was harsh but Andrew knew it wasn't personal. "Ms. Malone scheduled a few events with friends here in the city. I ran recon on the locations and vetted those she was meeting with, but my guess is they might all know she's staying here."

"The flowers were delivered for Ms. Malone," Joey said. "But the note is directed to Mr. Malone. The suite is under his name."

Andrew nodded. "It could be anyone."

Doug scratched the back of his head. "If the ransomware attack was the first warning, this note suggests the threat against Ms. Malone has escalated."

A throbbing started at the base of Andrew's skull. His mind was working through the unsettling thoughts circling his mind. He had to be wrong. *Had to be.*

"You okay, Andrew?"

Setting the note on the table, Andrew faced Doug. "Outside of Mr. Malone's security team back at home, do you know if he mentioned to anyone about hiring us? Specifically, did he tell anyone I was going to be Ms. Malone's personal protection detail?"

Doug frowned. "I don't know but I can ask. Why?"

Pressing his hands on the back of the dining room chair, Andrew worked through the events of the day again—wanting to be wrong.

"Sir, I don't think the note is referring to Ms. Malone walking away." He met Doug's eyes, feeling Joey's concerned stare on him too. "Today, I was doing a favor for a friend. Taking his sister to the airport, or I was supposed to but she's got this list, and she's stubborn, and she decided she was staying in New York City in spite of her brother's concern. Anyway, I was about to leave her outside of her hotel when I caught sight of a man in a leather jacket tailing her. I figured he was just marking her for pickpocket or something, but she's the sister of a friend and I wanted to make sure she was safe." Andrew was gauging Doug's expression as he told the story. So far, the man didn't look upset. "Anyway, I got her an Uber to the West Side and was about to leave her to do her strolling—" he ignored the amused look Joey shot him—"when I saw the guy again. Or at least I thought it was him. I wasn't sure, but when I made it back to the bookstore, I heard a scream and it was her. The guy was standing over her in the back alley but he took off when he saw me."

The tension from that moment felt amplified in light of the pieces Andrew was now putting together.

"Was she okay?" Joey asked.

"Yes. She's fine and back at her hotel." Andrew swallowed. "If whoever sent this note knows I've been hired as Ms. Malone's PPD and was watching me, they may have assumed—"

"She was Ms. Malone," Doug finished for him. "Mistaken identity."

"Which means they've targeted your friend's sister," Joey said.

It sounded so much worse spoken aloud than it did in Andrew's head. He wanted to be wrong but the pieces fit. He'd endangered Ryan's sister.

Chapter Nine

Frannie double-checked the lock on her hotel door after setting the room service tray from her dinner in the hallway. The bowl of soup and salad were going to set her budget back but it felt safer to overpay than to head back out to find something to eat. *And I can skip lunch for a couple of days.*

Ensuring the bolt and the swing bar were securely locked in place, she upped the temperature in the room, grateful for the cozy warmth but unable to shake the chill that seeped into her bones.

"Are you sure you're going to be okay?"

Andrew's parting question had had her assuring him with more confidence than she felt but she feared that if she were honest about how shook up she was about the attack at the bookstore, he'd call her brother.

Climbing onto the bed, she pulled the covers over her legs and grabbed the remote in one hand and the cup of coffee she'd just made in the other. Flipping the channels, she landed on *Home Alone* and hoped the eight-year-old's shenanigans would lighten the mood.

Already part way through the movie, Kevin McAllister reveled in his ability to thwart two grown men's attempt to rob his family home as Marv gave an ear-piercing scream.

Psh, if only every criminal was as dumb as Marv and Harry.

The image of the man in the leather jacket flashed back to her mind. What were the odds she'd be mugged, or almost mugged, on her first day in the city? If Ryan ever found out, she'd never hear the end of it.

If Ryan finds out!

Frannie sat up, put her coffee down, and grabbed her cell phone. If Andrew called Ryan and told him ... *Oh my word.* But she couldn't call Ryan. He was out of the country. Where, she didn't know, or how many hours behind or ahead he was. He worked terrorism cases so all she could imagine was Ryan facing off with a terrorist and then holding up his finger to pause the mission so he could answer her call.

Of course, the chances Ryan would answer her call in the middle of some life-threatening moment were slim, but then, she'd thought the same thing about getting mugged in New York too.

Opening her contacts list, she hit the number for Vivian, and said a little prayer for Ryan's safety wherever he was and for whatever he was doing. Nothing had deepened her faith faster than her brother's dangerous career choice.

"Please tell me you've changed your mind and are calling me from Reagan?"

Vivian's unconventional greeting was jarring. "I'm not at the airport and I didn't change my mind," Frannie answered. "Hello, sister-in-law, good to know you're on my side."

Vivian laughed. "I'm a journalist, remember? I'm impartial."

"Ha! Except when it comes to my brother." Frannie snuggled into the pillows stacked behind her. "Did you know Ryan sent a *bodyguard* to escort me to the airport?"

"A bodyguard?" Vivian said around a bubble of laughter. "He did not."

"He did so." Frannie's gaze drifted to her purse, where Andrew's card was still tucked inside. She didn't need it anymore since he'd made her add his number to her contacts and that thought made her cheeks warm.

Kevin McAllister swung a paint can from the banister, smashing Marv's face. Frannie's lips twisted into a sneaky smile. "I pepper-sprayed him."

"You what!"

"I didn't know who he was and he approached me at my hotel room door and he's got these big, broad shoulders. And muscles." Vivian's soft *ooh* made Frannie roll her eyes even though she was smiling. "And," Frannie continued, "you know Ryan's given me all of these what-if scenarios. What if you're followed? What if you're carrying groceries? What if your shoes are untied?"

"Wait, what?" Vivian interrupted. "Your shoes?"

"That's from when I was a kid and never liked tying my shoes. As many times as he reminded me, I really thought I'd see more people tripping on untied shoelaces but once again he overplayed the threat."

Vivian laughed. "Okay, can we get back to the pepper spray?"

"It's not funny, Viv. I could've blinded the man. Or myself. Well, I could've if I had better aim but the bodyguard was ready and I ended up spraying the hallway."

"I don't think you can be blinded by pepper spray but at least you tried." Vivian exhaled. "I would've loved seeing it."

Frannie scowled. "I'm sure Ryan can use his FBI skills and pull the hotel security video."

"Oh, you're right."

"Viv!"

"I'm sorry, I'm sorry. My husband may have gone a bit

overboard with the whole bodyguard thing but hey, if he looks like Kevin Costner—"

"Who?"

"Kevin Costner. *Kevin. Costner.*" Vivian's tone was properly appalled and it made Frannie smile. "Please tell me you know who the OG bodyguard is? Whitney Houston." At that moment Vivian busted out in an off-key rendition of "I Will Always Love You."

"Mercy! Mercy!" Frannie pulled the phone away from her ear. "I give in. I know who Kevin Costner is."

"Whew! Because forget Christmas movies. I was about to pull out the DVD and force you to watch it with me. Twice—to really get the feel of the emotions."

"I think my emotions need more Kevin McAllister." Frannie watched as Kevin opened the door to his neighbor's house, thinking he'd outsmarted the dimwitted duo. Her stomach clenched in new understanding when Harry grabbed Kevin and snarled in his face.

Frannie turned the channel. She knew how the movie ended—Kevin would be rescued—but after today's events, the fear she was pretending didn't exist was twisting her stomach into knots.

"What's wrong?"

Pausing on a rerun of *The Office*, Frannie hesitated before answering Vivian.

"Frannie?"

If she told Viv what had happened, she would certainly tell Ryan and that was the last thing she needed. But then again, what if Andrew was already on the phone with him? Maybe if she gave Vivian a less-serious version, then—

"*Frankie.*"

"Oof, okay, okay." Frannie wrinkled her nose. "You sound like my brother."

"Then tell me what's going on. Tell me why you're not here in D.C. helping me prep veggies for homemade pizza night?"

A pang of guilt and longing warred inside of her. Frannie's shoulders sank deeper into the pillows.

"Okay, if you don't answer me in five seconds I'm going to send that bodyguard back to your hotel."

"Sorry." Frannie rubbed her temple. "It's just that something happened today and I don't want Ryan to freak out."

"You're starting to freak me out. What happened?"

"I was—" Frannie inhaled deeply, trying to figure out the best way to retell the story that wouldn't cause her sister-in-law to speed-dial Ryan. She let out a frustrated breath. *Might as well let the freak out ensue.* "First, I'm fine."

"Francis." Vivian's tone was nearly a growl.

"A man may have grabbed me earlier today at a bookstore."

"A MAN GRABBED YOU?"

"No. Well, yes, but not like how you're saying it." Frannie pushed off the covers, threw her legs over the side of the bed, and stood. Reliving this made her want to move so she began pacing her room. "I was at a bookstore and had to use the restroom but this man came up behind me and shoved me. At first, I thought it was a mistake, but then he told me not to scream before he pushed me out the emergency exit door and into an alley. I elbowed him and broke free of his grip and then Andrew was there and the guy took off. It all happened super fast and I'm fine."

Frannie bit her lip, hoping the main thing Vivian was focusing on was that she was fine.

"Are you okay?"

The backs of her eyes stung. Frannie had been poised to defend herself, play off the entire event as no big deal, but suddenly the weight of what happened felt heavy as she heard the concern in Vivian's quiet question.

Using the hem of her sweatshirt, she dabbed the corners of her eyes. "I wasn't hurt, Viv. I think the guy was trying to mug me, but Andrew scared him off."

Vivian's exhale came through the phone and Frannie was sure she was trying to figure out the best way to force her on a plane just like Andrew. But the truth was, she wouldn't have to try very hard. Over the last couple of hours, the adrenaline from the event had evaporated, leaving her feeling shaky and ... scared.

"What do you want to do?"

Leaning her shoulder against the wall, Frannie noted the difference between her brother's response and Vivian's. Ryan would've demanded she get on the plane under threat that he'd fly there to get her, but Vivian was respectfully allowing Frannie to come to her own decision. And she appreciated that about her sister-in-law.

"Is it bad if I admit that leaving the city makes me feel weak?"

"No, but you know you're not, right?"

Frannie walked to the window and stared up at the purplish sky. "I don't want to think I am but after what Calvin did and then at the bookstore, I just hate feeling like I don't have any control over my life. Like I'm just living at the whim of everyone else's decisions and beliefs about me. I wish I could be more like you. Strong. Independent. You went after your dreams and—"

"And it nearly cost me everything," Vivian cut in. "You know that. You know what I lost."

"I know, I'm sorry. I don't mean to dismiss what you went through." Frannie felt bad. What happened today was nothing compared to what Vivian had experienced and she knew it colored the way Ryan looked at the world, how he did his job, and certainly his concern for his entire family. When he found out about what happened today ... "Ryan's going to be mad at me."

Frannie pressed her forehead against the window. It was ice-cold but felt good against the heat of emotion pressing against her ribs. She hated proving her brother right, but worse was feeling like she was proving the hotel employees right. *And everyone back home.*

"No. He's not going to be mad at you. He's going to be worried. Just like I am. He loves you and only wants to keep you safe."

"I know but it would be nice if maybe he believed in me a little more."

"Honey, he does. We all do. If you want to stay in New York then I'll talk to your brother, make him understand." Vivian paused. "If that's what you want."

Frannie lifted her head from the window. "I think I want to come to D.C. If that's okay."

"It's more than okay." Vivian sounded like she was smiling. "Jisoo has to make a gingerbread house out of sugar cubes and I was volunteered to make four dozen cookies for the second grade holiday party."

"But you don't bake."

"The class mom said as long as there's enough icing, sprinkles, and candy the kids won't care."

Frannie laughed. A lightheartedness returned to her chest that told her she was making the right decision. "I'll call the airline and see about rebooking for the first flight to D.C."

"Sounds good. Do you need me to contact Kevin Costner to make sure you get to the airport?"

"I'm not sure you could convince Star-Lord to risk another bout with pepper spray." Frannie smiled again at the memory instead of feeling guilty.

"Star-Lord? I thought you said his name was Andrew?"

"It is but he kind of looks like Chris Pratt except taller, I think, and more ... real."

"So handsome and accessible?"

Frannie thought of the way Andrew's expression wavered

between inconvenienced and concerned. "I mentioned I practically pepper-sprayed him, right?"

"Yes, but you're not denying he's handsome."

Her lips split into a grin. "No, I cannot deny that."

"Ooh, I can't wait to get all of the details when you get here tomorrow. If he's Ryan's friend, maybe we can find out what he's doing for the holidays and—"

"Not sure the sting of rejection has worn off yet."

"Oh, sorry." But Vivian didn't sound all that sorry. "I've already moved on from ... what's his name again?"

Frannie was about to provide it when she figured out Vivian's game. "Ah, you're good." Yes. Going to D.C. to spend time with Vivian and Jisoo would be just what she needed to get over whatever-his-name-was.

"I'll text you with my flight details."

"Can't wait!"

Ending the call, Frannie tapped her phone against her chin and stared out the window again. Leaving was the right thing to do. Right? It felt right but it also felt like she was ... giving up. Giving in.

Why did that guy have to come after her today? If the whole thing hadn't happened, she had no doubt her decision right now would be different. She wouldn't be ready to fly to D.C. She wouldn't be hiding in her hotel room.

Staring up at the sky, Frannie saw small flecks of white falling from the sky. Snow? It was snowing.

"Well, to quote Clark Griswold"—Frannie glared at the snowflakes turning New York City into a giant, magical Christmas snow globe seconds after she decided to leave—"'If this isn't the biggest bag-over-the-head, punch-in-the-face I ever got.'"

Chapter Ten

Father Time was sadistic. Torturing with seconds that ticked into anxious minutes until they stretched into excruciating hours that had Andrew fighting against the compulsion to get back to Frannie's hotel and do whatever was necessary to get her to leave the city.

The only reason he hadn't taken off was because Doug had sent Mac to the 1911 to keep an eye on her, which should've eased the worry coursing through him. But for some inexplicable reason, he felt like the only thing that would make him feel better was if *he* was the one there with her. He couldn't shake the guilt of letting her down. Letting Ryan down. Being the one with her, he could at least redeem himself somehow.

Outside, the sky had darkened, but that didn't stop Andrew from letting his gaze roam the city streets below in an attempt to locate the general area of Frannie's hotel. Even with all of the light pollution from streetlights, neon signs, and hundreds of vehicles, he couldn't help focusing on the shadows that reminded him that danger could be lurking anywhere.

"Mr. Malone is on his way." Doug checked his cell phone.

"He's already aware of the note and we'll catch him up on what's happened but we need to discuss the plan going forward."

Andrew paused in his pacing. "What do you mean?"

"Whoever sent this threatening note thinks your friend is Ms. Malone." Doug pressed his lips together like he knew Andrew wasn't going to like what was coming next. "If we let them believe *that*, Ms. Malone is safe. Here with Joey. That buys the FBI time to figure out who's behind this and—"

"Wait." Andrew blinked. "You want them to go after Frankie?"

"Frankie?"

"Frannie," Andrew corrected. "Frannie Frost. She's the sister of FBI Agent Ryan Frost, the man who saved me from Angelo Evola."

Doug looked thoughtful for a second. "You said she was supposed to leave New York, right?"

"Supposed to," Andrew said. "But she's determined to stay."

"Why?"

Andrew inhaled slowly. Was this going to sound as crazy to them as it had to him when Frannie mentioned it? "She has a bucket list of things she wants to do in New York." Joey and Doug exchanged a look. "I've tried to convince her multiple times to leave but she wants to stay and finish her trip."

"Why is her brother concerned about her?" Joey folded his arms over his chest, giving Andrew a rare glimpse of the Secret Service agent he used to be.

This was probably going to sound worse than the bucket list thing. "Her boyfriend broke up with her when she got here. She's from a small town in Georgia and Ryan was concerned about someone taking advantage of her." Andrew gripped the back of the dining room chair again. "And I don't think he's going to be thrilled that we're allowing her to be confused for Ms. Malone, who now has an active threat against her."

"You know we have to be fluid in our plans when it comes to protecting our clients," Doug said. "Nothing ever goes perfectly and this is one of those times, unfortunately."

Unfortunately. It felt a lot more than unfortunate. If whoever sent that note to Ms. Malone intended to up their game, then what happened to Frannie today could be just the beginning.

"Unless"—Doug met Andrew's eyes—"you can get her on a plane out of the city."

A burst of air passed through Andrew's lips. "Sir, if we send her on the plane, what makes us think whoever is targeting Ms. Malone won't follow her?"

Doug frowned, thinking for a second before he exhaled too. "Then she stays in New York and you stay with her."

Andrew's relief was weighted with this new responsibility. The woman had a bucket list and a determination not to leave the city until she finished it. If he was honest with himself, her insistence to check off her list irked him. He had a job to do and her silly list had interfered with it. However, seeing her face light up at Levain and then when he recommended checking out Dyker Heights—that innocent joyfulness stirred something inside of him.

And she had a great smile. One he wouldn't mind seeing again.

That was the last thing he needed to be thinking about. He refocused his thoughts on finding out who was behind the note and who that man in the leather jacket was. "Does the FBI have any leads on the ransomware attack?"

"Agent Nash Martin from the Dallas Field Office is continuing to work with Mr. Malone's team," Doug answered. "But they don't have any new leads. The field office here is sending out Agent Geneva Simpkins to take a statement from Mr. Malone."

There was a knock on the hotel door and Joey walked over,

his hand on the weapon holstered at his hip as he looked through the peephole. Being that Joey was the newest guy to the team, Andrew hadn't really had an opportunity to work with him yet but he already appreciated the man's professionalism to take this threat seriously. Andrew hoped to find out more about why the man left the Secret Service but for now he was grateful Joey would be keeping an eye on Ms. Malone.

Simon Malone entered the hotel room with Oskar behind him. It was protocol for clients to submit photos of themselves and Andrew noted the man was aging about as well as any other billionaire. The photos showed he had dark hair graying at the temples in a clean cut and only a few lines near the corners of his eyes, but the man stalking into the room right now looked like he had aged beyond his fifty-seven years. The distress shadowing Mr. Malone's eyes reminded Andrew once more that having money might mean power but it didn't solve everything. In his line of work, he'd seen the other side of wealth—the fear and problems it could lead to that required armed security.

"Valentina?"

"She's safe and finishing up with her spa appointment in the main bedroom," Doug said. "She doesn't know anything about the note. Joe Caruso intercepted it."

Mr. Malone's shoulders relaxed but his hooded expression remained in place. "I didn't think it would come to this." He unbuttoned his suit jacket before dropping onto the couch, placing his elbows on his knees. "I had no idea they would threaten my daughter."

Doug shared a look with Andrew before he sat in the chair across from Malone. "Mr. Malone, we have a local FBI agent coming over, Geneva Simpkins. She's going to handle the investigation on this side and work with Agent Martin in Dallas, but I do need to ask if you know of anyone who might go after your daughter?"

"No." His response came out rushed but Andrew noted something else there. Did he believe that? "About a month ago, the news came out about Kline Capital's investment in Hope Village and a week later I got an email warning me I was making a huge mistake, but I didn't take it seriously."

"What is Hope Village?" Doug said.

"It will be a sister charity to Hope's Children, a nonprofit my wife was a part of before she died. They will provide services to single parents, moms and dads who need assistance finding affordable living, childcare, jobs, medical, and legal needs." He shook his head. "It doesn't make any sense to me why someone would be upset by the expansion."

Andrew couldn't think of a good reason either but that didn't eliminate the possibility. He stepped forward and introduced himself. "I was originally your daughter's personal protection detail but Joey Caruso will be handling it going forward."

Mr. Malone's worried gaze moved between him and Doug. "Why?"

After a permissive nod from Doug, Andrew gave a brief rundown of what occurred outside the bookstore. He watched Mr. Malone's confusion turn concerned as the pieces began to come together. "I think whoever is threatening you marked me and misidentified someone else as your daughter."

Worry creased Mr. Malone's forehead. "Is she okay?"

Andrew's respect for the man rose. "She is." He thought about the way Frannie worked hard to convince him she was perfectly fine, but she couldn't persuade him the tremor he'd felt sitting next to her on the ride back to her hotel wasn't from fear. He'd never forget the vulnerability tightening her pretty features, making him want to toss away professionalism and tuck her against his side. He rubbed the back of his neck, wishing he could shirk this attraction. He wouldn't fail her. Not again. "But it's our responsibility to make sure she remains safe considering the threatening message."

"Yes, of course." Mr. Malone stood. "I'll cover all of the expenses."

"You don't need to do that." Andrew and Doug spoke at the same time.

Andrew would've covered this out of his own pocket since it was his fault for putting her into this position in the first place.

The bedroom door opened and a woman with dark hair tied up in a bun exited, carrying a bag and a folding massage table. Other than a quick glance around, she continued to the door, pausing to address Joey, who met her there.

"Ms. Malone is getting dressed and said she'll be ready shortly."

Mr. Malone ran a hand down his face. "What a mess I've made of things."

Andrew felt some solidarity with the man. He'd made a mess of things as well, but he couldn't sit here and console the man whose money had likely made him, his daughter, and now Frannie a target.

"Sir." Andrew turned to Doug. "I'd like to get back to the 1911 and check on Frannie. I'll need to get in touch with the hotel's security team there and—"

"They don't have a security team," Mr. Malone cut in with a sniff. They all looked at him. He lifted his shoulders. "My head of security, Isaac Lawson, runs one of the country's biggest security firms. He's assessed multiple hotel chains' security risks and I can assure you the 1911 has never made his list. It's a boutique hotel and doesn't have the funding to support more than a four-man team monitoring security cameras."

That news churned Andrew's stomach. He needed to get back to Frannie ASAP.

"Move her here," Mr. Malone said. "I'll pay."

"We have a discretionary fund," Doug said. "We can take care of it."

"No." Mr. Malone squared his shoulders in a face-off with Doug that had Andrew and Joey exchanging a look. They were close in height but Doug had at least twenty pounds on the businessman in the Armani suit. And as often as he'd caught Doug coming in from a training session at Joe's Boxing, that extra weight was likely all muscle.

Mr. Malone's posture remained unmoving. The fact that he wasn't backing down told Andrew he probably didn't get refused often.

"This is non-negotiable. Get that young lady into the hotel here where at least I know the security is top-notch."

"If you insist on moving Ms. Frost to another hotel," Doug started, "then I must insist we move her to a different hotel. She cannot stay here where you and your daughter are staying."

Realization dawned in Mr. Malone's gray eyes. "Oh. Yes, I hadn't thought about that. Fine. Then The Peninsula."

Andrew's jaw dropped. The Peninsula was a five-star luxury hotel and it wasn't cheap, especially this time of the year.

"That's very generous of you," Doug started but stopped when Mr. Malone held up his hand.

At that moment, the door to the bedroom opened up and Valentina Malone stood there in a red dress that left nothing to the imagination. She tucked her blonde hair behind her ear, and her blue eyes, beneath lashes too long to be real, surveyed them.

Andrew did the same to her, trying not to be obvious. The hair and eye color were similar but the build—Valentina's thin and angular one was different from Frannie's soft, feminine curves. However, it wasn't hard to see why someone might confuse the two women on first glance.

"Hi, Daddy." She took a step in heels so tall Andrew didn't know how she could stay up on them. "Everything okay?"

"Hi, pumpkin." Mr. Malone circled the couch and pecked his daughter on her temple. "I think we're going to order in for dinner tonight."

"Daddy, I wanted to go out tonight."

Andrew sent a sidelong look to Joey at Valentina's childish whine. Dipping his chin, Joey hid his eye roll.

"Not tonight." Mr. Malone smiled. "Chef Léandre is delivering a six-course meal."

Expecting a tantrum, Andrew was mildly surprised when Valentina only exhaled loudly before turning to head back into her room. "Fine, I guess I'll change."

Andrew hoped Mr. Malone's influence would prove helpful when it came to convincing his daughter to stay in her hotel for the remainder of their trip. He was already trying to figure out what he could do to convince Frannie of the same thing.

Doug caught his attention and tipped his head in the direction of the door. When they arrived there, he paused. "Head over to the 1911. I'll send you the details once we secure Ms. Frost's room at The Peninsula." He exhaled. "You said Ms. Frost is the sister of an FBI agent?"

"Yes, Ryan Frost."

"You're going to need to let him know what's happened."

Andrew clenched his teeth. He knew he had to but it didn't mean it was going to be an easy conversation.

Doug looked empathetic. "Maybe the two of you can figure out how to get her back home safely. I'm not sure how long it'll be before someone realizes the mistaken identity but when that happens, I'm going to need you here."

Andrew flicked a quick look to where Joey stood off to the side, almost invisible. Probably had plenty of practice blending in as a Secret Service agent but he would quickly make his presence known if required.

As if reading his thoughts, Doug added, "Caruso can handle

Ms. Malone but something in my gut tells me this could go south real quick and I'd like to have a full team on this."

"Yes, sir." Andrew quietly exited the hotel suite and headed toward the elevator. Doug wasn't one to exaggerate and it made him curious if he knew something more from his conversation with the FBI.

If it was important to the safety of their clients, Doug would've shared whatever he knew, but it was still unsettling that Andrew was facing a faceless threat.

Not faceless. The man in the leather jacket. Andrew pulled out his cell phone and tapped out a message to Doug to see about getting the security footage from the bookstore to run the man's face through facial recognition. If they could get a name, then that would give the FBI a direction for their investigation.

Andrew stepped into the elevator and pressed the button for the lobby. He took a deep breath when he stepped out of the elevator and dialed Ryan's number. The muscles in the back of his neck tightened as he lifted the phone to his ear. Part of him prayed the federal agent wouldn't answer but instead Ryan's voice spoke into Andrew's ear, two furious words.

"What happened?"

Pinching the bridge of his nose, Andrew shook his head. Had Frannie already called her brother and told him what happened? That made him feel worse. He should've called Ryan right away. "Man, I'm sorry. I had no idea she was going to get wrapped up in this."

"Wrapped up in what?" Ryan's sharp tone dropped to a low growl.

Andrew headed for the rotating doors and was surprised by the thick, puffy flakes of snow swirling in his face and already collecting on the ground. He normally loved New York under a fresh blanket of snow but this conversation tempered his excitement.

Just rip the bandage off. Andrew hailed a cab and began filling Ryan in on the events of the day, starting with his arrival at the hotel. He left out the part about the pepper spray and because of client confidentiality, he couldn't give Ryan detailed information on the Malones, but he told him the rest.

"I'm on my way to your sister's hotel to move her to The Peninsula. It has better security and I'll explain everything." Andrew ran a hand through his hair. "I promise I won't let anything else happen to her until we get this whole thing figured out. And I will make sure she gets back home safely. I'm sorry I let you down."

Silence filled the line and Andrew hated the way that made him feel. He'd let down the man who had literally saved his life. This was his job. To protect people. And he'd messed up. Basically did the exact opposite by exposing Frannie to danger.

"You didn't let me down," Ryan said. "I knew Frannie wasn't just going to comply. That'd be too easy. But you were there when it mattered and kept her from being harmed further. It could've been a lot worse."

The quick forgiveness loosened some of the knots in Andrew's stomach. "I hope after I tell her what's going on she'll comply and discard that bucket list of hers."

"You can't tell her anything."

Andrew's head reared back. He was expecting Ryan to let him have it but instead he was asking him to ... "You don't want me to tell her that her life might be in danger."

"That's exactly what I'm telling you." Ryan sighed into the phone and Andrew could almost imagine the level of agitation pulsing on the other end. "She's already been through enough and based off what you've told me, it seems a little circumstantial that what happened inside the bookstore is related to ransomware threats against your client. I don't want to get Frannie worked up over nothing."

"What if it's not nothing?" Andrew didn't feel right keeping the threat a secret from Frannie. "If she knows, it might be easier to keep her in her hotel."

"Ha!" Ryan released a humorless chuckle. "Sometimes my sister's idealism gets in the way of common sense."

Andrew grimaced. "I wish you would've warned me." *And warned me about her appeal.* Those soft blonde waves of hair a man could tangle his fingers in. That alluring Southern drawl that gently floated into his ears and hooked him by the throat. *Yeah, a warning would've been nice.*

"She probably thinks," Ryan went on, oblivious to Andrew's struggles, "what happened today is normal for New York."

"She did mention you told her the statistics showed she was likely to be the victim of a crime here."

"Sounds like Frankie." Ryan sighed audibly. "Look, I talked to Vivian right before this and she said Frankie is going to fly to D.C. tomorrow. Keep her at her hotel for the night and I'll let a few buddies from work know what's going on and they can keep an eye on her and my family. If what happened today was more than a New York statistic, then I'd be surprised if whoever is behind the attack doesn't realize their mistake. There's really no reason to tell Frankie anything that's going to make her paranoid or scared."

The taxi pulled up in front of Frannie's hotel. Andrew swiped his card to pay and then got out. It still didn't sit well with him to keep Frannie out of the loop, but her brother probably knew best what she needed. And he felt better knowing that the FBI in D.C. would be there just in case. He just needed to get her on the plane tomorrow. Should be easy but after this morning ...

"What if she insists on doing something else on her bucket list before she gets on the plane?"

"I wouldn't worry too much about that." Ryan's voice was cutting out. "Vivian just texted me the flight information and

Frankie will be out of your hair by noon tomorrow. My sister's never been a morning person. So just keep her safe until then."

Ending the call, Andrew shoved the phone into his back pocket. He walked into the hotel and shook off the snow that had collected on his head and shoulders. He checked into the room Mac had rented on the same floor but two doors down from Frannie's room.

He paused by her door, listening. The sound of the television was the only thing he heard. He checked his watch. A little after seven. Seventeen hours. He just needed to keep Frannie safe for seventeen hours and then make sure she boarded a plane taking her safely out of New York City.

Chapter Eleven

There was nothing like waking up to Michael Bublé crooning "Winter Wonderland" in your head. Frannie shielded her eyes from the bright light pouring into her hotel room window. She'd left the curtains open the night before to allow the silent snowfall and Christmas music from her cell phone to carry her to sleep.

She'd feared the man in the leather jacket would invade her dreams but emotional exhaustion played defense, tugging her into a rather peaceful slumber. Rolling out of bed, she went to the window, and her mouth dropped open at the sight.

It wasn't only a dusting of snow but a full-on blanket covering the city, and it was absolutely beautiful.

It rarely, if ever, snowed in Walton, Georgia. The humid climate was just too warm, only giving her glimpses of snowflakes on the very rare occasion the temperatures dipped south of freezing, and the flurries usually melted long before they ever hit the ground.

Her gaze moved to the street, where a few people were bundled up and weathering the cold. Light traffic was moving slowly but at least there were vehicles on the road, which meant she should be able to get a cab to the airport. Though she imagined she'd need to leave a little earlier than she'd planned, just in case.

The wistfulness of the moment slipped away as Frannie went to her phone to double-check her departure time. She frowned upon seeing several text messages from the airline.

"Flight cancelled." Frannie gasped. "What?"

She quickly scrolled through the messages that began with delays until the last one at three this morning confirmed her flight to D.C. was cancelled due to inclement weather and told her to contact the airline to reschedule.

Frannie dialed the number listed and it went straight to a busy signal. Of course. She tried for another fifteen minutes before finally reaching a message that asked her to give her name and phone number for the airline to call her back.

Staring out the window, she rubbed her arm. Well, now what? Her suitcase lay open, her clothes for the plane ride set aside. Wait. She'd already informed the hotel she was going to be checking out. Grabbing the hotel phone, she rang for the front desk.

"Good morning," Frannie said when someone named Alicia answered the phone. She hoped this wasn't one of the employees from yesterday morning. "I was just notified my flight was cancelled and I'd like to—"

"I'm sorry but your room has already been reserved for another guest," Alicia cut in. "And we are currently fully booked."

Frannie sank down on the edge of her bed. "No rooms? Where am I supposed to go?"

"I can give you some names of hotels nearby but you'll need to call right away. LaGuardia, JFK, and Albany are shut down due to the weather."

Suddenly the snow didn't seem so magical. "I'd appreciate that." Frannie grabbed the hotel pen from the desk and ended up only jotting down two out of the five recommendations. There was no way she could afford a Hyatt or Hilton or The Plaza. Leaving her with the Holiday Inn and Days Inn. "What's the late checkout time?"

"Normally two but since we are fully booked and half of our housekeeping staff is delayed, we're asking all guests to check out no later than twelve."

"Twelve?" Frannie's accent always deepened when she panicked and Alicia huffed, making Frannie believe she might be one of the women she'd spoken to the day before. If so, she wouldn't give her the satisfaction of thinking Frannie couldn't take care of herself. "Twelve is fine. Thank you."

She hung up the phone quickly, not feeling fine at all. Using her cell phone, she searched for a few more hotels in her price range and called them plus the numbers she was given. All were fully booked due to the storm.

The muscles in her throat ached with emotion but she would not cry. She would figure this—

Her cell phone pinged with a message from ... Frannie's brows pinched. Dale McGill? He once was her co-worker at Way Station Café back in Walton but she hadn't heard from him since he confessed his feelings for her, but she was—or thought she was—in a long-distance relationship with Calvin so she kindly rejected his date request.

> Hey, Frannie. Just wanted to check on you.
> Sorry about Calvin.

Check on her? Calvin? Frannie's eyes rounded. How did he know— "No. No. No. No." She swiped open her Instagram account and pulled up Calvin's profile. Her hand flew to her mouth. "No!"

Through blurry vision, Frannie stared at a photo of Calvin and a beautiful brunette, both dressed to the nines and smiling like they were models for Colgate. The woman's left hand was extended toward the camera, showing off the perfect view of a giant solitaire diamond.

Engaged already? Frannie peeled her focus from the ring to look at the pride radiating on Calvin's face; his eyes sparkled almost as brightly as the diamond on the woman's finger. She read the caption and felt sick.

Couldn't wait to ask this woman to be my bride. #engaged

The photo already had over three hundred likes and nearly as many comments congratulating the happy couple. Frannie recognized many of the names and grew more nauseated. Their friends knew. Their family knew. Dale McGill knew. It wouldn't be long before half of Walton would know she'd been dumped in New York City.

Her cell phone rang and Frannie nearly lost it when she saw her mom's name on the screen.

"Hey, Mom, I don't have a lot of time to talk, I need to check out of my hotel and there was a snowstorm overnight so I need to either find a new hotel or I'll be camping out at the airport with all of the other stranded passengers."

"Honey." Her mother's soft Southern accent unlocked the dam and Frannie couldn't stop the tears from streaming down her cheeks. "Are you okay?"

Taking a minute to regain her composure, Frannie tried for casual, but not too casual, nonchalance because her mom would read right through it. "Yeah. I mean outside of my flight being cancelled."

"Francis?"

Frannie swallowed against the emotion. "Really, I'm fine."

"He wasn't the right one." Her mom's tone was gentle but firm. "He was a nice guy but he wasn't the one for you."

"How do you know that?" Her voice wavered and she swiped hard against her cheek to stop the flow of tears.

"He wouldn't have let you go if he was the right one."

Years of teasing from Frannie's childhood came roaring back. There were too many nights to count when her mom would return home after her second shift at work to find Frannie crying from the mean words of classmates. Her mom would offer her variations of the same platitudes, trying to comfort Frannie, but as Frannie grew older it became clear that her mom wasn't just saying it for her benefit.

He wouldn't have left.

He wouldn't have walked away.

He would know what a treasure you are.

The words were little solace to the pain of rejection and so Frannie vowed she'd do whatever it took to make sure a guy never did to her what her father did to her mom. She became extra picky when it came to dating, which, with a brother in law enforcement, wasn't too hard to do, but when she got to Anderson, she'd fallen for Calvin.

"Viv says you're flying to D.C.?"

"I was supposed to, but there was a snowstorm." Frannie was grateful her mother didn't push the subject. "I'm waiting for the airline to call me back to reschedule."

"Are you sure you don't want to come home? I'm sure Lane and Ms. Byrdie would love to have your help at the café."

Thinking about Dale McGill's text message made returning to Walton the last thing she wanted to do. "I'm excited to spend time with Vivian and Jisoo. They've already made plans for me and I think it'll be a nice distraction." *A necessary one.*

"Okay ... but promise me you won't let this keep you from coming home. Things like this happen and it doesn't—"

A knock at her door pulled Frannie's attention from her mom's words. "Thanks, Mom. I appreciate it but someone's at the door and I need to get ready to check out."

"Okay. Please keep me posted on where you're going to be and all of the flight details. I don't like the idea of you being there all by yourself."

And now Celine Dion was singing "All By Myself" in Frannie's head. She preferred Michael Bublé on all accounts.

"I will, Mom." She made it to the hotel door. "Talk to you later."

Ending the call, Frannie peeked through the peephole and then jerked her head back. What? *Not again.* She looked again, hoping she was hallucinating, but nope. Through the distorted view, on the other side of the door, Star-Lord had returned.

Chapter Twelve

A thump sounded from the other side of the door and Andrew's pulse spiked. "Frannie? It's Andrew. Andrew Bishop from Defensemen. Are you okay?"

Most of the night, he and Brayden switched between sleep and making rounds by Frannie's room. Around midnight, his attention shifted from her safety to the weather. By four, the airports in New York and New Jersey were closed. And any hope he had for Frannie flying safely out of New York had been buried under nearly nine inches of snow.

Frannie wasn't leaving New York today, which meant he was on duty.

The lock clicked and Frannie opened the door, standing there in pink thermal pajamas. He squinted. Were those reindeer … jumping rope?

"Ahem."

He yanked his gaze away from her pajamas but his embarrassment kept him from meeting her eyes. He focused on the soft strands of blonde hair that had slipped free from the braid hanging over her shoulder. "Sorry. Reindeer games. I get it."

She pulled the door to her hotel room closer, affectively hiding most of her body. "You can let my brother know I won't be needing an escort to the airport today. My flight's been cancelled."

The waver in her voice pulled his attention straight to her eyes. They were glassy and rimmed with red like she'd been crying.

"What's wrong?" There was no good reason for his defenses to go on alert because of tears but that didn't stop him from placing his palm on the door and taking a step closer. "Are you okay?"

She sniffled, using the hem of her sleeve to wipe at her cheek. "I'm fine."

Andrew didn't know what to do. He could see she wasn't fine but pushing her for answers felt invasive. And he was already walking a fine line after being caught ogling her reindeer pajamas.

Focus, Bishop. After his conversation with Ryan last night, he had practiced what he was going to say to Frannie this morning. He hoped his planned explanation would be enough to keep her from asking questions that would force him to either lie to her or break another promise to Ryan. "Your brother told me you were planning to leave today—"

"I was." Her tone turned sarcastic. "But in another ironic turn that is my life, the city decided to become a winter wonderland, trapping me here with no place to stay."

Andrew's lip twitched. He shouldn't smile but even her sassy attitude was enchanting. He cleared his throat. "Right, which is why I'd like to offer to take you to a new hotel, where a reservation has been made for you."

The door opened wider as Frannie leaned forward. "A reservation for me?"

He'd been expecting immediate resistance—or at least a bit of a fight—but her expression looked almost relieved. "Yes. After what happened at the bookstore, the Defensemen Agency would like to compensate you."

"Compensate me?" Her brows lifted with confusion. "What happened yesterday wasn't your fault. I'm lucky you were close enough to hear me scream." She rubbed her arms but he saw the tiny shudder ripple through her. "I should be the one compensating you for coming to my rescue."

That last bit opened a flood of mixed emotions. A warmth blossomed in his chest at being the one who came to her rescue, but the stress of not protecting her like he should have had his muscles knotted tighter than a string of Christmas lights. "If I had done my job correctly—"

"It wasn't your job." Frannie was suddenly inches away from his chest, her hand on his arm sending a current through him that reached his toes. She looked up at him and there was so much compassion in her expression it forced him back a step. She dropped her arm and her cheeks flamed red. "Sorry."

"No, it's me. I mean, I should be apologizing. To you. You didn't do anything. I, uh ..." Why were the words getting stuck on his tongue? *Take a breath, Bishop.* He did. "We have a room." He looked past her into her tiny room. The 1911 was nice but it wasn't The Peninsula. "One that has a whole lot of Christmas spirit." He'd done a little internet recon, checking to see what The Peninsula offered that might help him keep Frannie tucked safely inside. "Including reindeer."

"Reindeer!" Her brows shot up to her hairline. "Real reindeer?"

"No, New York City has wildlife laws. But reindeer sugar cookies," he added quickly, hating that he'd led her on. "And a giant gingerbread house that looks like the hotel, a candy cane scavenger hunt, and carolers who sing in the lobby."

"You should've led with the candy cane scavenger hunt." She

gave him a glare that was all tease and he had to admit he liked it. "I feel uncomfortable accepting the room as compensation, though."

"Don't." Andrew may have stretched the truth a little. Mr. Malone was covering the majority of the hotel room for Frannie but Andrew had convinced Doug to let him pay for the rest. "It's all covered."

"Are you sure?" She twisted the hem of her pajama shirt. "I have a list of hotels that I can stay at."

"Frannie, you're unlikely to find a room anywhere else in the city."

She glanced behind her to the window that was frosted at the edges. "Okay." She faced him. "But I want to talk with your boss or manager."

"Why?"

"To make sure they know what happened yesterday wasn't your fault."

Her insistence on defending him caused something in his chest to flicker to life. Man, another time, another place, and he might've explored that flicker but right now he just needed to get her to The Peninsula safely.

"I appreciate that but I don't think it's necessary." He tipped his chin at the suitcase sitting behind her feet. "What is necessary is getting you checked out of here and into your new room so you don't miss the candy cane scavenger hunt."

Biting her lip, Frannie smiled and clapped her hands beneath her chin. "Okay. I can be ready in like fifteen minutes."

"Fifteen minutes?"

Frannie pressed her hands on his chest like it was no big deal but the heat of her touch beneath his Henley said otherwise. "There are candy canes to be scavenged. I'll meet you in the lobby in fifteen minutes."

. . .

When Andrew and Frannie walked through the revolving doors of the 1911, Frannie inhaled on a gasp. "It's even more beautiful than I imagined."

Her scarf slipped to the ground and he scooped it up. Without thinking, he snaked it around her neck, taking care to lift her hair and not react to the way his fingertips buzzed brushing against her skin. It was far too easy to appreciate the alluring way her dark lashes contrasted against her creamy skin, highlighting her natural beauty. Her aquamarine eyes watched him with a spark that had his insides warming. The feeling was disarming and he shook it away, letting his hands drop back to his side and bringing his mind back to a safer place—the view.

Andrew glanced around. Except for the gray mounds of dirty snow that had been scraped to the edges by street crews, the rest of New York City was still decked out in a blanket of white worthy of Bing Crosby's ballad.

Inside the Uber, Frannie's nose was practically glued to the window, watching New York City show off. Her bubbly delight was infatuating, and he found himself wanting nothing more than to continue to watch her excitement, but he still had a job to do.

He swallowed, preparing for the next part of this plan. "So, um, when we get to the hotel, I was thinking of maybe sticking around. Help you scavenge those candy canes."

She sat back. "You don't have to do that."

"I want to."

Her expression darkened. "Is this because you feel bad about yesterday? Or did my brother put you up to this?"

"I do feel bad about yesterday." Safer not to answer that last one. Andrew sensed her hesitation and knew it was time to pour on the charm. He dug deep to those years he had to schmooze sponsor execs. Locking her in his gaze, he leaned closer, and registered her sharp intake of breath. "But I really don't have anywhere else to be today." He smiled at her, the one he reserved for his female fans. Was he manipulating her feelings? Absolutely. But he'd do anything to keep her safe. "That is, if you don't mind the company?"

Andrew wasn't sure whether it was Doug's connections or Mr. Malone's but he'd received a call from The Peninsula's head of security last night. They'd gone over a game plan to keep an eye on Frannie, allowing Andrew to monitor her from the security office. It would work for one night so long as the weather cooperated for the airports to reopen tomorrow.

"How good are you at scavenging?"

"I can't say that I've ever scavenged." He pressed his lips together. "Scavenged. *Scavenged.* Is that even a word?"

"It's a word and by the time we're done scavenging ..." She frowned. "Wait, now it does sound weird. *Scavenging*." She shook her head, giving up. "I've never lost a—" Her words froze as she pressed her face back to the window. "Is that Central Park?"

He couldn't help chuckling at her awe. When was the last time he'd looked at New York City like this? Once upon a time when he was playing defenseman for the Bandits, living here felt like an out-of-body experience. Michelin Star dinners, celebrity parties, signing autographs for cheering fans.

Now his life felt very ordinary. Not that his job was ordinary, and maybe that's why he said yes when Amanda asked him to consider the career. Ordinary felt like a disappointment to his family, team, friends, himself.

"What do you think?"

Her question pulled him back to the expectation in her eyes. "I'm sorry, what?"

"About the bucket list? If I'm going to be stuck here for the day, maybe we could check a few things off." Her eyes sank to the list she must've pulled out of her purse. "Then at least the whole trip won't be a total embarrassment." She mumbled that last part before clamping her lips shut, blue eyes finding his. "Ice skating at the park. Do you think they'll be open today?"

Andrew's gaze moved to the park. There were a few people already enjoying the snow, including several children. If someone was watching him, following him, to get to Ms. Malone, taking Frannie to the park was risky.

He was about to make up an excuse to avoid taking her out but her quiet words echoed loudly in his head. *"The trip won't be a total embarrassment."* She wasn't talking about what happened at the bookstore. At least he didn't think so.

Something had made her cry this morning and he was pretty sure it was the bozo who dumped her for reasons he couldn't yet figure out. Frannie seemed smart and funny and she was certainly beautiful.

"What am I thinking?" She folded her bucket list. "You probably don't want to play tourist with me since you live here."

"Rockefeller is overrated." The last time he'd been in skates was exactly that—the last time—but when her gaze swung back to him, his resolve began to slip. "Expensive and overcrowded."

Her smile brought the light back to her eyes. "Well, that's good because I read that ice skating at Bryant Park is the perfect way to kick off the holiday spirit with its European-style Christmas market."

"Do you have these memorized?"

"I've wanted to come to New York ever since I saw *Miracle on 34th Street.* The original with Natalie Wood, not the remake." She said this as if he needed that cleared up. He hadn't seen either version. "The movies made it look so magical and romantic." Her jaw clenched as she swallowed. "Anyway, I've kept a running list of things I would do if I ever got the chance to visit. It's probably silly but I don't know if I'll ever be back."

Those words stung for some reason and filled Andrew with the desire to give her the best day he could—safely.

"Ice skating at Bryant Park sounds like a great way to spend the afternoon."

"Really?" She nearly squealed, earning her a laugh from their driver. "But after the candy cane scavenger hunt and we'll need to see what time the carolers will be there because I don't want to miss that."

Her excitement seemed almost tangible, defying every natural law of physics as it curled into him with pricks of heat that burned his chest. He could give this to her. Candy cane hunt. Ice skating in the park. Carolers. As long as he didn't get distracted by—her hand clutched his arm.

"Are you kidding me?"

The Uber had pulled up to The Peninsula and a doorman was already opening Frannie's door for her. The driver popped the trunk as another doorman grabbed her suitcase. Andrew pulled a few dollars from his wallet and tipped both men before grabbing Frannie's bag as she gawked up at the historic hotel.

"This ..." Her voice was breathless. "This is incredible."

"It's even better inside." He took her gloveless hand and led her in, savoring the warmth of her palm against his. He probably should let go, but didn't. *Who knows when she'll be back?* He was tiptoeing in dangerous territory, but it was just for the day and he didn't want her to slip on the snow ... *that has already been scraped from the sidewalk by The Peninsula's staff.*

Leading her inside, he was nearly yanked backward as her feet stopped mid-step like she was cemented to the spot. Giant Christmas trees, the longest strands of garland he'd ever seen, and red and gold ornaments embellished the already ornate lobby. As promised, a replica of the hotel made entirely of gingerbread was roped off, with visitors taking photos nearby.

"I'll check you in."

Ten minutes later, Frannie had a bag of candy compliments of the Christmas Sweet Shoppe and they were headed to her

"Nights Before Christmas" suite. Andrew had no idea what that meant, only that he was sure Mr. Malone had made it happen.

Andrew started to hand her the room key but she was busy reading the list of holiday activities at the hotel, a candy cane hanging out of her mouth, so he swiped it instead and held the door open for her.

"The candy cane scavenger hunt is this afternoon but—oh ... my ... jingle-jangle stars."

Chapter Thirteen

"Please tell me I'm not dreaming." Frannie rushed into her hotel room—*no, suite!* She was staying in a suite with a sitting area and ... She stopped in front of the fully decorated Christmas tree placed perfectly in front of windows trimmed with garland, berries, and red bows. She slid her fingers along a branch. It was real. "There's a Christmas tree in my room."

"So, the room's okay, then?" Andrew said, and his hesitance spun her around.

"Are you serious?" She turned in a circle, arms stretched out. "The room is amazing."

Andrew's lips curled up at the corners, easing into a smile that made her blush. A low laugh rumbled out of him but it wasn't the kind that made her feel embarrassed by her over-the-top enthusiasm; rather, it left her feeling a bit giddy. Or maybe it was just the beautiful room she was standing in that was giving her that feeling. Not the handsome bodyguard. *Oh yes, nothing makes a girl weak in the knees quicker than tinsel.* She averted her attention to a plate of cookies sitting on the coffee table next to a note.

She grabbed the note and read it.

Ms. Frost, I know this doesn't make up for the trouble but I do hope you will enjoy your stay. Sincerely, Mr. Malone.

"Mr. Malone?" She set the note down and removed the plastic wrap from the plate. "Who's he? Your boss?"

"In a way, yes." Andrew lifted her suitcase. "Where would you like me to put this?"

Heat flamed up her neck. She'd been so enamored with the hotel's luxurious decorations that she'd completely forgotten she'd left him with her suitcase. "I'm sorry." She bent to take the suitcase handle from him at the same time he bent to pick up the purse she'd dropped and their foreheads collided.

"Ow." She rubbed her head. "Sorry."

"Sorry," he said at the same time, his gray-blue eyes moving over her face as his thumb brushed across her forehead, sending a tingling sensation through her. Her neck grew hot, reminding her of the way he'd slipped her scarf around it back at the hotel. Man, was it just her or was the room getting hotter by the second? "Are you okay?"

"Yes." She blinked. Did that come out breathless? Stepping back, she needed distance and a distraction from the man whose touch was recalibrating her internal temperature. Trying again, she reached for her suitcase and rolled it to the closet, where she took out the stand. "I'd really like a chance to thank your boss for allowing me to stay here. I would've been happy with any room."

"I can pass along the message."

His tone sounded weird and a flicker of something Frannie couldn't name passed through his eyes as he lifted her suitcase to the stand. Did he feel obligated to hang out with her—she looked at the stunning room she was in, one she could never afford in a million years, and then back to Andrew.

"Look, you really don't have to hang out with me today. I'm sure you have better things to do."

He straightened and met her gaze. "The candy cane scavenger hunt starts after lunch. There's a restaurant downstairs or you can order room service, it's all covered."

Frannie didn't know why but she wanted to take back the permission she gave him to not hang out with her. She didn't know if it was Calvin's engagement post, her co-worker's *concerned* message, or her mom's reminder that she could basically tuck tail and return home, but her emotions were all over the place and left her not wanting to be left alone right now.

Andrew's eyes roamed her face like he could read her thoughts, and his expression softened. "There's something I have to do for work but I promise you I'll be back in time for the scavenger hunt."

There was no reason why his promise should mean so much to her but it did and she couldn't stop her smile. "And ice skating, right?"

The corner of his lips lifted. "Yes, ice skating too."

Nothing in the way he was looking at her now made her feel like he was under obligation and the idea that maybe she could have at least one fun day here in New York City, checking off a few bucket list items, made the world seem right again.

At a quarter past two, Frannie was in her own version of a Hallmark Christmas movie. And it had nothing to do with the sugar high she had from the candy cane scavenger hunt she and Andrew nearly won before considering their under twelve competitors.

Frannie smiled. Bryant Park was more than she imagined.

Positioned in front of the New York Public Library was an ice-skating rink surrounded by the cutest Christmas market. At the front was a giant Christmas tree. Andrew confirmed it wasn't nearly as big as the one at Rockefeller Center but she didn't mind because he also mentioned Rockefeller didn't have a carousel and this area did.

The snow hadn't kept anyone away. New Yorkers and tourists, young and old, were shopping, sipping hot drinks, skating, and with the Christmas music playing overhead, it was hard not to let herself get caught up in the magic of the moment.

Frannie took some photos with her cell phone while Andrew was getting their skates. It wasn't a competition but if Calvin was going to blast his news all over social media, she'd at least have photos to prove she wasn't hiding in her room, mourning a broken heart.

It was strange, but the initial sting of the breakup felt like it was wearing off. She'd replayed Calvin's words over and over, and it was becoming increasingly more embarrassing to admit that maybe he was right. When he'd left for London, he hadn't committed to a long-distance relationship. That was her.

"I've got bad news," Andrew said, walking over without skates. "Ice skating is over for the day." Her disappointment must've been obvious because Andrew quickly waved two tickets. "But, there's bumper tubes."

"What are bumper tubes?"

In answer to her question, a loud cheer erupted around her and she looked to where the Zamboni was tugging a chain of large, brightly colored tubes with a seat in the middle of them. The staff unhooked the tubes and Frannie watched the first round of riders select their tubes. A couple of minutes later, the riders began maneuvering their tubes, bumping into others, sliding across the ice, and spinning in circles.

Next to her, a small group of boys was practically jumping out of their coats, they were so excited.

"What do you think? It's not ice skating but it looks fun. And if you really want to skate, I can take you to Rockefeller."

There was something kind of hopeful in Andrew's voice and there was no denying the way his eyes tracked the riders with restrained boyish excitement. He wanted to do this probably as much as the boys in front of them.

"Let's do it."

The smile on Andrew's face made her heart flutter. They queued up in line for their turn behind the boys, leaning their arms on the rink's wall as they watched the bumper tubes ping-pong back and forth on the ice. She tried really hard not to think about the way her insides were reacting to Andrew's closeness. Or the awareness that it had been a long time since she'd had these skittish feelings around a man.

She rubbed her gloved hands together. It was frigid outside and the layers of clothing she wore didn't seem to be cutting the chill—or helping with her self-confidence. Hard to feel pretty when there were extra inches of thick clothing rounding out her frame.

Not that there was a particular reason she wanted to feel pretty. After grabbing a bowl of soup, the cheapest thing on the restaurant menu at the hotel, Frannie forced herself to recognize that the strange way Andrew made her pulse race was likely due to several complicated factors. The first being, she'd just been dumped. Heartbroken and single were a recipe for a disastrous rebound. Second, the feelings were probably spurred on by the fact that he'd basically rescued her and that kind of heroism led to relationships that only worked in the movies. And lastly—she gave him a sideways glance—he was her brother's friend. Definitely off-limits territory.

Icy wet droplets splattered her face. She looked down to find the boys in front of them swiping their hands against the snow accumulated on the railing, sending it flying at each other. A boy in a red knit cap looked back at her with a mischievous glint in his eyes until they rounded on something behind her.

"You're ..." The boy hit his friend to get his attention.

Frannie turned and saw Andrew standing there, wiping snow off his nose and giving the boys one of those looks that should've been intimidating ... if not for the tiny flakes of snow sitting on his eyelashes.

She might've made a smart comment about his frosted look if the boys, once in front of them, weren't now surrounding ... Andrew?

The boy in the red hat pointed. "You're Andrew Bishop!"

Andrew flashed an appreciative smile at the boys now chanting his name but Frannie saw discomfort as he glanced around at the attention turning in his direction.

"He's The Beast." A boy in a yellow jacket elbowed the first boy. "Andrew 'The Beast' Bishop, right?"

"Hey, guys." Andrew gave the boys high-fives and handshakes. "Keeping your chiclets in place?"

The boys gave him toothy smiles. Frannie eyed Andrew and he gave her an awkward shrug. Who was this guy? A personal bodyguard wouldn't warrant this kind of attention, especially from kids. *And what are chiclets?*

"Can you sign my jacket?" A boy with red cheeks and nose held up his arm. He was wearing a knit cap with a patch that read *Rangers*. "My mom might be mad but my dad will think it's cool."

"How about I find some paper and sign that for you"—the boys erupted into cheers—"*after* our turn on the ice?"

Ahead of them, the line moved and while there was some mumbling, the boys seemed agreeable to the terms and skipped ahead, handing their tickets to the staff member, chatting excitedly about *The Beast*.

"Okay, explain, Mr. Beast."

Andrew walked Frannie forward. "I used to play for the Bandits."

Frannie shrugged. "I have no idea who they are."

Andrew chuckled, handing their tickets over. "It's an NHL team."

Her eyes moved across his broad shoulders, remembering the strength she'd felt against her body the day before. All hard muscle ... except for the soft touch of his hand on her forehead. His gaze locked on hers at that moment and she quickly turned her attention to finding an empty bumper tube.

Andrew reached for her hand and pointed her toward two near the rink wall. He carefully led her across the ice and helped her into her tube.

"We're coming for you, Beast!" The boy in the red hat pointed at his eyes and then at Andrew.

"You're going down, Freckles." Andrew pointed back at him, laughing as the kid bragged to his friends about the Beast giving him a nickname. "I knew that kid was going to be trouble."

Frannie laughed and read the instructions for the controls to operate her tube. Andrew climbed into his and, after a quick seatbelt check, the staff member gave the go. She thrust her joystick forward but her tube began spinning, pressing her body into her seat like she was on the Tilt-A-Whirl at the county fair. She giggled, unable to control the joy bubbling inside of her.

Releasing the joystick, she caught her breath and let her tube come to a stop so she could reorient herself. Andrew was in front of her and waving just as a little girl bumped into his tube. It barely moved him but he crumpled to the side in an act that made the girl laugh.

He started toward her when she caught sight of three tubes aiming for him.

"Bishop!"

Her warning was too late as the three boys rammed their tubes into Andrew's, sending him gliding sideways in a dizzying spin that had her laughing so hard her eyes teared. She wiped at her eyes in time to see she'd somehow become the new target. Grabbing for her controls, she sent her tube backward and accidentally bumped into a grandfather whose glasses slid to the tip of his nose.

"Sorry."

"Get Bishop's girlfriend!"

She turned her head to see the boys closing in but if she moved, they'd hit the grandfather, who was still struggling with his gloves to push his glasses back up. Bracing herself for impact, she was ready to take one for the team when Andrew's tube slipped in at the last second, catching two of the three tubes, causing them to spin sideways and bump into the third one, sending them slipping in different directions.

Andrew flashed a grin at her. "There's a reason I'm called The Beast."

When she narrowed her eyes on him, Andrew's own rounded. "Let's get him, boys."

"Charge!"

It was then that Andrew noticed the three boys had circled back and were coming at him from three sides, and her tube would close in, essentially trapping him. He shook his head and sent a pleading look to Frannie, who smiled innocently before pushing her joystick forward.

All four tubes crashed into Andrew, bouncing everyone around like a pinball machine. Frannie was laughing so hard she began to hiccup. Andrew narrowed his eyes on her in confusion, which only made her laugh harder, happy tears streaming down her cheeks and freezing against her skin. Finally, the horn sounded and everyone's tubes slowly came to a stop.

The boys crowded Andrew's tube as he got out. He told them

something that sent them off the ice as he headed her way. Still hiccupping, Frannie stepped out of her tube but forgot she was still on ice. She started to slip but Andrew was there and weaved his arm around her waist, saving her from a fall.

His firm hold helped her find her balance. "You okay?"

"Yeah, thank you." Her gratitude came out on a puff of air between them. Was her heart pounding because she almost ate it or because Andrew Bishop had his arm around her? She hiccupped and blushed. "I get the hiccups when I laugh too hard."

Keeping his arm around her waist, Andrew walked with her off the ice and toward a bench. "I saw the look in those kids' eyes —I was trying to protect you."

Frannie looked up at him. "It was the look in *your* eyes when we targeted you." Frannie laughed on a hiccup. She looked up at him. "Besides, you protected me yesterday. You're off-duty, Beast."

Her teasing attempt to assure him seemed to float right over him like the smoke spiraling from one of the food kiosks. Andrew's hold tightened on her and his gaze turned pensive. His jaw locking made her wonder what had changed the mood. Why his gray-blue eyes pinged back and forth like the tubes they were just on.

Chapter Fourteen

Heat pulsed hot beneath Andrew's wool coat, making him want to shed it, but how would he explain that to Frannie? *Sorry, but I can't seem to get a grip on the teenage emotions I thought I had outgrown.*

Thankfully, the boys had found them after the bumper tubes, bringing paper and a pen for him to do autographs as he'd promised. It had been more than a year since he'd signed anything for anyone. It wasn't that he hadn't been asked. He'd run into fans occasionally and chatting with them about his time on the ice was fun, but as time passed, it was becoming rare.

"I think you made their year."

"They're good kids." Andrew followed her gaze to where the boys were showing off their copies of his message to each of them. He'd made sure to praise them for their team work on the ice.

"I take it you were pretty good to earn the name Beast."

He gave a shrug. "It was a fun season of life."

Frannie's blue eyes squinted up at him. "How long did you play?"

"A few years."

Her brows scrunched together beneath blonde bangs hanging loose beneath her pink knit cap. She pulled out her cell phone and began typing on it. A second later, her blue eyes flashed up at him and he knew what she was reading.

"According to *USA Hockey Magazine*, you were named one of the NHL's top defensemen. *And* one of hockey's most eligible bachelors."

Her tone was teasing, as was the coy look she was giving him. He pulled off his cap and ran a hand through his hair, unsure which topic he wanted to avoid more, his career in the NHL or the unexpected way he was drawn to the woman sitting next to him.

You're protecting her. It was his job to be drawn to her, to keep her safe.

"Are you hungry?"

Frannie blinked a few times, looking startled by his random question. "I could eat something."

Food was a safe subject. They stood and he led her to the area where several food kiosks were set up. He stopped in front of Dulcinea Churros. "This place is known for their Nutella-filled churros. Or"—he pointed to a popcorn stand across from them—"there's a salty option. And The Lodge"—he pointed to a glass-top building—"has more sustainable choices."

"How badly will you judge me if I confess my belief that cinnamon sugar dough and Nutella seem like sustainable life choices to me?"

Andrew's lips slid into an easy smile. Frannie wasn't like any of the female groupies he'd been surrounded with while in the NHL. While he and his teammates could devour the entire menu at restaurants post-game, the women sipped their calories out of a glass. "No judgment here."

After paying for their Nutella-stuffed churros, Andrew walked Frannie through the holiday market, keeping an eye on her and their surroundings as she browsed the little shops. It was hard not to become distracted by her enthusiasm for all things Christmas in New York, but he still had a job to do.

He was definitely not off-duty.

When he'd left Frannie in her hotel room at The Peninsula earlier, Andrew met with the hotel's security team and was able to track Frannie when she left her room for lunch. Agent Simpkins was able to get the surveillance footage from the bookstore but the angle of the cameras gave them no usable images to run through facial recognition.

So, for now, Andrew was keeping an eye out for a man in a leather jacket.

"How did you and my brother become friends?" Frannie said once she paid for an ornament. "Did you work with him on some secret FBI mission?"

Andrew stepped around a couple walking a German shepherd wearing elf ears. *Poor dog.* "It wasn't a secret mission ..." His attention moved to a man up ahead. He was wearing a leather jacket similar to the one on the man the day before and Andrew's nerves fired up.

Positioning himself closer to Frannie, he barely took notice of the sweet scent of her hair as his assessed the quickest escape route through the crowd.

"You okay?" She glanced up at him and then down to where he'd unconsciously taken hold of her hand.

Andrew tried not to read into the way her eyes sparkled in surprise. Instead, he let his attention flick back to the man who had turned around and—*was not the same guy.*

"Sorry." He released her hand. This wasn't a good idea. If someone was going to physically come after Ms. Malone and had mistakenly identified Frannie as her, bringing her out in public like this wasn't smart.

"So, not a secret mission." Frannie's statement drew his gaze back down to her. Whatever spark he'd seen in those blue eyes had dimmed. "You used to play for the NHL and the admiration in those boys' eyes tells me you had superstar status on the ice but when I asked you about your game, you were humble." She paused in front of another kiosk selling coffee, hot chocolate, mulled wine, and cider. She met his eyes. "Genuinely. So, Andrew Bishop, what's your story?"

He liked the way his name rolled off her lips in that Southern accent and that thought brought his gaze straight to them. *Focus, Bishop.* The words of his childhood hockey coach snapped him back to the woman eyeing him almost suspiciously as she waited for his answer.

"Would you like some coffee?"

A bubble of laughter spilled out of her, but he kept his eyes on hers and found himself enjoying the way her whole face lit up with her smile. "No way you were ever a Fed."

Andrew widened his stance and folded his arms across his chest. He raised an eyebrow. "What makes you say that?"

Frannie stepped into the coffee line. "Your diversion tactics are lacking."

He stared at her, wondering if she'd caught the way he'd been looking at her lips. It couldn't have been longer than a second. Two max.

"What would you like?" Frannie nudged him with her shoulder. "And I'm paying so don't even think about pulling out your wallet, Bishop."

That was the second time she'd called him by his last name and it didn't feel anything like the way it did when his coach or teammates said it.

"I'll take a medium coffee, black." He whipped out his wallet and slapped a twenty on the counter. "And I'll be paying for whatever Frankie is having."

Her gasp was all the confirmation he needed to know he'd

won this round. He smiled, turning, and was met with a glare so teasing there was no way his heart didn't feel the flutterings of flirtation driving his pulse up.

"My brother is the only one who gets away with calling me Frankie."

Her attempt at seething fell short and the mention of her brother refocused his attention back to why Frannie was standing there with him in the first place. *Keep her safe.*

"Frankie!"

The barista called her name and Frannie shook her head. They grabbed their coffees and began walking again, only this time, rather than letting Frannie lead them through another aisle of shops, Andrew led her toward the street, where he could order an Uber.

"Would it be okay if we sat for a minute?"

Frannie didn't wait for his answer and headed toward the table that had just opened up, near the Christmas tree, forcing his decision. At least the giant tree provided coverage on one side. Andrew sat, positioning himself facing out to keep an eye on the remaining open area. He had a job to do. Frannie was part of the job.

"So you worked together?"

Andrew's cell phone chirped with a message. "Excuse me." He pulled it out of his coat pocket. His muscles tightened when he saw the message was from Doug.

> FBI was finally able to get a clean image of the man from the bookstore. Jimmy Strazza. Connected to Adonis family. Did time for aggravated assault with a deadly weapon against a judge. Agent Simpkins is working on locating last known address.

The Adonis family. Andrew didn't need any more details. New York had seen a decline in large-scale activity from organized crime families but the Adonis family was still making headlines for illegal activity, including extortion and the attempt by Angelo Evola on Andrew's life.

Palming his phone, Andrew rose to his feet. "We need to go back to the hotel."

"We do?" Frannie looked up at the Christmas tree. "I was hoping we could wait until it got a little darker so we can see the lights."

The afternoon sky had become darker with the thick cloud cover but Andrew wasn't willing to wait. "No, I should get you back. I don't want you to miss the carolers, remember?"

"Oh yeah." Frannie gathered her coffee and her small shopping bag but instead of walking with him, she headed toward the front of the Christmas tree.

"It'll be easier to pick up the Uber if we cross the street back this way."

"I just want to take another photo of the tree."

Frannie retrieved her cell phone from her coat pocket. She positioned herself, or tried to, for a selfie capturing the tree but from the wrinkle in her nose, she wasn't getting what she wanted.

"Here, let me take it for you." The quicker he helped her get the photo, the quicker he could get her off the street.

"Thanks." She handed him her cell phone, set down her bag, and then moved backward.

Andrew stepped back to get as much of the tree in as he could as she struck a pose, raising her hands in the air. She sent him a million-dollar smile that easily dimmed the beauty of the tree behind her.

He snapped two shots and then moved toward her. "I think those will work."

"Just one more."

Frustration moved through him. "We really should—"

"I need a photo with you." She cut him off and took hold of

his hand, pulling him to her. "My sister-in-law wanted a visual of the man I pepper-sprayed."

Andrew was about to argue that she didn't actually spray him but the words were quickly forgotten when Frannie moved in front of him, pressing her back against his chest so close he was sure she could feel his heart pounding.

"Say cheese, Bishop."

"Cheese Bishop."

Andrew looked at their image on the cell phone reflecting back as Frannie snapped a photo of the two of them smiling, but instead of looking at the camera she'd caught him looking down at her.

"Oh, um, you weren't looking."

Oh, he was looking, all right.

"Do you want to take another one?" Frannie looked up at him. "We could ask someone to take the photo." She lowered her voice. "Unless you think someone would take off with my phone."

"I don't think—" Out of his peripheral, Andrew's gaze locked on a man tucked by some trees, looking in their direction. He moved to the side to try and get a better look but the crowd had grown thicker, filling Bryant Park with tourists and New Yorkers taking advantage of the snow day.

"Something wrong?"

Andrew waited for a break in the crowd but when it came, the man was gone. "We should go."

Leading her toward 42nd Street, Andrew pulled his cell phone out but kept actively searching those walking around him. He checked for the closest Uber ... three minutes away.

"This way." Andrew had started to lead Frannie to the corner of 42nd and 6th when his eyes stopped on a man in a leather jacket. He was too far away to get a good look at the man's face but Andrew wasn't going to stick around for confirmation. "This area is too congested for an Uber to pick us up. Let's walk this way."

Turning them around, Andrew subtly picked up his pace. They moved toward the New York Public Library. It was closed but there were some stores on the other side of 5th Avenue where they could duck inside and wait for another Uber driver.

"Something you should know about me, I'm not really into exercise." Frannie reached for his arm and gave it a little tug. "Can we slow down a little?"

He wanted to tell her no. Tell her that she might be in danger. Tell her—twenty feet back, Andrew's eyes locked on the man before he took a quick side-step out of sight. The distance and the dimming daylight—or maybe his own imagination—might've been playing tricks on him but the man looked eerily similar to Jimmy Strazza.

"Frannie, I need you to stay close to me." *Don't tell her.* Ryan's request seemed stupid right now. Frannie might be in serious danger and that made Ryan's concern about what she could handle matter less than Andrew's promise to keep her safe. "I think someone is following us."

"What?"

She tried to look over her shoulder but Andrew slipped his arm around her waist and pulled her into his side, catching the top of her head with his lips. The touch sent a sizzling zip through him but he ignored it.

"Just keep walking and if I ask you to do something, I want you to do it, no matter what." He glanced down and hated the fear he saw on her face. "Okay?"

Frannie hesitated but then pressed her lips together and gave a nod before pressing herself deeper into the crook of his arm.

With a quick look over his shoulder, Andrew couldn't see the man anymore. Had he been mistaken like he had earlier? He was about to convince himself he was being jumpy when movement ahead of him drew his eyes to three men who looked the sort to hang out with guys like Jimmy Strazza and they were heading straight toward them.

As he pulled up short, Frannie stepped on his foot at his sudden stop. Looking back, he saw the man in the leather jacket had reappeared. They were closing in on them.

"This way." Andrew pushed through the crowd on their right and circled back toward Bryant Park. He'd seen at least three police officers there. It was unlikely Jimmy Strazza would try anything with police there but if he was brave enough, it would at least even the odds some.

"Who is it?"

Frannie's voice sounded shaky, and he hated that he had done this to her. In front of them, the number of people doubled. The sight of families with children made him instantly regret his decision to bring the danger back this way.

Maybe if Andrew could lose them, Jimmy and his thugs would catch sight of the NYPD and make the wise choice to back down. Without a second option, Andrew kept Frannie tucked next to him and walked her toward the congested shopping area.

With a final look behind him, Andrew saw that Strazza was just far enough this could work but Andrew would have to be quick and Frannie would have to trust him.

"Where are we—"

Before Frannie could finish her question, Andrew spun her up against his chest and pushed her three steps backward and into the narrow gap between Santa's Workshop and North Pole Nordicwear.

It was just big enough for the two of them with Frannie pressed up against him, her cheek and palms resting on his chest. His arms wrapped protectively around her as long strands of garland provided just enough cover from shoppers as they passed by.

Andrew felt like they were both holding their breath, his heart ticking off the seconds until the man he'd identified as Jimmy Strazza walked past. Except ... Andrew's forehead creased. It couldn't be.

"What do we do now?" Her warm whisper reached the base of his neck.

"I need you to stay here for a second." He maneuvered out of the tight space. "I need to check something."

"I don't want to stay here by myself."

"Just two minutes. I won't be far."

Andrew stepped into the fray, looking left and then right for the man. It didn't take long before he spotted him at the ornament store Frannie had shopped at. He wasn't more than ten feet away when Andrew realized his mistake at the same time the man looked directly at him.

"That's the guy." The man pointing at Andrew wasn't Jimmy Strazza. He took a bag from the confused salesclerk and walked over. "I was trying to find you. My wife saw your girlfriend leave this on the ground by the Christmas tree when you were taking a photo. I tried to follow you but then I lost you in the crowd."

"Thanks." Andrew accepted the bag with Frannie's ornament. "Sorry for the trouble."

"No trouble at all." The man smiled. "Merry Christmas."

"Merry Christmas," Andrew replied.

"Oh, Bishop."

He turned to find Frannie standing near the space he'd just squeezed the two of them into for apparently no good reason. Her hip was jutted to the side, arms folded, and chin tipped up.

"You've got so much explaining to do."

Boy, did he.

Chapter Fifteen

Something has changed.

Frannie didn't know if it was her teasing remark but the man she'd watched engaging with the boys, laughing on the bumper tubes, and giving her the kind of looks that reminded her what she'd been missing from Calvin—was not the same man who'd just escorted her back to her hotel.

She wasn't sure what to make of the guarded expression on his face except to note that the only time she'd caught it slip was when they were pressed together hiding from the man trying to return her forgotten bag.

At first, she was confused and a little scared, bringing up the memory of the man from the bookstore, but when it turned out to be nothing, she couldn't help but find the humor in the whole situation. But Andrew's tight expression on the Uber ride back to the hotel said his reaction to the unknown man wasn't a joke and it left her dying to know what was going on in his head. Why had he reacted the way he did? What had Andrew so rattled about someone trying to do a good deed? On the surface it seemed innocent but maybe with Andrew's background in personal protection, his instinct went to the worst-case scenario.

Just like my brother.

"Pardon?" Andrew paused to let Frannie enter the hotel ahead of him.

Had she said that out loud? She gave him a half-smile before walking into The Peninsula, and once again her breath was captured by the beautiful décor. The ornaments shimmered against the twinkling lights adorning the Christmas trees that had to be more than twenty feet tall. Huge swaths of garland hung from the railing and banisters, making the ornately designed lobby feel even more magical.

"Do you think we made it in time for the carolers?"

Andrew pointed at a sign near the Sweet Shoppe that said due to the weather the carolers were cancelled for the evening.

Frannie frowned. "Oh, that stinks."

And she felt that sentiment down to her bones. Especially when Andrew started for the elevators. She didn't want the day to end, or maybe she didn't want Andrew to leave. Or maybe she just really wanted to know more about the man sending her head on a seesaw of feelings she wasn't quite sure what to do with. It was wrong to be entertaining thoughts of Andrew when she'd just gotten out of a relationship with Calvin less than forty-eight hours ago, right? Although, technically, Calvin had checked out of their relationship more than a year ago and so really she'd been in a pseudo relationship with herself.

Oh, how pitiful is that?

Was that why she wasn't lamenting over Calvin's engagement? Sure, she cried this morning but was it because of love lost or because she didn't want to face the gossip back in Georgia? Something in her gut told her she knew the answer, but she wasn't ready to admit it.

And despite the lingering current left pulsing through her

from being wrapped up in Andrew's protective embrace, her heart was probably just desperate to feel the affection she'd been missing from her ex.

"You don't have to walk me to my room."

Andrew looked over his shoulder before stepping onto the elevator. "It's no problem."

Except it felt like a problem. Like she was a problem. *Ryan set this up.* He asked Andrew to do him a favor and that's all this was.

"Thanks for taking me to Bryant Park," Frannie said when they got to her floor. "It really was a great way to spend my day stuck in the city."

"Have you heard back from the airline?"

"Oh." She'd completely forgotten. Pulling out her phone, she cringed. "I missed their call."

"If you let me know what time they reschedule your flight, I'll make sure you get to the airport."

Unexpected disappointment weighed her steps. She was sure Andrew's offer to get her to the airport was out of kindness ... so why did it sound like he was in a hurry to be rid of her?

The side of Andrew's body brushed against hers when she swiped her room key and unlocked the door. He leaned around her so that his arm reached across the door, holding it open for her. His lips tilted into a smile that could melt chocolate. "And you won't need the pepper spray since you know me now."

And just like that, the flirty dip in his tone wiped away her reluctance to believe Andrew wasn't upset with her. She stepped into her room, her eyes widening. "Oh, look at that."

The hotel staff had come in for a turn-down service and the Christmas tree sparkled against the backdrop of New York City's darkening sky. On her pillow was a narrow rectangular box of Godiva holiday truffles. And the television had been turned on to a scene with a crackling fireplace.

Frannie inhaled and spun to face Andrew, who stood just inside the threshold of her room. "Is it me or does my room smell like gingerbread?"

"I'm not sure I know what gingerbread smells like."

Shedding her coat, Frannie breathed in the sweet and spicy scent. "It's how I imagine Santa's kitchen would smell."

A smile broke free on Andrew's face. "You believe in Santa?"

"You don't?"

"I got socks and batteries in my stocking every year."

Frannie pressed her lips together to keep from laughing. "How naughty were you as a child?"

His smile widened. "More than I care to admit."

"That sounds like me. My brother was the saint up until he hacked himself into the sights of the CIA."

Andrew's eyes widened. "He what?"

"You didn't know Ryan's a computer genius?"

Andrew rubbed the back of his neck. "I don't know much about your brother outside of his job in the FBI."

"Which reminds me that you haven't explained how you know my brother."

When Andrew shifted on his heels, a thread of tension spread between them that she couldn't quite understand ... unless ... Was the reason why Andrew wasn't forthcoming with an explanation because at the end of the day, he was just here as a favor to Ryan?

Of course that was the only reason. A favor. Nothing else. This man no doubt made millions on the ice. He could have his pick of women. Probably HAD his pick of women. Which made her wonder how he even saw her. A small-town girl who was pathetically needy after a breakup? But then ... the way she'd caught him looking at her. Or how he found ways to touch her. She could have sworn his gaze dipped to her lips at the ice rink. Maybe she was imagining it. She braved a glance his way. Or maybe not. Because his gray-blue eyes locked her in his intense sights and her breath cinched in her chest. The roar of the television fire had nothing on what was crackling between them.

Then as if in a trance, Andrew blinked. "Hey, are you okay?" He was at her side in three quick steps. His gaze softened on her. "I'm really sorry about today. I didn't mean to frighten you."

"Oh, it's not that at all." She walked over to her bed, picked up the box of chocolates from her pillow, and made quick work of opening the box. Maybe if she stuffed her mouth full of truffles, she wouldn't have to face the fact that today had been what she'd wanted with Calvin—minus the near scare, but even that would've had them laughing. *Kissing.*

Stop. She needed to stop making more out of a relationship that had ceased existing right under her nose. Setting the box of chocolates down, she went to the desk and picked up her bucket list and a pen. She crossed off *ice skating* and wrote down *bumper tubing* and then put a check mark next to it. Her throat tightened with unexpected emotion. This should've felt good but instead it left her feeling disappointed.

"Frannie?" His tender tone pulled her gaze up to meet his. "What is it?"

She exhaled, frustrated with herself. "It's nothing. I'm just feeling sorry for myself." She picked up the chocolate again, ready to drown her pathetic sorrows in the indulgent treat. "And frustrated that after what was an amazing day, I'm still thinking about what a fool I was for being blinded by some romantic notion I had with a guy for an entire year that, just like Santa, was pretty much a figment of my imagination." Her fingers fumbled with the wrapper until she gave up and tossed it aside.

Andrew was kind enough to keep his expression neutral as she unleashed her crazy. He removed his gloves, picked up the discarded piece of chocolate, and carefully unwrapped it, handing it back to her.

"Sorry." She bit into the chocolate. "It's been a strange and emotional couple of days."

"Part of that is my fault." He walked over. "I ruined your day today and you deserve an explanation for why."

Frannie suddenly wanted to take back her request for an explanation. She didn't know the extent of Ryan's work with the FBI but when he was a deputy in Walton, she witnessed what he was required to do in the line of duty. It didn't feel right to ask Andrew to explain anything.

"You really don't have to explain. I'm sure your job puts you on edge."

"It does." He inhaled and then led her to sit on the couch. He removed his jacket and set it on his knee. "I told you I played for the NHL. I was a defenseman for the Buffalo Bandits and three years ago our team was in the Stanley Cup final. My job as a defenseman is to keep the other team from reaching the goalie to score. We were down to the last seconds in the game and I should've been watching, should've been prepared for the hit, but I turned and didn't see it coming until it was too late. Roman Jágr was like a bull but his hit felt like what I'd imagined getting plowed by a semi-truck might feel like." Frannie shuddered at the thought. "As soon as I hit the ice, I knew my career was done but the pain of that was nothing compared to watching my teammate Dan Spencer get blindsided. He had to be taken off the ice on a stretcher. We found out later he had spinal damage that ended his career that night too."

"Oh, Andrew, I'm so sorry." She touched his hand but then second-guessed her decision, but before she could pull back, his fingers wrapped around hers. "Is that why you don't like talking about your career?"

"Partly, yeah." It looked like it pained him to admit it. "It was the worst feeling in the world to know I should've been paying attention, defended my position, but I made a mistake." His focus turned on her. "I met your brother because my mistake didn't just cost the Bandits two players; it cost us the championship. I was accused of throwing the game, which had been heavily gambled on, and started receiving threats. A man named Angelo Evola was a bookie who hedged bets for some pretty dangerous people. He came after me and threatened to kill me if I didn't give him the money to pay off his debt."

Frannie's eyes rounded. She couldn't help it. This was like an episode of *Law & Order*. "What happened next?"

"The FBI, including your brother, were already investigating Angelo Evola and when he hired an undercover agent to kill me, they stepped in, but not before Angelo hedged his own bet by hiring a second hitman. Your brother intercepted the final message, sending the hitman to a location where the FBI and NYPD were waiting for him. Ryan saved my life."

"Wow." Frannie leaned back into the couch, careful not to disturb the hand still wrapped in Andrew's tender grip. "I don't always think about the danger Ryan puts himself in doing his job but I'm glad he was there."

Andrew squeezed her hand and then released it. "Me too." He stood and picked up his coat. "So, today, at Bryant Park I thought I saw someone who's worked with Angelo and I ..." He pressed his lips together. "I guess after what happened to you at the bookstore, I overreacted."

"It's completely understandable."

Frannie stood and rubbed her arm. She didn't want him to leave. Not yet. The day had started off so good and now it was ending on this heaviness that didn't feel Christmasy at all. Next to the television was a piece of paper with a list of the evening's Christmas movies and which channel they were playing on.

"Do you want to stay?" she said quickly and then pointed to the movie schedule. "To watch Christmas movies with me?" His expression told her he was about to give her an excuse. "Just one, please. And I'll order us dinner. It's the least I can do for forcing you to spend the day with me."

"Frannie, stop." His gentle tone pushed her eyes to meet his. "You didn't force me to do anything. Today was a lot of fun. More fun than I've had in a long time and if you'll forgive me for my lapse in professionalism ..." He hesitated, and she thought she caught his eyes drift to her lips for a split second before he continued. "I'd be happy to watch a Christmas movie with you."

"Really?"

"Yes." He frowned. "Unless you're going to subject me to a Hallmark Christmas movie. Then I'm gonna split."

Frannie wrinkled her nose. "Definitely not Hallmark."

His brow lifted as he eyed her suspiciously. "You're not into movies with plaid-wearing men who quit their jobs in the city to take over the family Christmas tree farm and help the granddaughter of the town's only baker who he used to have a crush on but now has to convince his old boss not to tear it down or the children's home will be shut down right before Christmas?"

Now it was her turn to eye him suspiciously. "You're sure you don't prefer Hallmark movies? You seem to know a lot about their plots."

"Same plot. Same issues. Sometimes same characters."

Frannie laughed. "I can't argue that but I actually prefer men who live on the dangerous side, have a gripping backstory, and are willing to put themselves into tight spots to protect the ones they love."

Andrew's body stilled, gray-blue eyes locked on her for what felt like the longest second in her life before she smiled.

"And nothing puts me in the holiday spirit faster than Bruce Willis facing off with Hans Gruber."

A spark lit Andrew's eyes before he tossed his head back in a low chuckle that instantly brightened the mood. She enjoyed the sound of it and was happy to ease some of the tension she'd seen him carrying.

Frannie tossed him the remote control. "*Die Hard* is on channel nine or you can pick something else so long as the man's not wearing flannel and there's no Christmas tree farm, inn, or bakery being rescued." She looked up nearby restaurants on her cell phone. "Do you think places will still deliver with the weather?"

Andrew sent her a look. "It's New York." He held up his own cell phone. "But I've got it. You call the airline back and I'll get us dinner." He sent her a hard stare when she opened her mouth to object. "You're in my town and"—he leaned over the table and picked up her bucket list—"I'm helping you cross off *eat authentic New York–style pizza, the kind only locals know about.*"

"Fine, but I'm paying." This time she sent him a hard stare but instead of intimidating Andrew like she'd hoped, it only caused something to flicker in the depths of his eyes that caused a delicious shiver to dance down her spine.

Yes, *Die Hard* was the absolute best choice. No chance for romantic notions to stir while John McLane picked off the terrorists in Nakatomi Plaza one by one.

Chapter Sixteen

Andrew made quick work of ordering a pizza from Geno's and then sent another message to the Defensemen group. He'd sent one in the Uber on the ride back from Bryant Park asking for the FBI's status on locating Jimmy Strazza but all he got back was "**They're working on it**."

He glanced over to where Frannie was talking to someone at the airline She was staring out the window, which gave him the opportunity to figure out what he was doing. He didn't need to stay here to keep an eye on her. He could easily slip into The Peninsula's security office and monitor Frannie's safety from behind a bank of television screens and the hundreds of security cameras around the hotel.

Guests needed a hotel key to access the hotel floors but if someone wanted to get to Frannie bad enough, they'd find a way. He prayed that wasn't going to be the case. He prayed that his jumpy behavior that had them squished together in a less-than-appropriate way for two people who just met was due to an overactive imagination on his part.

But was it overactive? Sure, the man he'd seen following him and Frannie did have a similar build to the guy in the leather jacket, but what about the other three men? Doug had always told them to trust their gut when it came to personal protection. The body's innate sense of danger was rarely wrong ... except today.

And even though Andrew didn't hate the feeling of her body next to his, or the way her touch stoked a fire in him, his mistake didn't lend to professionalism.

Andrew dropped his gaze to his cell phone again. He really needed the FBI to figure out who was behind the threat to the Malones and whether the Adonis family was involved.

"I'm stuck here until Monday." Frannie plopped down on the couch and sighed.

There was a buzzing noise in his ears. "You're not leaving tomorrow?" She looked up at him and he saw a flicker of hurt in her eyes, which he immediately regretted causing. "Is the airport expected to be closed tomorrow?"

"No." Her expression cleared. "I just don't carry enough status to warrant the first available flight to D.C., and since I missed the call earlier, they filled all of the available seats for Sunday and the next available isn't until Monday night."

"Oh man, I'm sorry." Andrew moved next to her, careful to keep a respectable distance between them. His fingers still tingled from the way she'd reached out to comfort him earlier, but he needed to keep the line securely drawn in the sand ... er, rather the snow. "You don't need to worry about a place to stay. Your reservation here is for as long as you need it."

"It doesn't feel right. This place is expensive and—"

"And nothing, Frannie. You're staying here and tomorrow we're going to see about checking off more of your bucket list."

Her eyes lit up. "Wait, really?"

There wasn't much of a choice on his part but even if there were, in this moment, the way she was looking at him, he was certain he'd be unwilling to tell her no. "What's next on your list?"

Frannie reached to pick up the bucket list, and moved in close to his side, and he had to stop himself from reading into the way his insides came alive at her closeness. Her mood had certainly lifted and maybe it was arrogant on his part but there was no denying the pleasure it gave him to be the one to bring back her joy.

"Okay, so I originally scheduled these activities for the entire week but, um"—her voice lowered—"I guess I'll just pick the things I want to do most and, uh—" Her fingers covered the bottom of the page, but not before Andrew read what was there.

Christmas tree kiss.

It was just the reminder he needed to put an end to whatever unwise feelings he'd allowed to fill his brain. Frannie had just gotten out of a relationship. Unexpectedly. He had no idea why except that whoever she'd been dating had to be three screws loose in the head to let her go. And that was his opinion after only a couple of days.

"What about Santa Claus?"

He raised his brows. "Santa Claus?"

"At Macy's." Frannie tugged her lower lip between her teeth. "And then there's the holiday train."

Andrew had lived here for the better part of five years and could count on three fingers the number of Christmas-related activities he'd done and then only because his mom and dad came into town. "Are you talking like *Polar Express?* Because I'm not really the wear-pajamas-in-public kind of guy."

Frannie's nose wrinkled with her smile. "Not the Polar Express. These are vintage trains from the New York Transit Museum that only get put on the rails once a year for Christmas and they're decorated with wreaths and ribbons. No one will be wearing pajamas and not everyone dresses up, but some people do wear period clothing from the era."

"Are you?"

She hesitated but he could see the sparkle in her eye that said she was all-in before she even nodded. "Yes!"

"Well, then I guess we're going on a train ride tomorrow after we visit the North Pole."

"Yay!" Frannie clapped and then wrapped her arms around him in a quick hug that surprised him, and from the doe-eyed expression she gave him when she released him, it had surprised her as well. "Sorry. Sometimes my exuberance gets the better of me."

"Exuberance is good." *Especially if it results in that kind of physical contact.* That thought was just the kind to get him put on Santa's naughty list. "The world could use more exuberance."

That put a sparkle in her eyes and Andrew forced himself to look away. "Pizza is on its way. I'm going to find a vending machine and grab some drinks. What's your preference?"

"Sprite if they have it or a Coke."

"I'll be back." Andrew slipped out of Frannie's room and rested his back against the wall. He was simply doing his job. She was stuck in the city Sunday and half of Monday now. Just another day and a half, which meant he needed to be here with her. "Keep telling yourself it's just a job."

His voice echoed back at him in the empty hallway, and he pushed off the wall and headed toward the alcove with a vending machine and ice maker, repeating the words with the hope they'd keep his focus where it needed to be.

It shouldn't be too hard, right? *Die Hard* was a safe Christmas movie. Nothing romantic about Bruce Willis killing terrorists, right? Or visiting Santa with dozens of parents forcing their kids to smile while sitting on a stranger's lap—torture for all involved. And a train ride passing by the best of New York City's graffiti art, no matter how many wreaths and ribbons you put on it, certainly didn't stoke the flames of passion.

Nope, nothing romantic here at all.

Spending the day with Frannie tomorrow was going to be just fine.

WHEN ANDREW LEFT Frannie's room after the movie, he went straight to the elevator but kept his pace slow enough to make sure he heard her door close and the bolt latch. When he did, he released a long breath. At the elevator he pressed the button for the second floor, where the security offices were and where he'd wait for Mac to take over and keep an extra eye on Frannie so he could get some sleep. After his overreaction earlier that day, he needed the rest to be on his game for tomorrow.

Showing his ID, he entered the office and was introduced to two other security officers, Milo and Bart, both of whom were older than he was by at least twenty years and didn't seem put out by his presence. Neither man seemed all that interested in why he was there and left him to an empty chair behind a desk with a view of the screens.

Andrew settled in, his attention focused on the cameras watching the hallway of the twelfth floor. Pulling out his cell phone, he sent a message to Doug updating him on Frannie's flight. He started a message to Ryan, wanting to update him just in case Frannie decided to spill the details of their day. Would she tell him about the guy *following* them? Or about Andrew pulling her into a tight space where their bodies were so close he was sure he would've heard her heart beating if his hadn't been pounding louder?

Sisters didn't tell brothers those kinds of details ... did they?

His pulse jumped beneath his skin. If Frannie did tell Ryan

everything and Andrew excluded that little detail, Ryan would pick up on it and he had no idea how he might react.

The phone in the office rang and Milo answered it.

Focus, Bishop.

Andrew started his text again but was interrupted when Milo called over.

"Your partner is here." Milo pointed to a screen that showed the inside of an elevator and Andrew recognized his Defensemen colleague Mac riding up.

When Mac got to the door, Andrew let him in and gave a quick introduction before leading him to a small room off to the side that served as a break room. There was a Nespresso machine, snacks, a refrigerator, microwave, small table with chairs, and a couch. A large television screen mounted on the wall was divided into grids, giving them a visual on all of the surveillance cameras, including the twelfth floor once he set the screen to it.

"Amanda wants me to make sure you get some sleep."

Andrew had a courier bring his overnight bag to the hotel for him while he was with Frannie. The security manager also gave him the key to a much more understated guest room than Frannie's and Andrew was certain Doug or Mr. Malone was behind the accommodations.

"I'll be fine for a few more hours," he said to Mac now.

Mac nodded. "Amanda said you'd say that and told me to warn you that she would pull you from your next two assignments if you complain."

"What she doesn't know won't hurt me."

Mac lifted a blonde brow in a look that said exactly what Andrew already knew—Amanda would know. "I have some news on the Malones."

That grabbed his attention. "Have they figured out who's behind the ransomware attack?"

"No." Mac shook his head. "They're insisting Mr. Malone

not go through with the investment in Hope Village and if he does they will release all of Kline Capital's financial information for their clients. They have not claimed responsibility for the attempted attack on who they believed was Ms. Malone but Gerald Kline, Mr. Malone's partner and Valentina's great uncle, reported that he too received a threat of physical harm so the FBI believes they're connected."

The band between Andrew's shoulders tightened. "Which means, Frannie's still in danger of being mistaken for Valentina Malone."

"It's strange." Mac sat on the couch, elbows on his knees. "You'd think someone skilled enough to send out a ransomware that has the FBI scratching their heads would be wise enough to know they went after the wrong girl."

"I doubt they're personally involved in the attack." Andrew paced the small room. "I don't know much about hackers or tech terrorists, but I don't think they're the kind to get their hands dirty."

"Doug agrees with you. The FBI haven't figured out how Jimmy Strazza's connected to Kline Capital. Might just be a fast-paying job and Strazza got the call."

"That doesn't make me feel better." Andrew blew out a breath. "What about Mr. Malone? Is he going through with this deal?"

"As far as I can tell, yeah. He doesn't seem like the kind that bows under pressure or threats."

Andrew didn't get that impression either but for the safety of his daughter—for Frannie—if they could make the case that this threat was serious, maybe he could postpone the deal?

"Doug said Gerald Kline is arriving tomorrow evening for Monday's meeting and wants to hire us to protect him as well."

"Do we have the manpower?" Their small agency was already stretched with him having to keep an eye on Frannie.

"Amanda's calling in some favors. Brayden's busy with another client, so Oskar and Doug will remain with Mr. Malone, you and I maintain watch on Frannie, and Joey's stuck with the heiress." He released a humorless chuckle. "He's convinced he's being put through some sort of hazing initiation."

"Because being stuck in the penthouse at the Waldorf is terrible?"

"It's not the White House but ..." Mac grinned. "Let's just say Ms. Malone has been testing Joey's patience with her demands."

Andrew groaned. He'd worked with his fair share of divas. "One of those, huh?"

"Oh worse, man, so much worse. She asked Joey to find her alkaline water at exactly twenty-one degrees because that's what Beyoncé drinks."

"What's alkaline water?"

"No idea." Mac shrugged. "All I can say is that I'd rather stay up all night watching nothing happen here than put up with that." He looked at Andrew. "How's your day been? Boring, I hope."

Andrew swallowed and averted his attention back to the screen. Boring in their world was a good thing. It meant everything was going smoothly—according to plan. But given the way the last several hours spent with Frannie had turned him inside out, *boring* was not how he'd describe it at all.

"She's not asking for alkaline water."

"Lucky you," Mac said before joining Milo and Bart.

Andrew threaded his fingers behind his neck and squeezed his eyes shut for a second. Frannie wasn't asking for alkaline water but if she did—he'd find a way to get it to her.

Chapter Seventeen

Frannie snuggled beneath the luxurious covers for as long as she could before forcing herself out of bed. It wasn't that hard. Her room still smelled of gingerbread, the Christmas tree twinkled, and she'd slept as soundly as a Who in Whoville on Christmas Eve.

Okay, that's a little too dorky even for me. She sipped her coffee—this hotel had one of those fancy Nespresso machines and even had holiday flavors—from which she chose peppermint—and smiled to herself.

This was the life.

After a quick call to both her mom and Vivian, Frannie gave them her updated flight information and confirmed she was fine and living like Eloise, the precocious little girl from one of her favorite childhood books. Except she wasn't at the Plaza and she was not causing mischief.

At least not on her part—she smiled again. She really shouldn't find the incident yesterday so humorous, especially after what Andrew told her about his past. His instincts to protect her were both appealing and comforting. And not in the way Ryan was protective.

Frannie wrinkled her nose, not wanting to put Ryan and Andrew in the same category. Although ... maybe if she did, she'd have a better chance of keeping her mind from wandering to places it shouldn't go.

Checking the bedside clock, Frannie finished her coffee. She had just enough time to shower, dry her hair, and get dressed for her day with Andrew.

Andrew.

Her brother's friend.

A man who protected her. Twice.

She'd count the second time even if it wasn't a real threat.

A man who had a great smile and was going out of his way to make sure she checked off some items on her bucket list, even if that meant taking her to see Santa Claus.

Frannie turned on the shower and smiled once more. Today was going to be fun.

Just before ten, Frannie heard the knock on the door and she forced herself not to squeal like Buddy the Elf, only instead of saying "Santa is here!" she was thinking "Andrew is here!"

She gave herself a final look in the mirror, feeling nervous at her reflection. Today's outfit required months of searching vintage shops online but it was worth it when she found a rose-colored shirtwaist dress made of corduroy that paired beautifully with her grandmother's cornflower-blue belted wool coat. She'd even chosen a darker shade of lip gloss to give her lips a pop.

On second thought, she quickly grabbed a tissue from the bathroom and wiped her lips. Maybe this was a little over the top? Andrew knocked on the door again. Her lips were still a shade darker than natural but she was out of time.

Opening the door, she saw Andrew's eyes widen and then skim over her outfit before meeting her gaze. Her cheeks warmed but was it from embarrassment at her decision to go vintage or from the appreciative look he was giving her?

"Wow." He gave her another once-over. "You look—"

"Silly?" she supplied. There was still time, she could change.

"Like you stepped out of a movie."

Well, that wasn't exactly a compliment. Frannie took a step back. "I wasn't sure if we'd have time to come back here to change for the train and ... just give me a minute and I'll put something else on."

She started to let the door close but Andrew's palm landed on it. "No." He tipped his chin, looking into her face. "I mean, you don't need to change. I like what you're wearing, I think it's lovely."

Relief washed through her and she couldn't help but smile at the awkwardness of his compliment. The last person she remembered using a word like *lovely* to compliment a woman was her grandfather to her grandmother but she'd take it.

Frannie spent the next twenty minutes in the Uber running her palms down the dress, making small talk with Andrew that felt stiff and unlike their easy conversation the night before. Was it her? Was it him? Was she reading into this? Was she still thinking about his *lovely* compliment? Yes, yes, she certainly was but that was partly Andrew's fault because in the back seat of this Prius it was impossible not to inhale the woodsy scent of his cologne that had her wondering how he would look in a plaid shirt.

In between small talk about how she slept, if she had breakfast, how Georgia would've shut down for weeks if they'd seen this much snow, Frannie was trying to make sense of her feelings.

This felt like one of those teenage crushes she'd heard friends talk about when they liked the friend of an older brother. Unfortunately for Frannie, Ryan maintained high-level nerd status, which left her very few options when it came to crushing on his friends. She was not into late-night chats about castles, or dragons, or who the next tech genius might be.

But a late night watching a Bruce Willis flick with a former NHL superstar who is pretty much an action hero himself ...

Frannie's cheeks warmed, and she stared out the window to keep Andrew from noticing. After he'd left her room last night, she did a little internet digging and found plenty of articles about Andrew's career in the NHL and the headlining story that followed the devastating incident at the championship game. Her heart ached for all that Andrew had lost in his career while simultaneously crushing on the man who—from the dozens and dozens of photos she browsed through—didn't seem to take a bad photo.

But crushes were nothing more than brief, unattainable, or inappropriate feelings for someone. She'd looked up the definition because it didn't feel right to be having feelings for someone so soon after her breakup. There had to be an explanation for why her heart seemed open to the possibility of getting hurt all over again. Which was what would happen here, right?

"We're here."

Frannie's focus moved from the question she didn't want to answer and up the side of the Macy's flagship store on 34th Street. The first-floor exterior was covered in thousands of white lights while giant wreaths hung in smaller windows over the larger window displays. A large, brass clock was displayed over the entrance, where a huge reindeer sat in a field of snow mounds and pine trees.

"It's magical," she whispered, getting out of the car.

. . .

Andrew held out his elbow and Frannie slipped her hand into it as they walked inside the department store. She was a writing tutor, helping her students pen descriptive stories and here she was at a loss for the right words to describe how she was feeling at this very moment—protectively tucked into the side of a man who didn't make her feel silly for wanting to dress in her grandmother's old coat to see Santa Claus.

But she didn't have time to dwell on how Andrew was making her feel because the inside of Macy's looked like a twinkling, magical woodland complete with tree stumps and boughs of pine branches covered in lights. Animated forest creatures in scarves and hats peeked down on shoppers. Giant metal orbs circled overhead with different Christmas scenes such as Santa flying his sleigh around New York City or tiny replicas of the balloons from the Macy's Thanksgiving Day Parade marching down the street with words like *believe* and *dream* on them.

Andrew pointed toward the escalator. "This way to Santaland."

"Do you feel silly doing this with me?"

"I've lived in New York for five years and I've never done this before." His smile was genuine and reassuring. "It's kind of cool."

Cool didn't even begin to describe how Frannie felt when she walked through the store toward Santaland. The high-decibel sound of children laughing, talking, and some crying, filled the air but it didn't diminish the awe moving through her at the sight of the store transformed into a Christmas village.

A rainbow of lights shimmered around them like the northern lights, there was a choir of snowmen, Santa's sleigh brimming with toys, his workshop, and elves that were really store employees, but they smiled and waved as if this really was the best job in the world.

"This is incredible."

Frannie thought she heard some wonder in Andrew's voice and it delighted her. He might say he wasn't being forced to hang out with her but he was a guy and this probably wasn't the most manly thing to do and she wanted him to at least have fun.

"I love your dress," an elf with red glittery eye shadow said, scanning the reservation barcode Frannie showed her. "Take the lane on the left."

"Thanks." Frannie moved along the pathway with Andrew by her side. "Jisoo would love this."

"Jisoo?"

"My niece. Ryan and Vivian's daughter." Frannie smiled just thinking about her niece. "Do you think we could do a little shopping in the toy department after this?"

"Sure."

Another elf stopped them at the end of the trail and told them Santa was excited to see them in just one minute. Next to her, Frannie noticed a little girl wearing a glittery pink tutu over her pink denim overalls and her shirt had little ballet slippers and ballerinas all over it. She was wearing a pair of purple headphones and was rocking up against her mom and an older lady who looked like grandma.

"You have a cute ballerina."

The mom looked up and smiled. "Thanks. She loves the *Nutcracker* and wanted to show Santa her tutu."

"Oh, has she seen the ballet at Lincoln Center?"

"No." The little girl twisted around and the edge of her tutu caught on one of the posts and the sound of the tear brought a wrinkle to the mother's brow.

Immediately her daughter began to get upset, rocking, as her mom tried to soothe her. The elf manning the line looked confused as the little girl's distress drew the attention of other guests standing in line.

"I'm going to find a spot and see if I can get her to calm

down." The mom slipped out of the line with her daughter in hand. "Can my mom stay in line until we get back?"

The elf, looking unsure of herself, simply nodded.

"Sometimes the stimulation is too much for Kate," her grandmother said, looking apologetic. "My daughter, Kate's mom, was a ballet dancer and used to perform in the *Nutcracker*."

"At Lincoln Center?"

"No, smaller productions outside of the city and in New Jersey but it was her dream." The grandmother looked back to where her daughter and granddaughter had disappeared. "She's the most amazing mom and works so hard to give Kate the best life possible."

The sweet sentiment made Frannie think of her own mom and while Kate's mom was a warrior mom of a different sort, Frannie's mom was also pretty amazing. A pang of guilt rose in Frannie's chest at how embarrassed she'd been of her family situation growing up, and even now, as an adult, she still allowed her father's decision to negatively influence her.

"I have two tickets to the *Nutcracker* for tomorrow night." Frannie pulled out her cell phone. "I won't be able to go but do you think your daughter would use them?"

The grandmother's eyes widened. "What? Those tickets must've cost a fortune and are nearly impossible to get."

Frannie was very much aware of those two facts. It had taken her weeks of monitoring the website and setting alarms to be able to purchase the tickets, but with her flight leaving tomorrow night, they would go to waste.

"I have the tickets here." She held up her phone. "I can text them to you."

The woman's eyes glistened as she pulled out her phone, but then she hesitated. "Are you sure you ..." Her gaze moved between Frannie and Andrew. "Are you sure you and your beau aren't going to use them?"

"I'm sure." Frannie's cheeks warmed and she dared not look at Andrew. "If you give me your number, I'll text you the tickets."

Two minutes later, Frannie had given away her tickets, the grandmother thanking her for giving her daughter the best Christmas gift ever, and was now following an elf to see Santa Claus.

"I hope you've thought about what you're going to ask Santa for," Andrew whispered over her shoulder. "Because you are definitely on the nice list."

Chapter Eighteen

There wasn't supposed to be *anything* romantic about visiting Santa. He was a fat man in a red suit who tempted children to believe he could fly a sleigh with eight tiny reindeer to deliver toys across the planet in one night.

Nothing romantic about it at all.

Except Andrew hadn't been able to keep his heart from pounding against his ribs from the second Frannie walked in to meet the very, in his opinion, realistic Santa perched on a red velvet chair. His white hair and beard were real; even his cheeks were rosy beneath a pair of round golden glasses. But it was Frannie who kept his attention, the sheer joy glowing in her expression as she talked with Santa and then whispered what she wanted for Christmas in his ear—an action that had Andrew ridiculously jealous of the jolly saint.

Frannie radiated this light, an energy that was impossible to ignore. And it had become increasingly clear that he'd underestimated his ability to remain neutral—especially when she gave away her *Nutcracker* tickets.

"Is this really what little girls want to play with?" Frannie held up a doll that was marketed for girls ages three to seven but the doll was all curves, pouty lips, and in a cringe-inducing outfit. "Whatever happened to astronaut Barbie?"

Santaland conveniently exited into Macy's toy department and based on the shrill of whining, he didn't know if it was advantageous to sales or just torture to parents. Probably both.

Andrew pointed to a table of board games and puzzles. "Is she too young for games?"

"She loves to play games."

Frannie browsed through the selection and while she was distracted, Andrew kept a vigil on their surroundings. Mac's update the night before didn't sit well with him and as he tried to obey Amanda's directive to get some rest, he couldn't stop worrying about what could happen today.

He didn't want anything to make the smile on Frannie's face disappear.

"Way to keep it professional, Bishop," he mumbled.

"What?"

"There are, um, books." Andrew walked to a short shelf. "Does Jisoo like to read?"

"I think so. I know Ryan and Vivian read to her." Frannie's eyes sparked. "Oh, look, it's *Eloise at Christmastime*. This is perfect!"

Andrew studied the illustrated cover. "Yeah?"

"Yes. This is about a little girl who lives at The Plaza in New York City and her name is Eloise, which is my middle name. Even though I'm not staying at the same hotel, it'll be fun to show Jisoo photos of The Peninsula as I read her the book. Don't you think?"

Her smile was infectious and it reached deep inside of him. "I think it's perfect."

They spent some more time picking up a few more items before Frannie seemed satisfied that she'd spoiled her niece sufficiently. With bags in hand, they walked through the store and Andrew found it hard not to keep sneaking looks at her.

It was like she'd stepped out of one of those black-and-white films his grandma used to make him and his sister watch. There was always something intriguing about those leading ladies but his eight-year-old self wasn't mature enough to identify the allure of their spark for life—their moxie, as his grandma used to say—as the reason behind the heroes' inability to avoid falling for the dames.

And here Frannie was in her vintage dress, ruby lips, blonde hair falling over her shoulder in waves, her blue eyes flashing up to him beneath dark lashes ... Andrew blinked.

"You didn't hear anything I said, did you?"

Heat climbed his neck. "No, sorry. I was thinking about" —*you*—"my grandma." Frannie's eyes widened and he grimaced. "That came out wrong. I'm thinking of how you look like Trudy O'Connor."

Frannie's brow crinkled. "Trudy O'Connor?"

They walked around a congested area near the cologne section where tourists were taking pictures of the décor overhead. "I was remembering how my grandma used to make my sister and I watch old Christmas movies." He watched her expression soften. "There was one called *It Happened on Fifth Avenue*, and this military veteran gets evicted and befriends a homeless man who is squatting inside of a mansion. It's a good movie, funny, and the heroine is Trudy O'Connor."

"I've never seen it." Frannie paused by a table filled with men's ties. "Is she sassy? I like sassy heroines."

Andrew did too. "Yes."

Her eyebrow lifted in his direction. "Is she unapologetically independent?"

"She is." Why did it feel like Frannie was describing herself?

Frannie lifted a blue tie and held it next to her eyes. "Are her eyes the color of Midwest skies in the summer?"

Andrew moved in, tilting his chin down, and he thought he heard her breath hitch. His breathing felt heavy. *Bishop!* The elongated warning his coach used to practically growl whenever he came close to earning a spot in the penalty box echoed in his head. And just like on the ice, the warning caused him to pull back.

"The movie is in black and white so I can't comment on the color of her eyes but I remember she had a kind heart and my grandmother said—" Andrew stopped. His grandmother had encouraged him to find a woman with a kind heart because kindness was a special sort of beauty. One that grew more radiant with every passing year. He'd had no idea what she meant until now ... and it was *way* too soon to admit these kinds of thoughts or feelings when he barely understood them himself. "Um, I actually can't remember what she said after that but I think you'd like the movie."

Frannie looked like she knew he wasn't being entirely honest. She set the tie down. "I'll add it to my movie bucket list."

"How many bucket lists do you have?"

She paused at the tree rack and began pulling off hats. "A few. *My* grandma always reminded us that life is short. I didn't really believe that until I got older. Ryan was a deputy and he and his now-wife, Vivian, had a pretty close call that opened my eyes to the reality of what my grandma was saying." Her voice dipped, blue eyes darkening with an emotion he couldn't name.

"I'm sure that was scary."

"It was but everything turned out fine. Ryan saved the day. Joined the FBI. Married Vivian." She inhaled, rolled her shoulders back, and the light tone returned to her voice, but it didn't sound natural. "And my whole life is dictated by crime stats, warnings, and cautionary tales to keep me safe and sound in

Walton, which is really ironic when you think about it because Walton is where the whole my-baby-daddy's-wife-wants-to-kill-me-and-anyone-who-tries-to-tell-the-secret-thing went down."

There was no mistaking the sarcasm but he couldn't help the laughter escaping his lips.

She frowned at him. "You think I'm joking but if you compare the population of Walton with New York City and then compare crime stats ..." She bit the inside of her lip and then shook her head. "Well, I can't remember the statistics but it basically proved I'm just as safe here as I am in Walton."

"Your brother really didn't want you to come to New York, did he?"

"No." Frannie held up a gray fedora like she was sizing it up for him. "But I think it was partly because of ..." Her eyes flicked to his. "Did Ryan tell you about my, um, the reason I came here in the first place?"

He didn't want to lie to her but he also didn't want to embarrass her. "All he said was that your trip didn't turn out the way you hoped and he wanted to make sure you were okay."

Frannie picked up a herringbone newsboy cap. "It definitely didn't turn out the way I thought it would but—" She handed Andrew the hat. He started to put it back on the rack but she took it from him and reached up to place it on his head. "My grandma said that sometimes the best moments in life aren't planned or expected."

"I think I'd like your grandma." Her fingers brushed against his temple and his heart twisted against his ribs. "Am I buying a hat?"

"No." She tipped her chin up and adjusted the cap over his brow. "I'm buying you a hat."

"Why?"

"Because I'm dressed for a vintage train ride." She stepped back and appraised his outfit. "The dark jeans aren't exactly vintage but the wool coat—" she ran her hands over his shoulders and down his arms, unknowingly making his chest squeeze—"is timeless and you have the jawline of Jimmy Stewart. The hat pulls it all together."

"If I'm Jimmy Stewart, are you Donna Reed?"

"I can be." She gave him what he could only describe as a flirty smile. "If you lasso the moon for me," she said catching his reference to *It's A Wonderful Life.*

There was supposed to be *nothing* romantic about today. Santa. Shopping. Train ride. He'd left the security office this morning understanding his role: keep an eye on Frannie, protect her, if required, and make sure she made it on her flight tomorrow evening.

An ordinary day on the job, except Frannie was making it extraordinarily hard for him to find reasons why he should ignore the feelings brewing inside of him.

Chapter Nineteen

Andrew used the whole twenty minutes in traffic heading to the F Line on Second Avenue to remind himself of *all* the reasons why acting on the feelings Frannie stirred up in him was a bad idea.

One, she just had her heart broken. Romance 101 made it clear that rebound relationships never work. Two, her brother. Andrew wasn't sure where Ryan stood on his sister's dating life but as a brother himself, he understood the high standard a potential suitor must meet before being offered temporary and revocable permission to date his sister—conditions subject to change at any time. Three, Frannie didn't live in New York. This felt like a minor issue compared to the first two, but he'd tried long-distance once when he moved to New York to play hockey. His ex-girlfriend wasn't willing to leave Michigan or her family or accept that the only photos paparazzi liked to publish were the ones that stirred up gossip.

Andrew didn't blame her. Even he was shocked at the headlines accompanying his image. Their breakup was mutual, amicable even, and it freed him up to focus solely on hockey.

Which worked out fine until he watched his teammates with their families before games, getting hugs and kisses from their wives and children, celebrating wins that seemed so much sweeter with their loved ones next to them.

Andrew sent a side-look at Frannie. It didn't take his brain long to imagine her smile, her cheers, and the feel of her arms wrapped around him at the edge of a hockey rink.

"We're here!"

The Uber pulled to a stop in front of the steps leading down to the F Line train. Andrew got out and checked his surroundings before offering his hand to Frannie. He carried her shopping bags as they descended the stairs and Andrew was shocked at the number of people waiting for the train. And even more surprised by how many were wearing vintage attire like Frannie.

"That man is wearing a top hat, a monocle, and has a cane."

"I know," Frannie whisper-squealed. "He looks like a young Teddy Roosevelt."

The overhead speaker crackled to life and an announcement was made for the approaching holiday train. Passengers cheered and clapped. Frannie rose up on her tiptoes, trying to get a peek but her small stature was no match for the crowd—or their hats.

Taking her hand, he led her down the track a bit until he found an open spot. They made it just in time to see the dark green train screech to a stop. A wreath with red ribbons was mounted to the front and on the side *City of New York* was written in gold lettering. When the conductor stepped out, he was wearing period clothing that immediately had Andrew thinking of the Polar Express.

Frannie handed him a ticket and they moved to board the train. Andrew's insides stirred with a strange sensation. This ticket was supposed to be for someone else. Everything they were doing together ... she was meant to do with someone else.

"Ticket, sir?"

Andrew handed the conductor his ticket and then followed Frannie to an open seat. Her face glowed with excitement. Did it bother her that he was here instead of her ex? A part of him felt a pinch of jealousy that she might be thinking of him in this moment.

The conductor announced their departure and soon the train vibrated with movement as it pulled out of the station. Christmas music played on the speakers and passengers took selfies and photos, their voices full of excitement.

A couple, somewhere in their upper seventies or maybe older, sat on the wooden bench seat across from them. The old man rested a cane against his knee, one age-spotted hand on it and the other holding onto the hand of the woman next to him. She smiled up at him beneath a velvet hat with a flower on the side of it.

"I like your hat." Frannie had to speak up over the chatter and train sounds. "It's lovely."

"Thank you." The woman's rheumy gaze moved between Frannie and Andrew. "Are you two local? Or tourists?"

"I'm a tourist." Frannie's shoulder leaned into his. "He's from here."

"New York at Christmastime is magical," the woman said, her eyes moving to the passing high-rises outside the train's window. "No mistletoe needed, right, Benny?"

"No, my love." Benny, the man next to her and presumably her husband, leaned in and kissed her on the cheek.

Andrew and Frannie exchanged a smile, their eyes lingering for a second too long, and something electric passed through him. He saw Frannie swallow before turning to the window. New York City zipped by and he was left wondering what harm it would do to just man up and ask her about her ex. He didn't want to upset her or ruin what had turned into a really fun day. There'd been no run-ins with danger, although a little disappointment swam in his chest that he couldn't hold her close again. But bringing up her ex seemed like he was sliding headfirst into dangerous territory.

He blew out a breath and shifted in his seat. His attention snagged on an announcement for St. Patrick's Christmas Mass services. The graphic showed the inside of the church decorated with evergreen wreaths, red bows, and hundreds of poinsettias. It was beautiful and awakened a longing inside of him he hadn't felt since he was a kid.

"It's beautiful, isn't it?" Frannie had followed his gaze to the poster. "I wanted to get tickets to tour the church but ..." Her voice grew shallow. She pressed a hand over her dress and straightened. "I couldn't get Calvin to commit to a date."

So, the idiot had a name. Andrew's fingers itched to pull up Frannie's social media and search out this Calvin and figure out what kind of man dumps a woman who flew all the way to see him and planned an entire week of holiday events that culminated in—he blinked. *No.* He wasn't going to think about that last line on Frannie's bucket list.

"It should've been my first clue, I guess." Frannie let out a soft puff of air. "Nothing makes you feel more foolish than figuring out all of the clues were there and you were just too blind to see it."

Andrew wanted to say something but kept his lips closed. He wanted to hear her out. Wanted to find out what happened. Wanted to know if the glimmer of attraction he thought he'd seen in her sapphire-blue eyes might be real.

But Frannie pressed her lips together too and Andrew wasn't willing to let this go.

"I'm sorry it didn't work out." He swallowed over the dryness in his mouth. "Do you want to talk about it?"

She looked over at him, a curve to her lips. "Won't that be weird?"

Andrew shrugged. "Only if you're embarrassed to admit you dated an ogre."

Frannie laughed out loud and covered her lips when a few people looked over at her. "Calvin wasn't—isn't—an ogre." She sighed and Andrew watched her slip back to memories that had his insides churning with unfounded envy. "He just recognized what I couldn't see, or maybe refused to see, before I did."

"I get that. I mean, not in a relationship-type scenario." He settled against the seat. "I hurt my shoulder early in my career and ignored the surgeons and physical therapists when they told me I was pushing too hard, too fast. I refused to accept their warnings that if I didn't allow it to heal properly I risked permanent injury that could take me out of the game forever. I didn't want to see a future outside of hockey until that last game forced me to." He looked at her. "Maybe that isn't such a great analogy."

"No, it is, actually." Frannie leaned into his shoulder. "Just a different kind of heartbreak."

The idea that Calvin possessed enough of Frannie's heart to break it left a bad taste in his mouth. It was probably just what he needed to rein in his feelings. He'd likely misinterpreted whatever he thought he saw reflecting in her eyes and she most likely wasn't looking to put her heart out there again.

The momentum of the train slowed and the floor beneath their feet rumbled as they pulled to a stop at Grand Central Terminal. Andrew extended his hand to help Frannie up and earned a wink from the older gentleman as he helped his wife up.

With her hand in his, Andrew led Frannie up the stairs into New York's famous train station. Her lips parted, eyes wide as she took in the barrel ceiling and elegant marble-and-stone structure that even inspired him.

"It's just how I imagined it."

The low gong of a bell rang out overhead, silencing the

passengers inside the terminal and stopping them as they looked for the reason behind the chiming tone. A group of people dressed like Frannie walked to the center of the floor. A second later, a song played overhead and the couples began dancing.

"Oh, it's the Christmas waltz!" Frannie squeezed her hands beneath her chin.

Next to them the guy in the top hat led the woman he was with to the floor, and they began dancing. The older couple who *didn't need mistletoe* sat on a bench nearby. The woman caught his attention with a tip of her head, sending him a message he understood clearly.

Andrew pivoted to Frannie and held his hand out. "Would you care to dance?"

Her eyes rounded. "I don't know how to do what they're doing."

Picking up her hand, he smiled. "It's called dancing and you just need to follow my lead." With a quick stop by the older couple, Andrew received enthusiastic consent to leave Frannie's shopping bags with them before walking her to where the group of dancers was continuing to grow.

Frannie's grip tightened on his. "I'm apologizing right now for stepping on your toes. Possibly tripping you. Maybe even causing severe bodily injury."

He laughed. "The waltz is a simple dance. Just remember step, side, slide." As he positioned his hand on her waist, a smile broke free on his face at the feel of her close to him again. "Let me move your body."

She blushed before shifting her gaze to her feet. "Step. Side. Slide."

Andrew waited a beat and then took his first step, leading Frannie back a step and then to the side before his feet came together, her foot landing on his toe. She looked up at him apologetically but he gave her an encouraging nod and repeated the step.

"Just relax." He squeezed her hand and after a few more missteps, Frannie's movements synced with his.

"I'm dancing the Christmas waltz. In Grand Central. In New York."

He could feel the flex of her back muscles as she moved in time with him. "Was this on your bucket list?"

Frannie looked up beneath dark lashes. "No."

His heart pounded in delight at her answer and an idea came to mind. "Do you mind if I take control of your bucket list for the rest of the night?"

Her lips parted into a smile, eyes sparkling. "Not at all."

Chapter Twenty

Frannie had no idea what to expect when Andrew asked to take over her bucket list, but going to a two-hundred-year-old church in Lower Manhattan was not even close to being on her radar.

The Uber dropped them off in front of the gray stone structure, and with its stained-glass windows and large arched doorway, all decorated with boughs of holly and ribbon, it felt like she'd stepped onto the set of a Christmas movie.

"What are we doing here?" she whispered when Andrew opened the door for her.

"I know you wanted to tour St. Patrick's but I thought you might enjoy St. Augustine's."

Thick red carpet muffled their steps as they entered the cathedral that arched over long pews. At the front, the altar was decorated with twinkling trees, poinsettias, and an empty manger off to the side.

"Mr. Bishop." An older lady in jeans and a Christmas sweater with cats on it stepped out of a hallway. Her eyes moved to Frannie and then back to Andrew. "We weren't expecting you tonight."

"I know." He hugged the woman in a familiar way before he put his hand near the small of Frannie's back. "Loretta, this is my friend Frannie. She's from Georgia and wanted to see St. Patrick's but I told her that place was overrated. St. Augustine's is where the real spirit of Christmas exists."

Loretta's face squished into a smile that made Frannie smile too. "The Holy Spirit dwells wherever His children are." She turned and waved at them to follow her. "Come, we're just getting set up for the kids."

"Is this where you go to church?" Frannie whispered as they followed Loretta, who was humming "O Come All Ye Faithful."

"When I can."

Frannie felt guilty. Today was Sunday and he'd probably missed church because of her. "We could've come here this morning."

"You would've come to church with me?"

Even though the hallway was dimly lit, she could still see the flicker of interest in his eyes that was becoming more recognizable the more time she spent with him. "Yes."

He smiled and it was the kind of smile that turned her insides around. She'd lost count of how many times that had happened since meeting Andrew and quite frankly she wasn't sure how to react.

Frannie didn't have a chance to entertain the thought further when they were ushered into an open space that looked like a gym. It was decorated for Christmas with trees and long tables covered in red cloths where several adults of all ages were wrapping gifts.

"Are you two hungry? We have some soup, fresh bread, and hot chocolate." Loretta pointed to a kitchen pass-through where a few senior adults were enjoying dinner.

Andrew looked at her and she nodded. Soup and fresh bread on a cold day sounded wonderful.

"We'll take two bowls and then"—he looked at Frannie again —"we'd like to help."

"Yes." Frannie answered the question lingering in his blue-gray eyes. "We'd love to help."

Loretta got them settled at the table with their soup, a creamy chipotle chicken, with a side of the yummiest-looking rolls that gave her no shame when she asked for two. She hadn't realized how hungry she was until they started eating. From their companionable silence, it appeared Andrew was just as hungry.

Frannie wiped her lips. "Are these for the kids here at the church?"

"No. St. Augustine's runs a prison ministry and these gifts"—Andrew set his spoon down—"were donated by church members for the children with a parent who has been incarcerated."

Stacks of gifts were lined up on tables marked by signs indicating appropriate age groups. Another long table at the back held rows of laundry baskets containing boxed and canned food items.

"What are those for?"

"Those are for the families to take with them." Andrew collected their bowls. "Are you still hungry?"

"No, I'm good, thanks."

After Andrew dumped their trash, Loretta led them to a table to help with wrapping. For the next thirty minutes, Frannie listened to stories about the children who would be arriving and the inmates who had come to know the Lord through their ministry.

When they had finished wrapping all the toys, Loretta directed everyone to their stations for the arrival of the children and their families.

"Will you two be able to stay?"

"I'm sorry, Loretta, but we have somewhere to be."

Frannie frowned at Andrew. *We do?* But all he gave her was a charming half-smile before heading off to collect their coats and bags.

"Thank you so much for the wonderful soup and bread." Frannie looked around the room at the excited faces of the volunteers. The kids weren't the only ones being blessed tonight.

"Well, it's our way of thanking you for helping us tonight." Loretta released a happy sigh. "Let me go get you and Andrew some hot chocolate to take with you."

Andrew walked over and started to help Frannie into her coat when she looked down at her shopping bags at his feet. Instead of reaching her arm into her coat sleeve, she reached for the bags.

"Give me a minute."

Frannie hurried to a table, emptied her bags, and quickly wrapped the items.

"What are you doing?"

"I'm donating these." Frannie stacked her packages on the table for children the same age as Jisoo. "My niece has more than enough."

"But what about the Ella book?" Andrew picked up the book. "That was special."

"Eloise." Frannie took the book and placed it on a square of wrapping paper. "I can get her another one in D.C. Besides"—she taped the last edge and set the gift with the others—"my luggage was already close to the maximum weight."

This time, Frannie slipped her arms into her coat and caught a glimmer in Andrew's eyes that looked very close to adoration and it made her heart beat a bit faster. She fumbled with her scarf, placing it around her neck to hide the climbing heat.

"Two hot chocolates to go." Loretta met them at the door and handed them two foam cups with lids. "I know we're not St.

Patrick's but I hope you felt the Presence of joy and peace while you were here."

"I did." Frannie's entire body felt light and while she could credit part of that to the way she'd caught Andrew watching her, she knew that the real lightness had everything to do with the unexpected gift of being able to bless those in need. "Thank you for letting me help."

Frannie and Andrew said their good-byes and exited the church. Outside, the frigid air stung her cheeks but she didn't mind. The sun was setting, leaving the city in the glowy haze of twilight, and Christmas lights were already beginning to twinkle from the rooftops and skyline.

A black SUV pulled up to the curb and Andrew's eyes lit once more with a sparkle that turned the cold air around her into a balmy breeze.

"You ready for the next part?"

She had no idea what the next part was but she set her hand in Andrew's open one and let him lead her to the waiting vehicle. The driver stood by the door he'd just opened. This was not an Uber. Her nerves tingled with excitement as she climbed into the blissfully warm back seat.

"What's the next part?" Frannie blew on her cup of cocoa before taking a sip. The warm chocolatey drink slipped smoothly down her throat. "Mmm, this is good."

"Enjoy it." Andrew settled into the leather seat next to her, his knee grazing hers. He tipped his chin in the direction of the windshield and the sea of brake lights ahead of them. "We've got some time."

Frannie took another sip and sighed in contentment. "The red lights actually feel festive tonight."

Andrew chuckled. "Have you always had such a positive outlook on life?"

"Ryan calls it blissful naivete and says it's why he has

prematurely gone gray, but I say it's his fault for always trying to control everything."

"I have a sister, I get it."

Frannie eyed him and suddenly Andrew didn't look so confident in his decision to back her brother. "Ryan followed me on a date. In his squad car. And then used his speaker to embarrass me when my date leaned in to kiss me on my cheek."

The back of the SUV was dark but not so much that she didn't see something flash in Andrew's eyes before the corner of his lips curled into a smirk.

"It's brother code. Protect sisters at all costs from jerks."

Rolling her eyes, she playfully bumped him with her shoulder. "Chris wasn't a jerk. And now I hear he's at the top of his class at med school." She exhaled. "He was outside of my league."

"If a little brotherly intimidation scared him off then he wasn't even close to being worthy of *your* league."

Frannie's cheeks flamed at the compliment, her eyes searching Andrew's face for any hint that he was just saying that to make her feel better but the way his jaw muscle flexed and he swallowed, something told her he wasn't being flippant.

She didn't know what to do with that or the way it was fanning her mixed-up emotions.

"Did Ryan like Calvin?"

Running her thumb over the lip of her drink, she sighed. "He didn't *not* like him but I could tell Ryan was hesitant. It didn't really bother me because Ryan's never really cared for any guy I've dated so I just figured he would eventually learn to like Calvin. Especially if ... we got serious."

"And your family? Did they like him?"

A tiny rush of defense rose inside of her. "Does that matter? I'm the one dating him. The one who has to love him, not Ryan or my mom, right?"

Andrew pressed his lips together and she felt bad. He didn't deserve the brunt of her frustration caused by her finally figuring out what her mom and brother already knew about Calvin.

"Did you love him?"

Frannie's stomach knotted. She'd been asking herself that question ever since Calvin broke up with her. She licked her lips, unsure she wanted to admit the gnawing truth that Ryan was right about her blissful naivete.

"It's okay if you were." Andrew's voice was low, his gaze penetrating her defenses. "There's nothing wrong with putting your heart on the line."

"I don't think I loved him." Her words came out small and she looked out the window. "I think I loved the idea of him. Of being in a relationship that seemed impossible for someone like me."

"What do you mean?"

The cocoa turned heavy in her stomach and Frannie didn't want to ruin what had been a wonderful day with her sad story. "Nothing." She forced a smile to her lips but saw the doubt on Andrew's face. For a second it made her want to spill all of her secrets, but her confession was interrupted by the driver.

"Sir, we're here."

The SUV slowed to a stop and Frannie gasped. Through the window, thousands of bright lights dazzled in front of her for as far as she could see. Andrew's touch on her hand disrupted her staring just long enough for her to get out of the vehicle.

Dozens of people, bundled up, filled the sidewalk, taking in the overwhelming sight of an entire neighborhood that literally glowed from the innumerable amount of holiday decorations and lights covering their homes and yards.

Andrew smiled at her. "Welcome to Dyker Heights."

Chapter Twenty One

"This is incredible."

Andrew enjoyed the touch of her hand gripping his bicep. Her smile was enough, but the added closeness made his decision to bring Frannie to the most festive neighborhood in NYC worth it. "I think it's best experienced with a stroll and the driver will meet us on the other side but if you'd prefer or are too cold, we can drive."

"Pshh, cold shmold." She shivered against him and then smiled. "Toes are overrated anyway."

"I'm pretty sure they're the least appreciated appendage."

"Come on, Bishop." She squeezed his bicep. "Nothing's keeping me from the hap-hap-happiest Christmas experience."

He recognized the line from *National Lampoon's Christmas Vacation* and chuckled. They joined the crowd of tourists and New Yorkers alike who knew Dyker Heights was a bucket list sight to experience. The first house they stopped at looked like it was covered in a million colored lights stretching over the entirety of the home with Christmas inflatables filling every inch of the tiny yard. Frannie released his hand and pulled her cell phone from her pocket to take a photo.

She did this at every house and Andrew was starting to worry Frannie might actually forsake her toes in the name of Clark Griswold.

"How are your feet holding up in those shoes?"

"Bishop, I'm a Southern girl, we're practically born in heels and pearls."

Frannie's voice nearly purred in that Southern accent and it was all he could do not to reach for her and pull her close. Instead, he offered his arm again to keep her steady on the sidewalk as they walked around snow mounds scraped along the side.

At the next block, the owners of a home covered in glowing snowflakes, a full-size sleigh with eight tiny reindeer, and two twenty-foot nutcrackers standing sentry had a table set up with hot cocoa, cider, and homemade cookies.

If it wasn't negative arctic degrees, Andrew might've politely declined but his toes were already numb, which meant Frannie's had to be too. The hot liquid would at least keep them warm until they got to the SUV.

He thought about their conversation. She didn't love her ex and her defensiveness led him to believe it wasn't new information even if she admitted to only realizing it now. But what would it say to her if Andrew admitted his attraction and desire to get to know her better? He wasn't the type to date for fun. Those days were over, thankfully. Now, he was searching for someone who made him want to dream up a thousand ways to make her smile.

"You're awfully quiet."

"Sorry." He twisted the cup of cocoa in his hands, feeling the warmth seep into his gloved hands. No way he was admitting that the smile he'd begun to think about was hers. It was time to tread into safer snowbanks. "What do you do back in Georgia?"

"I work the after-school program at the community center tutoring creative writing and helping students with their English papers or essays."

Excitement laced her words and her career choice didn't surprise him. He'd seen the affection she had for the little girl and her mother at Macy's. "Have you always wanted to teach children?"

"No. Actually, I wanted to be a journalist, kind of like my sister-in-law, Vivian, but my brother was against it—too dangerous." She rolled her eyes but there was a flash of awareness that said she wasn't completely disagreeable to her brother's reasoning. "And then our professor brought in a guest lecturer, a travel writer, and she told us amazing stories of the places she'd seen all over the world. So, I thought maybe I'd do that but ..."

"What is it?"

Frannie's shoulders rose with her inhale. "Ryan." She exhaled. "After graduating I received an offer to intern for a small travel magazine in Atlanta but Ryan came in clutch with the crime statistics." Her voice lowered into a gravelly interpretation, he guessed, of Ryan. "For a single girl in the city." Frannie rolled her eyes. "It would've been an amazing opportunity but once again my brother's concern had me freaking out and second-guessing that maybe he was right."

Andrew led her around an icy patch on the ground. "I'm sorry."

"It's okay." Frannie released a humorless laugh. "Ryan means well but sometimes I feel like my life is in a holding pattern that I can't get out of until it's been approved by my safety-marshal brother." She released his arm and took a sip of her hot cocoa, her blue gaze turning glassy. "It feels like I can't escape this misconception that I can't take care of myself or have a life outside of what everyone expects."

The tips of Andrew's ears were ice cold a second ago but listening to Frannie had caused them to warm with a sense of irritation on her behalf. He understood protecting his loved ones, but at the expense of missed dreams and opportunities?

Frannie in her vintage dress and grandmother's wool coat, her cheeks rosy, looked every part the leading lady but she lacked their ever-present moxie. Did Ryan understand that his overprotectiveness was partly to blame?

"What kind of life do you want, Frannie?"

She blinked up at him for a long second before answering. "I want a life where I can make choices for myself without fearing the consequences of failure. I don't think anyone needs to know they can fail, they need to know that if they do fail, if things don't go the way they hoped or expected, that they have the support of the ones who love them most and will be there to help them find their way again." She pinched her lips together so that her nose wrinkled. "Was that too much?"

"Not at all." His voice was husky. "I think you deserve that kind of life."

Frannie did a half turn on the crowded sidewalk, her eyes sparkling under the Christmas lights. "Sometimes the risk of unexpected disappointments can lead to ..." Her blue eyes landed on him. "Unexpected surprises."

Even though it was freezing, the space between them sizzled. Warmth spread through him. *Do not look at her lips. Do not look at her lips.*

"I know the church wasn't St. Patrick's and"—he held up the Styrofoam cup of cocoa—"this isn't Serendipity's famous frozen hot chocolate but—"

"It's perfect." She stepped closer. "Today, tonight was—" A gust of cold air froze the words in a white puff of breath between them. Her chin tipped up and the anticipation he'd seen flicker in her blue eyes when she was waiting to see Santa simmered there and made him want to wrap his arms around her and pull her into his chest. "How long did it take?"

Her question jarred him from where his thoughts shouldn't be going. "For what?"

She looked up at him with wide blue eyes and it was far too easy to slip into them. "For you to figure out that you had a whole future outside of the one you'd planned for?"

Her question ignited a spark inside him that he didn't want to smother. A spark that made him believe—hope—that maybe she was already beginning to see a future without her ex. Was that too much to hope for?

Behind her, his eyes landed on a scrolled sign in red that simply read: *Believe.*

Andrew considered his answer, not wanting to push Frannie. "It took some time. My whole life from the time I was eight revolved around hockey. When I was told it was over, I felt like I was disappointing everyone who worked so hard; my coaches, parents, teammates, all of them sacrificed so much just so I could live my dream." Frannie's chin dipped and he saw uncertainty settle in her eyes. "But, all of my fears were for nothing. My family, teammates, coaches, they didn't stop loving me and supporting me. Turns out the only person who believed I had no life off the ice—was me. Never them."

With his hand at the small of her back, he guided her to the edge of the sidewalk so a family with a wide stroller could pass by. Another group of families walked by, crowding the sidewalk, and Andrew had to step off and into the street to give them room to pass.

A soft laugh slipped through Frannie's lips. "A few days ago, I was convinced my life had been flipped upside down, that everything I thought I wanted slipped away with Calvin, but he was right." She pulled back, her eyes moving back and forth, searching his. "We were in different places and I have no idea how long that had been true, but just like you said, I didn't want to consider what my life might look like without him."

"And now?"

A wave of marvel passed over Frannie's face but before she could answer they were moved along with the growing crowd. People filled in the spaces around them, chatting and laughing loudly as they pointed out the numerous and sometimes gaudy décor that made Dyker Heights memorable.

Andrew couldn't stop cutting glances in her direction. What was she going to say? And what was that look?

When they got to the corner, the vehicle traffic was heavy as cars maneuvered the intersection, being careful of the number of pedestrians darting into the street for photos. Andrew hesitated sending a message to the driver, hoping an extra minute or two might give him the answer to why his unanswered question had his pulse racing. But when he caught Frannie's lower lip quivering, he pulled out his cell phone and let the driver know they were ready.

Andrew took a fortifying breath and decided to take a chance he wasn't sure he should, but like Frannie said, sometimes the risk was worth it. Man, he hoped so. "For what it's worth, and I realize I've only known you for a few days, but, Frannie, I've never witnessed anyone who radiates as much joy as you. Being around you has—" *No stopping now, Bishop*—except he needed to stop. This wasn't about him or his feelings but about her. "I just wanted to tell you that being around you has shown me that your brother really has nothing to worry about when it comes to what you're capable of. I don't think you should let him, or anyone else, make you feel like you're stuck living the life someone else wants for you." He swallowed. "I hope you believe that you are strong enough and brave enough to chase whatever dream you set your heart on."

She tilted her chin, looking up into his eyes. "Even if that means losing all of your toes to show me the prettiest lights in New York City?"

Her humor came out breathless and it sent a tingle of warmth coursing through him. The corner of his lips tipped up. "I've heard toes are overrated."

Frannie inched closer, her gaze locked on his, and he couldn't stop the way his body reacted to her nearness.

"Hey, watch it!"

The jarring shout pulled Andrew's attention away from Frannie's face and over her shoulder to where a thick crowd had converged next to them in front of a house with a thousand toy soldiers.

Andrew started to turn when Frannie's body was thrown to the side like someone had shoved her. Her arms went wide but her heel caught in a crack, tilting her backward toward the busy intersection. The crowd shifted, separating them and keeping him from reaching her hands before she teetered backward, stepping into the street.

An older man nearby edged forward to lend his hand but his kindness wasn't fast enough for Andrew's liking and it was blocking him from getting to her first. The growl of an engine revving caused the hairs on the back of his neck to stand up. He looked to his left and saw the headlights of a car racing toward the intersection.

Andrew sidestepped the old man and jumped into the street. He reached Frannie in time to hear the tires screeching. Wrapping her in a bear hug, Andrew lifted her off her feet and swiveled so that his back was facing the oncoming car. His muscles bunched around her protectively as he braced for impact, but the car swerved into the middle lane, coming within a few feet of them as it sped by.

Sharp pain ached from where Frannie's fingers had pinched into his biceps. But he ignored the discomfort and tried to track the car to get the license plate but it was too dark to see anything. He glanced down at Frannie.

"Are you okay?"

"Yeah."

Andrew shouldered his way onto the crowded sidewalk, making sure there was enough space for him and Frannie. He looked her over, his eyes searching for any injuries before finally meeting her blue gaze again. "Are you sure you're okay?"

"I'm fine." Her nervous chuckle vibrated against his chest. "That was close."

Too close. His eyes searched the crowd around them. Had someone pushed into Frannie on purpose? Was the driver aiming for her or was that his own fears feeding his imagination?

"You just can't help yourself."

His attention drew down to her smiling face. "What?"

Her eyes flashed to his arms still firmly wrapped around her. "Protecting people even when you're not on the job."

Regret curled over his shoulders. He didn't know if what just took place was intentional or not, but instead of doing his job he'd allowed himself to get swept up in a daydream for a woman he was responsible for protecting.

Andrew released his hold on her and stepped back. The frigid air stung in the absence of her warm body nestled against his.

"I guess my odds were accurate." Frannie straightened the collar of her coat as if she hadn't almost been run over. "The chance of getting hit by a car in New York City is pretty high."

Andrew forced a fake smile to his lips as the SUV pulled up to the curb. He opened the back door for her to get in but kept surveying the area around them for any sign the danger wasn't over. Those odds might've been accurate for an average New Yorker but something told him that tonight's incident didn't have anything to do with statistics.

And despite Ryan's wishes, Andrew needed to tell her the truth.

"Frannie, I need to tell you something."

Her gaze swung to meet his and he could immediately see the implication of his tone. Her eyes seemed to be asking him if he was about to hurt her. He reached for her hand, hoping he wasn't about to do that.

"When your brother called, asking me to make sure you got the airport safely, I was already assigned to a protection detail. I was going to be picking up my client from the airport around the same time I'd be dropping you off so I figured it would be okay. And I felt like I owed your brother." Frannie's brows pinched and her eyes creased at the side. After all she'd told him about her overprotective brother, Andrew could only guess where her thoughts were going. "At first, when I met you, I thought your brother was probably right. Maybe you were a little naïve to the dangers of the city"—hurt flashed in her eyes and Andrew squeezed her hand—"but I don't think that now, Frannie."

The sound of a horn from somewhere outside pulled his focus to the windows. Was this the right thing to do?

"Andrew, what is it?"

There was a vulnerability in her voice, and it caused his heart to ache because he didn't want to hurt her.

He inhaled deeply and blew out a breath. "I saw a man following you when we left your hotel. I thought he was just some thug who saw you as an easy pick-pocket target and that's when I decided to make sure you got to your destination safely."

"That's why you took me to Levain's?"

"Yes. I figured if I got you out of his sights or allowed him to believe you weren't alone, he'd go away. And he did, but then when I left you at the bookstore I thought I saw him again but before I could be sure, I heard you scream in the alley."

"And you came to my rescue." The lightness in her tone sounded forced. "I already told you that wasn't your fault."

Andrew pivoted in the backseat of the SUV so that he was facing her. "Frannie, it was my fault. I was hired to protect a client who has an active threat against her life, and I was supposed to pick her up from the airport the day I came to your hotel. After you were attacked at the bookstore, my agency received a note that led us to believe you were mistakenly identified as our client and that what happened to you wasn't an accident. Rather, it appeared someone knew I was the one hired to protect our client and mistakenly identified you as my client. The note warned us that the client's life, your life, was still in danger. Even though it was dark, he could see Frannie's struggle to follow along in the flicking of the city lights. "You look very similar to my client."

Frannie sat back, her gaze grew distant as though she was replaying the moment from the bookstore and then she looked back at him. "The thing at Bryant Park, when you thought someone was following us ..."

"I thought the guy who attacked you had returned."

Realization spread over her face. "And tonight?"

"I don't think that was an accident."

"Why didn't you just tell me?"

Andrew worked his jaw. He rubbed his thumb across the back of her hand hoping she would understand. "After the bookstore incident, I called Ryan to let him know there was a chance you might be followed if we got you on the plane back to D.C. and you needed to be protected. Ryan said it would be better if we didn't tell you, so you—"

Frannie withdrew her hand from his and he saw the shift in

her posture. "What? You both decided not to tell me because I'm too naïve, too incompetent to take care of myself?"

"He didn't want you to worry."

"No." Frannie scoffed. "He wants to control my life." She shook her head. "I'm not a child. I'm not fragile. And my life is mine. Mine to experience, and make mistakes, and figure out." When her eyes found Andrew's, they shined with tears. "I thought that's what I was doing this weekend. Figuring out where I went wrong with Calvin and learning what it really is I want from my life and for my future. Our time together this weekend, you made me feel like I was capable of creating a future for myself but—" her frown deepened—"Did my brother make you hang out with me this weekend? To keep me safe?"

"No. I mean, he knew I would get you safely to the airport for your flight and my agency made accommodations so that we could keep an eye on you but Frannie, every minute I've spent with you has been my choice and not because I think you're fragile."

There was a hint of desperation in his tone to make her believe him. "At first, I had to trust Ryan's decision but these last couple of days have shown me that while his intentions come from a place of brotherly love, I don't think he knows how strong you are. You possess the kind of strength and courage that doesn't let fear rule you. I won't lie, I understand why it terrifies him." He wanted so badly to make her understand. "If anything happened to you, it would be devastating."

She turned to her window, hands folded in her lap and all he wanted to do was reach for them but his unanswered question from earlier wasn't the only thing lingering between them now. Would she forgive him for not being entirely honest? Because without that—it wouldn't matter how she answered.

Chapter Twenty-Two

Dickens should've written a fourth ghost. The Ghost of Missed Opportunity. Or was that the Ghost of Christmas Present? Frannie stared at her reflection in the bathroom mirror of her hotel room after Andrew had dropped her off for the night.

Something had shifted tonight. Actually, it was more than one thing. The whole day had been magical and unexpected in all of the ways a writer would script for a Hallmark movie. Minus the nearly-getting-run-over bit.

That was more Lifetime Channel.

Especially after Andrew's confession. She was furious with her brother, but it wasn't surprising. But with Andrew ... it was disappointing. For some reason, after only knowing him a few days, his opinion mattered to her. She didn't want him to see her as a damsel in distress, although being rescued by him did have its perks. There would be no confessing the number of times she'd sniffed her clothing that had picked up his spicy cologne. So, which is it? Was she upset with him for not telling her or was she falling for him? Could it be both?

She was afraid to answer either question and it caused her

head to throb nearly as badly as her ankle from twisting it on the sidewalk. Note to self for future trips to NYC: Forget what looks fashionable and go with comfort and stability. Being careful of her ankle, she stretched her toes in the pair of fuzzy socks that felt like heaven after wearing heels all day.

Frannie grabbed the box of chocolate truffles left by the hotel and folded her legs beneath her as she sat on the couch in her room. She'd left the lights off and allowed the glow of twinkle lights from the Christmas tree and the city outside her window to fill the room around her in an atmosphere of magic.

Future trips to NYC.

She unwrapped a chocolate and took a bite. A few days ago, this city was the last place she wanted to be and now ... now she was considering the possibility of returning.

And whether she wanted to admit it or not, it did have something to do with Andrew.

Frustration turned the chocolate sour in her stomach. All those moments when she noticed the shifts in Andrew's personality, she'd assumed it was because he was being forced to hang out with her—a favor to Ryan. Then at some point, she allowed herself to believe it was more. That the shared personal stories, deep questions, and looks that had her insides feeling perfectly gushy might mean something more.

Every minute I've spent with you has been my choice. And not because I think you're fragile.

The distress to be believed was clear in Andrew's voice when he spoke those words but the tiny whispers of doubt were clouding her ability to believe him.

If he only wanted to protect me, he didn't have to take me to Bryant Park or to see the Macy's Santa or to see the Christmas lights tonight. It had to mean something more, right?

She replayed the day over and over in her mind and it all led to Andrew's question that she'd left unanswered. *"And now?"*

What did life look like for her now—without Calvin? Frannie sank deeper into the couch cushions. How was she supposed to answer that? She had no idea how to assess the confusion twisting her insides into a knot. It was one thing to admit that Ryan was right about Calvin but he was wrong to ask Andrew not to tell her about the mistaken identity threat. And would Andrew still believe she didn't allow fear to rule her if he knew it had been she who had refused to accept all the signs that everyone else saw for an entire year—that her relationship with Calvin had long been over?

Frannie groaned. She needed to talk this out and there was only one person who'd be completely honest with her. Stretching to the coffee table, she grabbed her cell phone and dialed Vivian's number. It was past nine so there was a chance her sister-in-law would be asleep, and Frannie just hoped she wasn't going to wake up Jisoo.

"Hey, big-city girl," Vivian answered. "If you're calling to tell me your flight's been delayed or cancelled again, I'm going to make you tell your niece and feel the wrath of her doe-eyed disappointment."

"I'll be on the six-fifteen direct flight to D.C. tomorrow night."

"Whew." Vivian's sigh was dramatic. "I've lost count how many times I've had to explain to Jisoo why your flight was delayed, why the planes can't fly if it snows, and of course that only caused her to freak out because Ryan told her it was snowing where he was and she's worried Daddy isn't going to be home for Christmas." Vivian sighed again but Frannie heard the exhaustion in it. "When I pick you up tomorrow, I'm going to put my earbuds in and let you field questions on the drive home."

"I think I can handle that. I hope I'm not calling too late?"

"Nope. I just settled into bed with a glass of wine and was about to watch a biography."

Frannie wrinkled her nose. "Sounds fun."

"Mock me now, but you just wait until you're married and have a kid. The highlight of your weekends will be cancelled games, cereal dinners, and early bedtimes."

"Well, I already love cereal for dinner and I'm currently staring at the most comfortable bed in all of New York City, so I'm two-thirds of the way to boring adulthood."

"Hey now," Vivian teased before her voice grew serious. "So why are you back in your hotel room before ten? Wait." Her voice rose. "Please tell me you haven't been stuck in your hotel room this whole weekend?"

"No, actually, I've been crossing off things on my bucket list and just got back to my hotel room a half hour ago."

"By yourself?"

"Of course, by myself." And then she remembered Andrew sitting on this very couch with her the night before. She was sort of hoping for a repeat but she held back asking him after their uneasy ride back to the hotel. "It's just me, a box of chocolates, and a comfy bed tonight."

"I'm jealous about the chocolate but I wasn't referring to you being by yourself in your hotel room. I was asking if you'd been out in the city by yourself."

Frannie made a face. She was so tired of having to prove she was capable of being an adult. "Would it surprise you if I said yes?"

"Not really, but then again I married your brother and can't leave the house without him checking my tire pressure and making sure my cell phone is fully charged."

"Doesn't that get annoying?"

"Absolutely, but it's his love language. Protecting the ones he loves until it drives them nuts."

Frannie sighed. "Or keeps them from taking risks."

"What's wrong, Francis?"

Hearing Vivian call her by her full name never felt patronizing, unlike when Ryan did it. Still, she was worried whatever she said might get back to her brother. "First, you have to promise me that what I'm about to say stays within the confines of sisterhood. You cannot, under any circumstances, repeat anything I say to my brother, no matter what kind of FBI tactics he tries on you."

"Does what you're about to tell me put anyone's life in danger, potential danger, or is in any way illegal? I love you and your brother too much to disregard marriage vows, laws, or risk breaking your mom's heart."

"Sheesh, Vivian." Frannie chuckled. "It's not that deep. You didn't have to bring Mom into it."

Vivian laughed. "Okay, sister, spill it. What's going on?"

Frannie worked her lip, trying to find the right words until she finally gave up and blurted out, "I think I'm falling for someone."

"What?"

There were at least three emotions in that single word.

Confusion—check.

Concern—check.

Curiosity—check.

"I know, I know." Frannie closed her eyes. "I sound like one of those obnoxious bachelorettes who confess their undying love one second and then drool over a new bachelor that walks into the house."

"You do not sound like that but tell me, who are you falling for?"

Eyes closed, Frannie wrinkled her nose. "Andrew Bishop," she whispered.

"Who?"

"The bodyguard I nearly pepper-sprayed." There was an audible gasp that made Frannie hang her head. "I know. I know. *I know*. Calvin and I just broke up and these kinds of feelings are all probably rebound feelings or I'm just really pathetic, and there should definitely be a waiting period after breakups, right? Because what kind of girl does that make me look like if I'm entertaining thoughts about a man I've just met and then he admitted that Ryan told him not to tell me about the whole *your life is in danger*—"

"Whoa, whoa, whoa," Vivian interrupted. "First, take a breath."

Frannie did, but the jittery feelings she'd been having all day while breathing Andrew's spicy cologne didn't subside. And she would never admit that she'd sniffed her scarf more than once, inhaling the lingering effects of him coming to her rescue once more.

"Second, what do you mean *your life is in danger*?"

After a long intake of breath, Frannie spilled the details of her time with Andrew, about how he volunteered to hang out with her and cross things off her bucket list and how he asked to take over her list, unexpectedly surprising her with the church and their stroll through Dyker Heights. Vivian oohed and aahed throughout and released a happy sigh until Frannie got to the part about nearly getting hit by a car. She finished off her story with the details about the mistaken identity and Ryan's decision to keep it from Frannie and Andrew's confession.

"Whoa." Vivian exhaled the word. "Okay, I'm not excusing Ryan's choice to keep you in the dark but let's handle the easy thing first because I'm waiting for the part where falling for Andrew is a problem."

"Vivian. I barely know the guy. I shouldn't be daydreaming about the warm fuzzies he gives me every time he holds my hand."

"He held your hand?" Frannie pulled the phone away from

Vivian's shrieky gasp that echoed in her ear. "You didn't mention hand holding."

"It wasn't *hand holding* hand holding, it was him making sure I didn't slip and break my neck because I chose to wear heels in snowy conditions like an insane person." Frannie chose to keep the hand holding in the car to herself because she wasn't quite sure how to explain that one away.

"So, his chivalry gave you warm fuzzies. Again, I'm waiting for the problem."

Frannie rolled her eyes. "Maybe I should be talking to Ryan. He'd see the problem."

"Of course he would—he's your obnoxiously overprotective brother."

"Ah, so you agree with me that Ryan's obnoxious."

"No." Vivian snickered. "Okay, maybe he pushes the boundaries of what's normal but only because he loves us the way Buddy the Elf loves Santa."

"*Right.*" Frannie snorted. "That's problem number two. Andrew's just like Ryan. They both decided I couldn't handle the truth and I don't need another overprotective brother. One is enough."

"Let me ask you something. If Ryan was here in the States what do you think he would've done the second he found out about Calvin breaking up with you?"

"Quietly put a hit out?"

Vivian laughed. "He would've thought about it that's for sure, but my guess is that he'd have flown to New York and brought you home, either back to Georgia or here to D.C."

Frannie groaned. "You're right."

"If Andrew really wanted to keep you safe, if he was *really* like Ryan, he probably would've come up with a dozen reasons why you shouldn't leave your hotel. But he didn't. He took you out and helped you have what sounds like the most amazing weekend ever despite the potential threat. The only time I've witnessed Ryan take a calculated risk like that—it was for someone he liked. A lot."

The *someone* was Vivian and Frannie knew how much Ryan loved her, so the weight behind his decision to trust Vivian's ability to walk into a dangerous situation and take care of herself showed just how much faith he had in her. Was the same true for Andrew?

"Now that we've nixed the idea that Andrew is like Ryan," Vivian said, as though the answer to Frannie's question was crystal clear. "What's stopping you from at least admitting to yourself that maybe these feelings are something worth looking into?"

This answer wasn't so easy to explain even if she could accept Andrew's faith in her.

"Um, you heard I'm newly dumped, right?" She expected the words to be bitter on her tongue but instead they were rather bland, like she was almost numb to the feelings they should've brought up. "And let's not forget he lives here in NYC and if Ryan's Buddy the Elf, then this place might as well be as far as the seven levels of candy-cane forest and past the sea of twirly-swirly gumdrops."

"Your addiction to Christmas movies is frightening."

"Or impressive," Frannie teased back. "Be warned I will train Jisoo up to follow in my ways."

"What's impressive is your ability to change the subject. Let's just pretend for a second that your brother and you don't live in Candy Land, are you getting attraction vibes from Andrew?"

"Ew." She scrunched her nose. "I despise you putting the board game I play with my niece and the words *attraction vibes* in the same sentence. I'll never look at the game the same way again."

"Frannie." The playful irritation in Vivian's voice made her laugh. "Why are you avoiding the question?

A bubble of frustration filled Frannie's chest. She swung her legs off the couch and stood. "Because it feels weird. Three days ago I was expecting an engagement—"

"To a man you hadn't seen in a year."

"I'm *aware*." Frannie began pacing, careful of her sore ankle. "I don't need to be reminded of that to which I was clearly so blind to have missed, *sister*."

"You're right. Sorry."

Frannie blew out a breath. "It's fine. It's not your fault. It's mine." She paused by the window overlooking the city lights below. "I should've seen it coming. The signs were all there."

"Why do you think you missed it?"

She released another sigh. "Because I was scared." Once the words were out, she felt some of the pressure lift from her shoulders. "Calvin was my first serious boyfriend and our relationship felt like a security blanket. He was smart, successful, came from a strong family, and was everything others didn't think I'd end up with." Memories of her time with Calvin played through her mind like a movie reel and they ended in the same embarrassing conclusion. "I thought I had proved everyone wrong and all I needed to do was keep him from walking out on me like my dad did to my mom."

A few seconds ticked by. It was out. She couldn't take it back no matter how pathetic it made her sound and look.

"Frannie, you are not your mom except in all of the ways that make her brave, capable, and one of the kindest, generous humans I know. Your *dad* made a selfish decision and your *mom* made the selfless decision to work hard and raise you and Ryan up to be the amazing adults you are today."

Tears burned the backs of Frannie's eyes. Everything Vivian was saying, she already knew. She'd been so desperate not to end up like her mom, she overlooked the in-her-face fact that the relationship with Calvin had been over for more than a year. That her feelings for him had waned even before he left for London but she'd stubbornly refused to accept it was okay for the wrong man to walk out because then it opened the door for the right one to walk in. *Just like her mom.*

Her brave, independent, sweet mom had to face Walton and all of the rumors for years but it didn't stop her from letting her heart love again. To trust that she wasn't locked into the rumors but could rewrite her love story.

Frannie heard the muffled sounds of a little voice on the other end of the call before Vivian said, "Looks like my little elf needs some extra cuddles."

"I'm sorry I interrupted your evening." Her voice sounded raspy over the emotion balled in her throat. "I promise I'll make it up to you with free babysitting."

"Don't be sorry. That's what sisters are for."

Vivian let Jisoo say good night before ending the call. In the stillness of her room, Frannie sat on the edge of the bed. She looked down at the phone in her hand and considered everything that had happened over the last few days and then tonight. Vivian was right, Ryan would've convinced her to stay in her hotel room the whole weekend, but Andrew had taken a different approach. One that had her believing him and eager to answer his earlier question.

"And now?"

Andrew wanted to know how she saw her life and had she answered him right away she may have missed the significance of how this weekend truly transformed her perspective.

How did she see her life now? Without Calvin? Without the fear of being compared to her mom? Biting her lip, Frannie scrolled through her contacts until she got to Andrew's number. She quickly sent him her answer and hoped she wasn't too late.

Chapter Twenty-Three

Unknown Number: First, thank you for being honest with me. I'll be chatting with my brother about boundaries on his next break from fighting terrorists.

Second, thank you for a wonderful day.

Last, I have an answer to your question. And now … I'm experiencing the kind of life that gives me hope for something more.

This is Frannie by the way.

The last line still made him smile—even after the seventh time rereading the text messages. It wasn't like he typically received random text messages and the swirling in his gut when he read the first line told him exactly who it was.

Frannie wasn't upset with him. Based on previous experiences with women, Andrew had experienced the wrath of held grudges and withheld forgiveness but once again, Frannie was proving she was different. *And now …*

Hope for something more. Andrew's heart pounded at the

unspoken message he was reading between the lines. *Or...* maybe that pounding was due to the unexpected meeting Doug had called a few minutes after Andrew had sent him the news about the incident at the intersection.

Had it been a simple inattentive driver? An innocent bump on an overcrowded sidewalk? Andrew wanted to believe it was both but it all felt entirely too coincidental. And that was driving his blood pressure up because if it had been done on purpose, then it meant someone had followed them, or found them, and he had missed it.

And now he was waiting for the elevator at the Waldorf and not back at The Peninsula where he could keep an eye on Frannie. He would've argued with Mac, who was already waiting in the security office to take over for the night watch, but Doug's text made it clear they needed to discuss the potential threat since tomorrow was the ransomware deadline.

Andrew waited as a middle-aged couple stepped onto the elevator with him. He used the key he was given from Mac and swiped it to press the button for the twelfth floor. The couple was going to seven.

What would happen if Simon Malone followed through with the investment in the charity? Clearly the ransomware threat was serious because of the FBI's involvement, but how was it connected to Strazza and the Adonis family? Something didn't feel right. The attempts on Frannie, if that's what they were, while frightening, didn't come off as truly life-threatening. They almost seemed ... amateur. And that's the last word he'd use to classify the Adonis family.

The couple exited the elevator and Andrew rode it the rest of the way up, ready to discuss his concerns with Doug. When he got to the Malones' suite, he knocked once and a minute later Joey opened the door.

Andrew frowned at his friend. His gaze moved over him,

trying to figure out what was different about his colleague, and his gaze landed on Joey's dark brown hair. It was always combed into place but now stood askew on the sides, giving him a disheveled look that did not fit the normally composed former Secret Service agent.

"Everything okay?"

"You owe me," Joey mumbled under his breath before leaving Andrew at the door.

Stepping into the suite, Andrew surveyed the space that still looked as quiet and peaceful as the first time he'd been here. Doug was standing near the floor-to-ceiling window, talking on his cell phone with his back to them. Andrew followed Joey to the dining table.

"Where are the Malones?"

Joey sat at a spot where a glass of water and bottle of aspirin were. "Having a private dinner in the penthouse with Riggs Atwood."

"Riggs Atwood?" Andrew's brows rose. Riggs Atwood was Hollywood's current Chris Evans, landing him headlining roles in just about every action movie released in the last five years. "He's here?"

"Yep," Joey said, making the *p* pop. "He's on a break from filming and invited Ms. Malone to dinner, which gave me the infinite joy of spending the last six hours helping a fashion team figure out the perfect sexy-but-not-like-she's-trying outfit that would make him remember the night."

Andrew crushed his lips together to fight the laughter bubbling in his chest at Joey's dazed expression. "You, um, helped her fashion team?"

Joey shot him a hard glare. "I held up dresses, blouses, earrings, shoes, coats—she wasn't even going outside." His tone hardened. "But a coat might just be the accessory to pull off the look." He said the words in a high voice before rolling his eyes. "I was a human clothing rack for the world's most indecisive supposed fashionista. I don't know if my shoulder muscles will ever recover."

"Then you're probably not going to want to hear about the soup and bread I had at St. Augustine's tonight." Andrew couldn't help baiting him and he earned himself a look that transformed his exhausted friend right back into the severe posture of a Secret Service agent, daring Andrew to keep messing with him. "Sorry, man, I couldn't resist."

"I'm sorry to call you back here." Doug sat at the head of the table. "I'll make this quick so you can get some rest since Mac mentioned something about forcing you off the couch in the security office and to your room last night."

Andrew would have a talk with Mac about team loyalty. "I got a couple of hours in." Was that doubt shadowing Doug's eyes? It shouldn't surprise him that his boss was concerned given what happened with Frannie tonight. "Sir, I want to apologize for the incident tonight. I should've been more aware of our surroundings. Or taken Ms. Frost straight back to her hotel." He slipped a look to Joey. If he could keep Valentina entertained inside of her hotel, Andrew could've done the same. *Should have.*

Though spending time in the privacy of her hotel room watching Christmas movies on the couch with her probably wasn't going to keep him from getting distracted by his growing attraction. The only risk to Frannie was him doing something ridiculous like asking her out or ... The words of the cute older couple on the train came back to him. Kiss her—no mistletoe needed.

"Did you hear me, Bishop?"

Heat burned the tips of Andrew's ears. Doug was staring at him and Joey's face had come back to life with the smirk he was giving to Andrew. "Sorry, I mean, I just wanted to apologize for dropping the ball."

"You kept Ms. Frost from injury," Doug said, giving Andrew a curious look. "Outside of your hunch, we can't rule out that what occurred tonight wasn't more than an unfortunate incident." He flipped open the folder. "And we can be grateful that by this time tomorrow Mr. Malone and his daughter will be back home and under the protection of their personal security team and Ms. Frost will be on a flight to—" He looked up at Andrew.

"D.C." The answer sent an ache through his chest. Frannie was leaving tomorrow. He knew this but something inside of him didn't want to accept it. "She'll be heading to her brother and sister-in-law's home in D.C."

"Right." Doug nodded. "So, we have a little less than twenty-four hours to finish off this assignment without further incident." He spared a look at Joey and Andrew thought he saw the edge of Doug's lip curl. "Or providing fashion advice."

Joey's fingers threaded through his hair and he mumbled something about preferring to get his teeth drilled.

"Tomorrow morning Mr. Malone and Gerald Kline, will finalize their partnership with Hope Village."

Andrew frowned. "What about the ransomware threat?"

"The FBI has advised Mr. Malone to delay the transaction but his attorneys have informed him that any interruption would be costly and might possibly set the deal back or void it altogether." Doug released a breath. "I don't pretend to have the brains these suits do to understand the logistics of it all and it's not our job to figure out. We were hired to make sure we get everyone out of New York the same way they came in."

Joey let out an audible sigh that sounded very much like relief. Valentina Malone couldn't have been that bad. Personal shopping in the suite certainly wouldn't be as high stress as presidential protection.

Andrew stretched his fingers along his jeans. "I would think Mr. Malone is smart enough to heed the FBI's advice."

"I agree with you, Andrew, and I've given Mr. Malone my assessment." The lines at the edge of his eyes deepened. "You've worked with enough clients to know their adherence to our suggested security recommendations only happens when they don't get in their own way."

"I understand, sir, but if our goal is to get everyone back to their homes safely for Christmas, shouldn't Mr. Malone understand that there's still an unresolved threat against his daughter—or rather, an innocent woman? Even Gerald Kline received a threat. Going through with the deal tomorrow against the FBI's advice could escalate the danger."

"I've given Mr. Malone all the pertinent information for him to make the decision he thinks is best. Again, our job is to protect without interfering in our clients' lives. If we do our jobs right, we should all be on the nice list this year."

"For what I've been through I should have at least two years' credit."

Joey's dry humor cut the tension but Andrew was still concerned Mr. Malone's focus was being blinded by his pride. What if it had been his daughter attacked in the alleyway or nearly hit by the car tonight? Would that have put his pride in place?

"Tomorrow Oskar and I will provide detail for Mr. Malone and Mr. Kline. Caruso will stay with Ms. Malone since he's built such a rapport with her." Doug said it dryly but there was a spark of humor in his eyes. "You're good to stick with Ms. Frost tomorrow? Both airports should be in full operation tomorrow so there shouldn't be any reason for delay or distractions."

Doug Bowie was very similar to Andrew's own father when it came to trying to read him. Comments, looks, unspoken messages that left him wondering how much either man knew. Heat curled around his neck. "You have my word Frannie—Ms. Frost—will be at the airport on time."

"Very good." Doug pushed back in his chair and stood. "I'm going to head upstairs and check in with Mr. Malone." He looked at Joey. "I'll let you know when we're on our way back down."

Joey gave him a pleading look. "Please take your time."

Doug shook his head and snickered before grabbing the file from the table.

"Sir, is the FBI still looking into the Jimmy Strazza and the Adonis family connection?"

"Yes," Doug said, meeting Andrew's eyes. "And I've also got someone from NYPD looking into red light cameras from the intersection you were at and around Dyker Heights to see if we can grab the license plate on the vehicle."

The messages unspoken and spoken filled Andrew with confidence. Doug had his back even if Mr. Malone was making a dangerous decision. They just had to do their job and protect their clients.

"We'll debrief tomorrow night." Doug headed to the door. "If anything changes, you'll get a call from me immediately."

Andrew exhaled as Doug left. Most often, their clients complied with the security assessments, deferring to their experience and judgment to keep them safe but there were some who, like Mr. Malone, thought they knew better.

"It'll be all right."

Turning, Andrew eyed Joey. Once more, the man with the normally stiff posture seemed to sag in the seat. "Man, what did she do to you?"

Joey straightened, eyeing Andrew right back. "Should I be asking the same thing of you?"

Andrew folded his arms across his chest. "What do you mean?"

"Come on, man. I may be the new guy but I can recognize

the stunned look of being lovestruck just the same as Doug." Joey sipped his water with a raised brow as though he was waiting for Andrew to deny it. *Why am I not denying it?* His delay to do so led to a broad smile filling Joey's face. "Are you going to be able to do your job?"

"Yes," Andrew answered hastily and then he saw the mischief sparking in Joey's eyes. "I can do the job, just like I told Doug." He inhaled deeply, fortifying his confidence. "It's just she's ... caught me off guard."

"They usually do." Joey's blue eyes reflected someone who knew what he was talking about but he didn't give Andrew a chance to ask more. "Do you like her?"

"It's too soon. I'm supposed to be protecting her." Andrew stared at Joey. "Her brother is FBI. It's probably not a good idea. Right?"

"I'm probably the last guy you want to take relationship advice from."

Andrew caught a glimpse of emotion pass over Joey's face. "Why?"

"No reason."

The quick peek was gone but Andrew knew there was very much a reason. He hoped one day Joey would trust him enough to share the details of his past but Joey shook his head and the quick peek was gone.

There was a knock at the door and just like that, tired Joey switched into Secret Service Joey. He popped out of his chair, posture stiff as a board, eyes alert as he walked to the door.

Andrew followed a few paces back and stood to the side as Joey peered through the peephole. Joey stepped back and gave a shake of his head before opening the door to a man in a hotel uniform carrying a tray.

"Good evening, sir." The employee looked at the paper on the tray and then eyed Joey. "Michael Kors?"

Joey rolled his eyes. "Who is this from?"

The employee gave him a tired look. "From Penthouse Two, courtesy of a Ms. Jay L. Pez." He scrunched his brows together. "It's your dinner, Mr. Kors."

"You can set it over there, please." Joey stepped aside. The employee looked grateful there were no more questions as he quickly deposited the tray on the dining table.

"Enjoy."

"Thanks." Joey closed the door and met Andrew's confused look. "What?"

"Michael Kors?"

"The designer. Ms. Malone thought it was funny to start calling me that whenever she disagreed with my opinion on her clothing choices."

Andrew released a chuckle. "And Ms. Jay L. Pez?"

"Jennifer Lopez." He lifted his brows, looking guilty. "After the ninetieth outfit option I may have mentioned to the stylist that Ms. Malone was no Jennifer Lopez."

"You didn't."

"Not my finest moment but I had to draw the line when she asked me to model a feather boa." Joey cringed. "I knew she was messing with me but it happened right as her father and Oskar walked in."

Andrew cringed. "Oh no."

"Yeah, so I'll be living that down never." Joey looked over to the tray sitting on the table and then back to Andrew. "You hungry?"

"No." Andrew started for the door. "I need to get back to The Peninsula."

"You sure? Because I'm pretty sure whatever Jennifer Lopez sent down is probably poisoned."

"I'm sure it's not." He opened the door to let himself out. "But maybe call up to Doug and double check."

Joey let out a pitiful laugh before his expression sobered. "Hey, for the record, love doesn't have a timeline, sometimes it happens fast and unexpectedly. Ms. Frost isn't technically our client but it sounds like you've done your job keeping her safe. And her FBI brother trusted you enough to ask you to be there for her."

Andrew paused in the hallway. "You make it sound so simple."

"Man, you're not asking her to marry you." Joey scoffed playfully. "Just ask what her plans are for New Year's and go from there."

Chapter Twenty-Four

Frannie woke up feeling a little Grinchy. She packed her toothbrush and toothpaste in her toiletry bag and grabbed her brush. Running it through her hair, she stared at herself in the bathroom mirror.

She should be excited to finally be leaving New York City, about seeing her niece and spending time with Vivian. And she was. Mostly. But there was an ache inside her chest that felt like her heart had grown a size larger for the man who somehow managed to turn a disastrous trip into a serendipitous experience she didn't want to say good-bye to yet.

It was like the melancholy of the holidays. The buildup of excitement leading to Christmas Day and the joyful euphoria of making memories with her family that eventually dissipated in the days following the holiday that always left her feeling a little empty.

That feeling had come early this year—before Christmas—and there was no reason to feel this way, especially after Andrew's late-night text had her heart dancing like sugar plums in her chest.

Star-Lord: It's a good thing Christmas is the season of hope for the future. Would it be okay if I picked you up early tomorrow?

Her heart screamed even as her brain told her not to read into the sweet and simple sentiment. But it didn't stop her from kicking her feet beneath the covers on her bed like a child too excited to sleep on Christmas Eve.

This was bad. Frannie packed her toiletry bag into her suitcase and zipped it up, feeling the tightness in her chest grow. Andrew Bishop was just a nice guy. A friend of her brother. *A protective agent doing his job to keep her safe until she left the city.*

If she focused on those facts, then it shouldn't be hard to get on the plane to D.C. Yep, all she had to do was keep reminding herself of that and completely ignore the way her heart was kicking against her ribs harder than a Radio City Rockette.

She glanced down at her bucket list and the new items she'd added and checked off. Her lips curled into a smile as memories of her weekend with Andrew scrolled through her mind. The reel paused for dramatic effect worthy of a Nora Ephron movie when they were dancing at the train station, when their bodies were pressed together while they were hiding at the market, when their breaths mingled beneath the twinkling lights of Dyker Heights and she caught the hungry expression in Andrew's eyes that matched what was vibrating in her chest.

A knock startled her from the memory.

He's here! Frannie forced herself not to move. She didn't want to seem too eager and she needed a second to let the blush in her cheeks cool. Just ten seconds—nope, five. She hurried to the door and swung it open.

She locked gazes with Andrew before her attention drifted to his smile.

"Good morning."

"Morning." The word came out shy. Why was she being shy? Because something had shifted—at least on her part—and while she didn't want to read into his text, she couldn't help wanting him to define what *hope for the future* meant to him.

"Are we good?"

The hopefulness in his expression makes her want to fake a fainting spell just so she could feel his arms around her again as he caught her.

"Frannie, are you okay?"

Blinking from her fantasy, she gave a slow nod. "Yeah, we're good."

Before she knew what was happening, Andrew's fingers were brushing against her cheek. "You look a little flushed."

"Oh, um, I just finished packing my bag." She laughed nervously. "How come things never fit the same way they did when you pack them the first time?"

"I'm not sure." Was there a sadness to his tone? "I'll take it down to the car and I've already checked you out—" His eyes rounded. "Of the hotel," he added quickly. "So we can just drop off your room key in the box on the way out."

"Sounds good."

Ten minutes later, Frannie was sitting in the passenger side of a sleek black Chevy Tahoe watching Andrew navigate through New York traffic like a pro, though she had no idea where they were going.

"My brother would kill me for not knowing where I'm going."

The edge of Andrew's lip lifted. "You can give him your location ..." Andrew flipped his blinker and maneuvered the SUV behind a yellow taxi. "Now."

Frannie leaned forward, gazing through the windshield at the ornate building they were pulling in front of. "The Plaza!"

The French-inspired design drew her eyes up the marble-and-white-stone façade. Taxis, bellhops, and guests congested the entryway as a doorman opened the door for Frannie. She got out of the car and the energy surrounding the iconic hotel decorated in elaborate holiday dressing stole her breath.

"You can't leave New York City without a visit to The Plaza. Shall we, Ms. Francis Eloise Frost?"

Snowflakes. Not butterflies. Beautiful, dancing snowflakes fluttered around in her stomach as she let Andrew slip her arm into the crook of his elbow and escort her into the hotel.

Inside, Andrew walked her to a man in a dark suit standing behind a desk. He had sleek black hair, a pencil mustache, and the kind of sincere expression she could only describe as jolly.

"Good morning, Ms. Frost. Welcome to The Plaza. My name is Henry Klaus and I am going to give you a personal tour of our beautiful hotel before escorting you to your afternoon tea in the Palm Court."

Mr. Klaus snapped his fingers and another employee hurried over to take their coats, as another offered them a glass of champagne. Then with a click of his heels, Mr. Klaus began their tour.

"This is amazing," Frannie whispered in between Mr. Klaus's stories of the history of the hotel. "Thank you."

"The only way you can write about life is to experience it."

The warmth of Andrew's breath against her neck tickled but it was the way his words anchored their way into her soul that really impacted her. She met his eyes and for a few seconds couldn't hear anything Klaus was saying over the way her heart was beating for this man she'd only known for a few days and yet was encouraging her to move past her fears.

"The Oak Room you might recognize." Mr. Klaus's voice pulled her focus back to the tour but not before the side of Andrew's hand brushed against hers, their pinkies locking for a brief second while Mr. Klaus described the private room. "This is where Cary Grant's character, Roger Thornhill, was kidnapped in *North by Northwest*."

An hour later, after they had walked the same halls as The Beatles, Jacqueline Kennedy Onassis, and of course, Macaulay Culkin, Andrew gave her a spin in the Grand Ballroom, where Truman Capote hosted his infamous party with guests such as Andy Warhol and Frank Sinatra. They were then seated at a cozy, private booth for two inside the Palm Court.

Frannie gazed up at the stained-glass dome and the palm trees that were nearly as tall as the ceiling and sighed. "This is magical."

"Are you enjoying it?"

Meeting Andrew's eyes, she smiled. "Very much."

"It's your last day in the city and I wanted to make it special." And like a magician, Andrew produced an ornately decorated package. He set it on the table in front of her. "For the record, I didn't wrap it. My skills aren't this detailed."

The gift was wrapped in a red toile paper with scenes of Santa delivering toys under decorated trees and in his sleigh. Green and gold velvet ribbons tied in perfect bows made it look too good to open. "You didn't have to get me a gift."

Andrew shifted, suddenly looking uncomfortable. "Uh, it's not ... for you."

Frannie's cheeks flamed. "Oh." She glanced down at the tag hidden beneath a sprig of holly. "Jisoo? You bought a Christmas gift for my niece?"

"Kind of." He swallowed. "You gave away the Eloise book you bought for her and I just wanted to replace it, especially now that you've been to the hotel."

His expression was so vulnerable—probably because she had just turned his thoughtful gesture awkward for assuming the gift was for her.

"Jisoo is going to love it. All of this." Frannie inched her hand closer to his, wanting to feel the warmth of his touch again. "I hope I can bring her here one day."

"You think you'll come back to New York?"

"I very much want to." The air between them sparked and she leaned closer. "Though I'm not sure I can afford to hire you to keep me safe."

Something Frannie couldn't quite identify moved through Andrew's eyes before she caught them move to her lips. It wasn't a long look, just quick enough to send her pulse racing and cause her lips to tingle with anticipation.

"Welcome to the Palm Court."

Their waitress arrived with a cart and began setting up their tea service. Andrew flashed Frannie a secret smile before he directed his attention to the waitress explaining their menu. Frannie no longer cared about the tea options, or the tea sandwiches, or the cute little desserts ... okay, maybe she cared about those. *Are those miniature candied apples?*

Two *loooong* minutes later, Frannie had no idea what was on the little tiered tray in front of her and from the look hanging in Andrew's eyes, he didn't either. But, to be appreciative, Frannie filled her plate with a few items.

"Frannie, these last couple of days have been ... unexpected."

Well, that's not the kind of word to make a girl swoon. Her expression must've revealed her thoughts because Andrew's hand inched toward hers. His pinky brushed lightly against hers and it had all the power of a bolt of lightning for the current of electricity it sent buzzing through her.

"*Unexpected* because I had no idea that once I met Ryan's sister"—his pinky locked with hers—"that I'd be trying to figure out how my life will ever be the same when she leaves."

Swooning.

"I realize you just ended a relationship, but I'd be lying if I said I didn't want to shake the guy's hand for being too stupid to realize what he had in you."

Can you swoon from swooning? Frannie wasn't sure but was grateful she was already sitting down.

"With that said, I respect that you might need some time to figure things out and I don't want to rush you, but I hope that when you are ready, you might let me know."

Frannie knew there was no such thing as a perfect man but she'd heard Vivian and Ryan talk about being perfect for each other and she couldn't have picked out a more perfect man for her mom than Evan ... Was it too soon to consider that Andrew might be perfect for her?

There was only one way to find that out ...

Chapter Twenty Five

Andrew shifted in the booth at Frannie's silence. He'd laid it on the line like an adult. He wanted to date Frannie. When she was ready. He'd made that clear, right? He studied the woman sitting next to him—the pensive way her lips were puckered wasn't helping the direction his thoughts were taking him.

More than once he'd imagined kissing them.

And more than once he'd schooled himself to make sure Frannie was ready.

He grabbed a tiny sandwich and ate it. In one bite ... which from the quirk of Frannie's lips and the amusement sparkling in her blue eyes was not the way it was supposed to be done.

But before he could apologize, whatever he'd just consumed settled on his tongue and instantly initiated his gag reflex. He wrinkled his nose and covered his cough, willing himself not to spit out the food or worse.

Frannie's brow rose first in concern and then that spark turned into mirthful glee as she began giggling. "Are you okay?"

He grabbed for his glass of water and forced his throat to

cooperate as he washed the taste out of his mouth. His eyes watered and ears rang as he sat there a second to make sure nothing was going to come back up, and then he shuddered.

"You're not allergic to anything, are you?"

Wiping his mouth with a napkin, he eyed her. "And if I was, you just sat there laughing at me."

"Hey." She gave him a pointed look. "I'm pretty sure you laughed at me when I pepper-sprayed myself."

"I admit nothing." But she tipped her chin, lips parting in a way that brought his thoughts right back to kissing her again. He picked up the menu from the table. "What in the world did I eat?"

Frannie leaned into his shoulder to look and then began laughing again, the subtle shaking of her shoulders against his causing the perfume she was wearing to float around him.

"Foie gras with truffle kewpie and caviar." She glanced up at him. "I take it you're not a fan of the finer things in life?"

He was a fan of hers and making her smile and laugh was beginning to feel like it might become his new obsession. He'd eat a thousand of these—his stomach churned—okay, maybe not a thousand but he'd certainly do whatever he could to keep Frannie smiling and laughing.

Clearing his throat, he pivoted so that he was facing her. The small booth for two was surrounded by potted plants and palms, affording them a level of intimacy from the rest of the guests at nearby tables. His thigh pressed against hers, turning his stomach into knots as he waited for her response.

"Frannie—"

"Excuse me, Mr. Bishop?" A hotel employee was at their table. He tugged at the hem of his suit coat. "I apologize for interrupting your meal but you have a call at the front desk."

Andrew frowned. "I do?"

"Yes, sir." The employee gave Frannie a polite smile. "If you'll follow me."

Frannie gestured for him to go. "Don't worry, I'll be here enjoying my tea and foie gras caviar sandwich."

Andrew followed the employee to the front desk, grateful for his clipped pace because he wanted to get back to Frannie as quickly as possible. He took the receiver from the employee and answered. "Hello?"

"Bishop, I've been trying to get ahold of you." Oskar sounded flustered. "Are you still at The Plaza?"

Andrew searched his pockets and realized he'd left his cell phone in his coat pocket, which he'd left with the front desk concierge before the tour with Mr. Klaus. "Yeah. I left my phone in my jacket. What's going on?"

"Mr. Malone backed out of the deal." That should've been good news but something in Oskar's voice said that backing out of the deal hadn't resolved the threat. Andrew's shoulders tensed and he swung his gaze in the direction of Palm Court. He couldn't see Frannie but the urgency to get back to her set his nerves firing. "The FBI and Mr. Malone's IT team are monitoring the ransomware threat but so far nothing from the company has been released."

That should've given Andrew a small amount of relief but there was something tight in Oskar's tone. "What else?"

"A new threat came in a few minutes ago. A text message sent to Mr. Malone's cell phone containing his and Valentina's flight itinerary along with the names of the pilots and ground crew." Andrew felt like the foie gras was going to make a reappearance. "It's a twisted mind game and Doug is working with the FBI, TSA, and the police but Mr. Malone isn't willing to wait for them."

Andrew's eyes flashed back to where he'd left Frannie.

Everything in him called him to be back at her side. "What does that mean?"

"Mr. Malone has rebooked him and his daughter on several commercial flights leaving at varying times from both LaGuardia and JFK. Doug wants all of us to meet at the Waldorf in an hour to go over the plan to get the Malones to the airport safely."

An hour? Andrew glanced at his watch. It was mid-morning so traffic to LaGuardia shouldn't be too bad but he'd have to leave now if he wanted to get Frannie to the airport and back in time.

"Sorry to rush your date."

"It's not a date." Except that didn't feel true. Andrew had planned this morning especially for Frannie and now it was over before he'd even begun to figure out if he could be that person for her. He exhaled. "I'll be there."

On his way back to the table, Andrew paused just out of view. Frannie was taking photos of her plate filled with pastries that hardly looked real. Her lips were curved into a smile that lifted her cheeks so high it made the corners of her eyes crinkle. She looked happy. Beautiful. And it was completely unexplainable how much he was going to miss her.

Forcing himself forward, Andrew met her expectant gaze with an apologetic one. "I'm so sorry to cut this short, Frannie, but an issue came up for my job and I need to drop you off at the airport early if you don't mind."

Disappointment flashed through her eyes. "Oh, sure. No problem."

His chest was a mixed bag of emotions as he helped her to her feet. On one hand, it felt good that she was disappointed because maybe she didn't want to leave *him* early. On the other hand, he felt like a jerk having to cut her lunch short. He looked at her plate.

"Maybe we can get some of this to go?"

"That's okay." She eyed the other foie gras sandwich. "TSA might think that's a new form of explosive."

Frannie was joking but her words landed like a punch in his gut. Someone had openly threatened Mr. Malone and his daughter's flight. Andrew scanned his surroundings, aware that he'd let his guard down. Was someone still confusing Frannie for Valentina Malone?

They retrieved their coats from the concierge and Andrew made quick work of sending a text to Oskar.

Andrew: Status on the driver from last night?

Oskar: Doug's still working on it.

His sharp exhale pulled Frannie's blue eyes to him. "Everything okay?"

"Yes." He handed the valet the ticket for his car. "I'm just sorry to end your trip so suddenly."

"Me too." Her expression softened and for a brief second, he was certain he recognized the simmer in her eyes. It matched the one burning in his chest. Her hand found his and she gently guided them to a semi-private corner of the lobby next to the giant Christmas tree. When she glanced up beneath her lashes, there was a shyness in her gaze that had his heart beating a rhythm faster than the little drummer boy. "Thank you for this." Her eyes moved away for just a second, looking around, and he immediately needed them back on him. Thankfully, she must have read his mind because she was looking at him again, only this time with a saucy smile that didn't just make his heart beat faster, but stopped it altogether. "I would really like to get to know you better."

"I'd like that too." His voice was husky and it brought a smile to her face—one he couldn't remember not adoring. Stepping forward, he was almost at the perfect angle for his lips to meet hers but he didn't want to rush it. Frannie deserved to know he was in this for the long run. "I know there's the whole long-distance thing but my schedule is pretty flexible and I've got a ton of frequent flyer points."

Frannie inched forward and the curve of her body was so close it took all of his self-control to keep his hands to himself. Her teasing smile said she knew what he was thinking and that only made the heat between them climb another thousand degrees.

"And I can write and tutor students anywhere."

Was a sexier sentence possible? Andrew didn't think so. His gaze traveled down to her lips—mere inches away. The feelings he'd denied were dancing inside of him like a version of the "Twelve Days of Christmas" gone wrong. Milking maids, geese, swans, pipers, they were all getting jiggy with it.

"Sir, your car is ready."

And just like that, the music screeched to a halt and the moment melted away faster than a snowflake in Hawaii. Frannie bit her lower lip, eyes teasing to match the smile that told him if he'd gone in for the kiss, she probably would've reciprocated.

"Sir?"

"Yeah, I heard you." Andrew groaned. The valet was an older man with pink cheeks and nose chapped from the wintery weather. He felt bad. The man was only doing his job and from the line of guests waiting for their vehicles, he probably didn't need to spend the extra minutes trying to locate them. Helping Frannie into the Tahoe, Andrew tipped the valet a twenty and wished him a merry Christmas.

"My flight is still showing on time." Frannie looked up from her phone. "So, I only have to sit at the airport for a few hours."

"Again, I'm really sorry."

Her hand reached across the middle console and found his and interlaced their fingers together.

"Don't be. How many people get to say they twirled on the same dance floor as the Duke and Duchess of Windsor?"

"One more thing to add to your bucket list and then cross off." She squeezed his hand and there was a physical ache in his chest as he drove across the Queensboro Bridge. "It maybe wasn't everything you wanted to do but I hope it made your trip worth it."

"Andrew." She waited until he looked over. "It was one of the best trips of my life."

It was a good thing he was driving because the desire to sweep her into his arms was overwhelming. Never mind where his thoughts about kissing her were taking him. *Focus, Bishop.* On the road. On the traffic. *On the vehicles that might be following you.*

That last thought snapped his attention to the rearview mirror and side mirrors. If someone still thought Frannie was Valentina, she wasn't out of danger yet. He needed to talk to Doug. Make sure someone inside the airport kept an eye on Frannie until she got on her plane safely.

He turned left on 82nd Street and felt the foreboding needling its way through him. He was worried about Frannie's safety first and foremost but a part of him was also concerned that maybe these last few days were never supposed to be more than a fun weekend.

His gaze fell to their hands and he shook away that fear. He may not know everything about Frannie but nothing about what he did know supported the idea that their time together was trivial.

"Wow."

Andrew's focus sharpened on the airport gridlock ahead of them. He checked the time and didn't have much of it before he needed to get back to the Waldorf. A horn blasted from somewhere and Andrew edged forward. Agitated police officers were flagging drivers forward, blowing their whistles, or aggressively barking orders to New Yorkers who refused to comply.

"I'm flying out on American. Just up there." Frannie pointed to an area ahead where a bunch of orange barrels kept cars from the curb and had passengers unloading in the middle of the street, which was causing the congestion. "You can let me out anywhere and I can walk if that's easier."

It *would* be easier but he wasn't ready to say good-bye just yet. "I'll get you as close as I can and pull over to the side. Nothing brings out the best in drivers like holiday congestion at the airport ten days before Christmas."

A van pulled out ahead of him and Andrew navigated into the space just as a police officer eyed him. He gave Andrew the kind of look that said he'd better make it fast. Putting the Tahoe in park, Andrew carefully got out and met Frannie at the back. He retrieved her suitcase and set it on the curb.

"So, I guess this is it, huh?"

Andrew shifted on his heels. He wasn't quite sure what to do in this scenario. Hug? Handshake? High five? "I guess so."

"You have my number."

"I do." Why was this so awkward? "And you have mine. Will you let me know when you get on your plane? And when you get to D.C.?"

The corner of her lips lifted. "Sure."

An airport shuttle van pulled up behind the Tahoe and a large family speaking Italian unloaded and filled the space around them with animated conversation and gesturing hands as they tried to communicate with the driver who was stacking their luggage on the sidewalk.

"I guess I should go—*oof!*" An older gentleman from the Italian family bumped into Frannie, sending her forward. Andrew caught her against his chest and secretly wanted to high-five the man. Frannie peeked up beneath her long lashes and smiled. "Well, then."

Andrew brushed the hair away from her eyes, his thumb trailing a line down her cheek. "Well, then."

"Thank you for a really nice time, Andrew."

"It was my pleasure." Her eyes were bright and inviting—an invitation he wanted to explore but he hesitated, unsure. Any doubt he may have had disappeared when Frannie slipped her arms around his waist. He wove his arms around her waist too, bringing her close to him, and nothing had ever felt more perfect.

Well ... His gaze fell to her lips and he felt her lift onto her toes. He tipped his chin—

Fweeeet!

A shrill whistle rang in their ears and they turned to see the police officer who had eyeballed Andrew a minute ago standing nearby.

"Drop off only. Keep moving."

Frannie's arms dropped from his waist as she awkwardly stepped back and the emptiness he felt made Andrew want to shove the whistle—

"We were just saying good-bye."

"Make it quick and keep moving. No parking. Drop off only." The police officer continued to shout as he walked by them. "Ho, ho, ho, it's time for you to go."

Frannie wrinkled her nose. "At least he has Christmas spirit."

"Sounds more like Scrooge."

Grabbing her suitcase, Frannie rolled it around so she could pull it behind her. "I'll let you know when I'm on the plane."

"Merry Christmas, Frannie."

"Merry Christmas, Andrew."

Chapter Twenty Six

Gah. Frannie blinked away the wetness gathering in her eyes and stepped forward in the TSA line. This was silly. There was no logical reason she should have such feelings for a man she'd met only a few days ago.

Especially so soon after Calvin ended it. A part of her worried all of this emotion was because of Calvin but there was a larger part that said her feelings for Andrew weren't that shallow. She wasn't trying to fill the void left by Calvin.

She was certain of that. Calvin was a nice guy and the right guy to help her navigate her newfound independence in college but looking back at these last few days, it was becoming easier to see that she was the one invested in making sure he followed his dreams. She couldn't remember the last time Calvin even inquired about her job or if she was still writing.

And this whole last year?

Frannie snorted and the little boy in front of her laughed at her. She gave him a little wave before his mom and dad walked forward to the TSA agent.

The whole last year when Calvin was dating some woman at

his office and knew he was falling in love—he still didn't have the decency or courage to say something.

Somehow in just a few days, Andrew revealed to her what she'd been missing in her relationship with Calvin. Someone who didn't just consider her hopes and desires but who wanted to see her achieve them—even if they were as silly as a Christmas bucket list.

Frannie went through the TSA security checkpoint and collected her carry-on. She had four hours before her flight to D.C. She studied the terminal map for a comfortable place to hang out for a few hours and decided on *DiCampli Italian Bar and Grill.* She headed that direction and wondered how soon was too soon to send Andrew a message.

The hostess sat Frannie at a small table that shared a long bench with other tables and backed up to a tall planter that blocked out the busy terminal. After a quick look at the menu, she ordered a bowl of minestrone and a cappuccino recommended by the waitress.

Pulling out her laptop, Frannie opened a blank document and decided the best way to control the urge *not* to text Andrew right away was to spend the next hour or so enjoying her meal and writing about her bucket list adventure.

Thirty minutes in, she was second-guessing her decision to warm up with a soup and cappuccino. She'd barely made it to writing about the ice-tubing adventure before heat began to climb up the back of her neck. The sheer memory of Andrew squeezing her body against him as they hid from the good Samaritan still had her insides roasting hotter than chestnuts on an open flame.

She covered her smile with the tips of her fingers as she relived the way it felt to be in his arms, protected. She'd never felt so secure, and it made her heart dance with anticipation of possibility.

A waiter set down a glass of wine in front of her. "From the gentleman at the bar." Frannie followed the waiter's line of sight to a man sitting on a barstool. He lifted his glass in a toast. "He says you have a beautiful smile."

"I appreciate the compliment." Frannie handed the glass of wine back to the waiter. "But please tell him no thank you."

The waiter took her glass with a shrug and returned to the bar.

"That's a classy move." Two tables over and on the same bench, a man in a pinstripe suit, his coat hanging on the back of the chair, raised his own glass to her. His thick mustache twitched. "Some men need to learn women are worth more than a cheap glass of wine."

She wasn't sure if that was a compliment or a pickup line but given she guessed the man's age to be somewhere in the sixties, she accepted it as the former. "Thank you." She sipped on her cappuccino. "I didn't want him to get any ideas if I accepted."

"You have a boyfriend."

The man's eyes dipped to her left hand, making the correct assumption she was not married but Andrew also wasn't her boyfriend. She still didn't think the guy was hitting on her but to be sure, she answered, "I have *someone*."

The man flexed his own hand and she noticed the gold ring on his pinky. No wedding ring though ... and that's when she realized how her focus might be perceived. Her eyes shot up to meet his and his hiked left brow. "I can take care of that."

"What?"

"Your *someone*. I can take care of that."

Her eyes widened. Was this guy seriously offering to take Andrew out? Suddenly the tangy aroma of spaghetti sauce, the soft tenor of Dean Martin crooning from the speakers, and the mystery man with a plate of cannoli in front of him gave Frannie major *Godfather* vibes.

"What? No. Wait ... are you serious?"

"I can be."

Frannie stared and then the guy laughed. "I'm kidding."

Was he though? She tried to laugh with him but it came out sounding nervous. She turned back to her computer, pretending she wasn't watching his every move.

The way he wiped his mouth and looked at his gold watch—totally something a godfather would do. He opened his wallet and dropped a few bills on the table. She straightened, trying to get a look. Were those twenties? Definitely suspect. He picked up his jacket and briefcase before catching her eye. He tipped his chin and smiled. "Safe travels."

"Thank you." Frannie's gaze traveled to the nearby tables. A part of her was hoping someone had overheard the conversation because she still couldn't believe it happened. Watching him walk away to catch his flight, she felt a little silly. Did mobsters even exist outside of movies anymore? She wasn't sure but when the waiter came to collect the cash left on the table, Frannie couldn't help mumbling to herself, "And keep the change, ya filthy animal."

Okay, this had to be worthy of a quick text to Andrew. She had to warn him, right?

> Frannie: Hey. I'm eating at this Italian restaurant in the airport. I think I met a godfather. Might've accidentally put a hit on you. Watch out for the guys in suits carrying cannoli.

Chapter Twenty-Seven

How many people can claim they've had two hits put out on them in one lifetime? Andrew smiled and tapped out a quick text back to Frannie before he walked into the lobby of the Waldorf Hotel.

> Andrew: "I don't like violence, Tom. Blood is a big expense."

> Frannie: "It's not personal, Sonny. It's strictly business."

His grin deepened. Frannie's knowledge of *Godfather* quotes was impressive and was helping ease the tension that gripped his shoulders when her first text came in. Thankfully, she followed up with a voice text explaining her strange run-in at the airport restaurant.

> "I'm gonna make him an offer he can't refuse."

Don Corleone's voice echoed in Andrew's head as he stepped

onto the elevator. He stared at his phone, his insides humming with anticipation from the game they were playing. Was it flirting disguised beneath the surprising pretext of *Godfather* obsession? It had to be because he was staring at his phone like a lovesick teenager who had just passed a note to the girl he liked and was waiting for her to answer—did she like him? Yes or no?

The elevator doors spread open on the twelfth floor. He checked his phone again but there was no response. Disappointment followed him to the Malones' suite. After Andrew's quick knock, Oskar opened the door.

Andrew's cell phone vibrated. It took every ounce of self-control to pocket his phone without looking at the message. "Hey."

He stepped into the suite and found Joey near the window, arms folded over his chest and legs in a wide stance. Doug was sitting in an armchair next to the couch where Mr. Malone and Valentina sat.

Ms. Malone was considerably underdressed compared to the last time he'd seen her. Today, she wore a fitted pair of cream slacks and matching sweater that looked like cashmere. Her blonde hair was pulled into a ponytail and her makeup was understated and natural, making her look a lot more like Frannie than he remembered. That thought concerned him.

On the coffee table, Andrew spotted what looked like GPS printouts with routes, he guessed, for the airport. He walked over to Joey. "What's going on?"

"Agent Simpkins is on her way with some news," Joey said, keeping his voice low. "Told us to sit tight until then."

Slipping his hand into his pocket, Andrew pulled out his cell phone. Something about the tension in the room made him want to check on Frannie. Relief filled him when he saw her text.

"In Sicily, women are more dangerous than shotguns."

He smiled to himself and caught the attention of Joey, who snuck a peek at the message and then gave Andrew a curious look.

"Is that a threat?"

"No," Andrew whispered back. "Not unless cannolis are involved."

Joey rolled his eyes. "*The Godfather*, really?"

There was a knock at the door and Andrew used the time to send out a quick message.

I guess "we're going to the mattresses."

There was a nudge on Andrew's shoulder from Joey. He looked up from his phone and watched Doug being followed by FBI Agent Geneva Simpkins and three additional federal agents, all with grim expressions.

Andrew's cell phone vibrated and he glanced down at the message.

"Keep your friends close but your enemies closer."

He didn't know if it was the room full of federal agents but Frannie's message sent a curl of dread over his shoulders.

Agent Simpkins's dark brown eyes zeroed in on Mr. Malone. "I'm sorry to delay your plans to leave the city but we've discovered some things that I'd like to ask you about."

Stay safe.

Two words were all he had time for as Simpkins continued. He sent up a prayer and hoped it would be enough.

Not bothering to introduce the other agents with her, Simpkins opened up her briefcase and pulled out a folder. She withdrew a sheet from it and handed it to Mr. Malone. "Do you recognize that document?"

From where Andrew and Joey were standing they couldn't see what it was.

Mr. Malone appeared confused but nodded. "It's a registration document for a nonprofit corporation called Tanner Group."

Deep lines carved a groove between Simpkins's brows. "Are you familiar with the charity Passion and Purpose?"

"Vaguely. It sounds like one of the charities my wife might've worked with before she passed."

"No, Daddy." Valentina spoke quietly to her father. "It was started after mom died." She met the watchful gaze of Agent Simpkins. "After the accident it was too hard to stay home so I went to the office and helped out wherever I could just to stay busy." She looked back at her dad. "Uncle Gerry said a few of mom's friends wanted to start a charity in her memory. He helped them organize it and file the tax forms."

Mr. Malone gave a tight smile but there was painful emotion in his eyes as he looked to Simpkins. "Why?"

"And Michael Tanner, the executive director of Passion and Purpose, do you know him?"

"I can't say that I do." Mr. Malone shrugged. "After Patricia died, it was hard for us." Valentina reached over and held her dad's hand. "I wasn't in the right head space to take over the work she did with the charities and Gerry, my wife's uncle, was there for us. He's kept all of it running so that there was no gap in her absence."

"So, you've never met Mr. Tanner? Have you talked with anyone from Passion and Purpose?"

The skepticism in Agent Simpkins's tone was undeniable and caused a flash of frustration to darken Mr. Malone's eyes. "I've already explained to you that my wife's philanthropic work was hers, not mine. After my father-in-law passed away, I took over his role as CEO of Kline Capital. I don't understand—"

Doug's cell phone cut him off. "I'm sorry." He stepped away and answered it.

"Is this Michael Tanner responsible for the ransomware threat or something? My IT guys told me everything is still secure."

"Our cybercrimes unit traced the ransomware threat back to an IP address for an employee at Passion and Purpose." Agent Simpkins tapped something on her cellphone and then turned it around to show Mr. Malone. "Do you know who this is?"

Mr. Malone looked at the photo and frowned. "Yes, that's Barbara Thompson. She's Gerry's secretary. His eyes lit up with recognition. "Wait a minute, I do know who Michael Tanner is. I approved a fifty-million-dollar donation for the charity. It was so soon after Patricia's death and those days are a blur but I remember Barbara came to the house for me to sign the paperwork on behalf of Michael Tanner and she kept apologizing for the bad timing. I didn't realize the connection until now but what does Barbara have to do with this?"

"Michael Tanner is currently being investigated by the SEC for investment fraud and using shell charities to launder money." Agent Simpkins said. "Passion and Purpose is one of those charities. Did you know Mr. Tanner is also listed as the director of Hope's Children?"

"Stop." Mr. Malone shook his head and looked like he was trying to put the pieces together. "Hope's Children was my wife's charity. She started it nearly thirty years ago. It's not a shell company and—"

"You said your wife's uncle took over her charities when she passed?" Simpkins cut in and Mr. Malone gave her a nod. "And you've kept track of the charities' monies since then?"

Mr. Malone hung his head. "That's really Gerry's area of expertise." He looked to his side at Valentina. "He knew how important this new charity, Hope Village, was going to be to our family. It was supposed to be an extension of Hope's Children that Valentina would eventually manage." Worry framed his eyes in deep creases. "Are you saying Michael Tanner was laundering money through our charity?"

Before Agent Simpkins could answer, Doug rejoined them but didn't sit down. "That was the NYPD. They picked up the driver from last night's incident." Doug's eyes found Andrew's. "It's Solomon Adonis."

Solomon Adonis? Andrew's pulse stalled. Anyone in the tri-state area who bet on the ponies was familiar with the Adonis family. They owned the famous Golden Thoroughbred, one of the largest horse-racing tracks in New York, and were big investors in tracks around the country. Solomon had a reputation for collecting on unpaid bets that leaned on the more violent side though he always had a way of keeping his hands clean. He was also the one Angelo Evola owed money to when he came after Andrew.

One of the unnamed FBI agents stepped away, pulling out his cell phone to maybe pass along the new information that had Andrew concerned for an entirely new reason. He caught Doug's attention. "Was I the target last night?"

"No. The detective questioning Solomon confirmed Ms. Malone was the target."

Valentina sucked in a breath and Mr. Malone rose to his feet. "What do you mean? Valentina was with me last night."

Doug motioned for Mr. Malone to take his seat. He did and Valentina gripped his hand. "You're aware that Ms. Frost was mistakenly identified as your daughter. Last night someone took aim with their vehicle to run her down."

Mr. Malone muttered an expletive. He looked over at Andrew. "Is she okay?"

"Yes." Andrew appreciated the genuine concern but everything in him was anxious to race back to the airport. Was that man Frannie met in the restaurant as innocent as she believed?

"So, you have the man now? Ms. Frost and my daughter are safe?"

"Unfortunately, no."

A ringing noise filled Andrew's ears as Doug continued.

"According to Solomon, the threat against your daughter isn't over. Jimmy Strazza was hired to go after your daughter while she was here in New York. When Strazza failed to get to her, whoever was behind the contract upped the ante."

Mr. Malone frowned. "What do you mean, upped the ante?"

Doug looked between Mr. Malone and Agent Simpkins. "It's a full contract job."

"What does that mean?" Mr. Malone's voice pitched high but understanding tightened the lines on his face. "Are you telling me someone is going to try and kill my daughter?" He wrapped a protective arm around Valentina's shoulder as she buried herself into her father's side. "That's not going to happen."

He's right. Andrew's stomach churned. "Sir, Frannie ..."

"Agent Simpkins." The agent who'd been on the phone walked over. He showed her something on the cell phone and she turned to face Mr. Malone.

"Mr. Malone, where is Gerald Kline?"

"Gerry?" He frowned and then panic hit his eyes. "Is he in danger too?"

"Gerald Kline and Michael Tanner have been illegally funneling charity monies into investment accounts that don't exist." Simpkins spread out more documents in front of Mr. Malone. "And it's not just the charity money. The SEC and our fraud division have uncovered that Kline was also fraudulently investing money from hundreds of wealthy individuals that include some who have criminal backgrounds or connections. If they've uncovered the truth, that their money is gone, some might be more than willing to harm innocent victims to send a message to get their money back."

Mr. Malone rubbed his brow. "They're coming after Valentina because of the money Gerry owes? How much? Maybe I can figure out a way to pay them back."

Simpkins shook her head like the message wasn't clear. "He owes the man who hired Solomon Adonis forty-two million dollars."

"Gerald owes forty-two million dollars?" Mr. Malone looked stunned.

"Mr. Malone," Simpkins sounded agitated. "Gerald Kline owes more than that and to some very dangerous people. We need to find him."

"Sir." Andrew couldn't stand back any longer. His nerves couldn't take it anymore. Was Frannie still in danger or had Solomon Adonis figured out they'd been going after the wrong person? "If the contract has been changed to hurt or kill ..." He felt bad when he saw Valentina cower back into her father but there was no softening the blow when lives were at stake and right now Andrew needed to know if that included Frannie's life. "We need to know who else is working the contract."

"No," Mr. Malone shook his head again. "Gerry would never hurt Valentina."

"Daddy, do you believe that?" Valentina faced her dad. "Uncle Gerry wasn't happy when the will was read and

Granddad gave Mom's share of the company to me." Her voice trembled. "Remember what the lawyers said? If I die, everything goes to him. If he's desperate enough ..."

"Shh." Mr. Malone drew his daughter to him and pressed a kiss to her forehead.

"Mr. Malone." Frustration and fear pulsed through Andrew as he fought to keep his cool. "People like Solomon don't mess around. Whoever hired him is serious. Your family, your daughter, Ms. Frost," he swallowed back the emotion rising in his throat. "Gerald Kline has put all of you in danger. We need to find him before anyone gets seriously hurt."

One, two, three seconds passed and Andrew was about to lose his cool before Mr. Malone looked up at Agent Simpkins, his expression apologetic.

"Gerry is gone. He left for the airport an hour ago, I think."

The airport. Andrew was already moving toward the suite's door. Oskar caught him with a hand to his chest. "I'd suggest you let me go if you want to keep your chiclets."

Oskar raised his brows, his gaze moving past Andrew. Turning, Andrew stared at Doug, who was back on his cell phone. The other agents moved in different directions, two left the suite and another pulled out his phone and walked to the dining area.

"I need to get to Frannie."

"You'll get to your girl," Oskar said before letting his hand drop. "But we need a plan. Just one second."

One second? He didn't have one second. It was probably going to take him an hour to get to the airport, fighting the traffic.

"I need to know now!" Doug's voice rose as he spoke into his phone. "Was Solomon Adonis the only one contracted to go after Ms. Malone?"

Painful seconds passed before the look on Doug's face gave Andrew his answer. He needed to get to the airport now.

Chapter Twenty-Eight

Watching a thousand videos of dogs playing in snow was probably not the smartest thing to do before her flight. Frannie searched the crowded gate area for an open outlet she could use to charge her cell phone. It died just as a cute Huskie puppy was about to frolic in the snow.

She blew out a frustrated breath. There wasn't a single free outlet and it didn't look like any of the passengers plugged into one were going to let go of their precious commodity.

Maybe there was another gate that was less crowded? She glanced in both directions of the terminal and decided to head toward the end. Unfortunately, this side was still filled with the post-construction materials used to combine C and D terminals that hadn't been completely cleared up yet, forcing passengers unable to find a seat near their gate to stand shoulder to shoulder.

This wasn't going to work. Frannie turned around. She needed her cell phone. Her boarding pass was on it. She could just go up to the gate and have them print her one, but she'd need a way to let Vivian know when she arrived in D.C. And then there was Andrew.

Their game of *Godfather* texts required some digging on her part. She'd seen the movies a couple of times but had to Google movie quotes to find the perfect responses. That probably hadn't helped her battery situation.

Ahead of her was the terminal's new food hall. Finding a charging station there might be her best bet. She checked her watch; she had thirty minutes before her flight began boarding. That should be enough time to get a decent charge and since she was in boarding group C, she'd have a few extra minutes before she had to be on the plane.

"Ma'am."

Frannie turned at the sound of the male voice and found a TSA officer approaching her. "Yes?"

"We're going to need you to come with us, please."

There was another TSA officer a few feet behind him, his gaze monitoring the passengers nearby whose curiosity had drawn their eyes to her. Her cheeks warmed. "Is something wrong?" She glanced down at her purse and carry-on suitcase. Had she remembered to get her ID? She looked up. "Did I forget something at the security checkpoint?"

"We just need you to come with us." The first officer—his silver name tag read *Leonard*—took another step toward her. He was a few inches taller than her and nothing about his average build was intimidating but his serious gaze made her nervous. What had she done?

The second officer, Kirby, walked forward. "Ma'am, it won't take long." His thick accent matched the sharp lines of his jaw and deep-set eyes, and his nose looked like it had seen the fists of a few people. He was the perfect stereotype of New Yorkers she'd seen on movies. "This way, please."

Frannie swallowed, feeling the growing number of people staring at her. She forced a smile as she followed them past the food hall and the security checkpoint. Their steps felt urgent as they hurried her down a hallway. With each rushed step, her heart pounded harder. Her mind immediately went to Ryan. If something had happened, the FBI would probably try to call her cell phone but it was dead so maybe they sent these guys to find her? She forced herself to breathe. It may not be as serious as that. Maybe Vivian was worried when she couldn't get ahold of Frannie ... although, sending TSA to find her seemed a little excessive. Unless something else was wrong.

"Um, can you tell me what this is about?"

They were halfway down the hall when a female TSA officer exited from a doorway up ahead and the two officers slowed down suddenly, causing her suitcase to hit the back of her heels.

"You guys need a hand?" the female TSA officer asked as she approached.

"We got it," Leonard said, sliding a hand to Frannie's elbow that instantly made her feel uncomfortable. She moved her arm away from his touch and tried to meet the woman's eyes but was blocked when Kirby stepped in the way.

"It's a mess out there," Kirby added with a laugh. "Holiday crowds are crazy."

The female officer walked by, grumbling, "I hate this time of year."

"This way," Leonard directed Frannie, keeping his hands to himself this time, but something didn't feel right.

Staying where she was, Frannie stared back at Leonard. "I would really like to know what's going on."

"You'll know in a few minutes." Leonard started to reach for her but she backed up a step and bumped into Kirby's solid frame. "Let's go, Ms. Malone."

Frannie's eyes widened. "Who?"

Leonard rolled his eyes but not before he sent Kirby a silent message that Frannie understood the second his meaty hand wrapped around her bicep.

"Making this difficult only hurts you." Kirby gave her arm a tight squeeze that made her whimper. "Move."

"But I'm not Ms. Malone. My name is Frannie, Francis Frost."

Kirby yanked her forward. "Whatever you say."

Blood rushed in Frannie's ears. She tried to wiggle her arm free but Kirby only tightened his grip with a snicker. They didn't stop at the door the female TSA officer had come out, and Frannie's panic climbed. *What is happening?* Where were they taking her? Her thoughts flew back to the moment in the bookstore. She looked between Kirby and Leonard. Were either of them the same man?

"Where are you taking me?"

Leonard opened the door to a stairwell. "A family reunion."

Frannie stopped. Family reunion? Ryan. She had no idea where he was or what he was doing for the FBI but could he be in trouble? *Think.* Ryan's voice echoed in her head along with a dozen warnings of the tricks criminals would use to gain trust or threaten. She didn't know which tactic this was, but she wasn't just going to let them take her without a fight.

"Excuse me, officers, I think I'm lost."

Leonard glanced past her shoulder, his gaze sharpening on the lost passenger who spoke up behind them. Frannie looked back and wanted to cry in relief. It was the man from the restaurant—the godfather who offered to *take care* of Andrew.

His eyes found hers for just a second before he swung his briefcase and nailed Kirby in the side of his head with a thickening thud. Kirby released her arm, falling to the side for a step before lunging at the man. Frannie screamed to warn him but the man was ready and sidestepped before his fist connected with Kirby's side. Leonard jumped in to help his friend and grabbed the man from behind, pinning his hands to his sides.

The man's wide eyes locked on Frannie. "Run, Francis!"

He knows my name? Kirby punched the man in the mouth and blood spurted out and Frannie fought against her longing to help him and backed into the stairwell. She raced down the first flight of steps but the door above her slammed against the wall and she picked up her speed, using the stair rail to keep her upright. The pounding footsteps and hard breathing said someone was gaining on her.

She made it to the bottom floor and was about to push the door open when her body was slammed against it. Leonard's arms wrapped around her, squeezing her so tightly she couldn't breathe.

"Please," she gasped. "I'm ... not ... Malone."

❄

"She's in the east D stairwell." The NYPD officer who met Andrew at the curb where his Tahoe had screeched to a halt jogged next to him, his ear to the radio attached to his uniform. "Suspect is in a TSA uniform."

Great. Andrew scanned the baggage claim area, suddenly seeing what felt like a hundred officers in that familiar blue uniform walking around. *Like finding Waldo.* "Which way to the D stairwell?"

"We have to go back outside." The officer listened to the radio chatter. "Airport maintenance says construction barriers redirect the exit outside of baggage claim."

Andrew ground his molars. The airport congestion from holiday travelers and those delayed from the snowstorm forced him to weave around passengers and luggage. He saw the closest exit and started for it.

Outside, the cold air bit at his cheeks and he followed the NYPD officer through the throngs of passengers unloading from their vehicles. His frantic movements and the panic he couldn't hide from his features seemed to be putting fear into those watching him. He didn't want to scare them, especially since most New Yorkers still carried some level of understandable apprehension after 9/11 but Andrew *was* scared.

He'd all but delivered Frannie into the lion's den when he dropped her off at the airport and there would be no excuses he'd accept if something happened to her.

"This way." The officer led him around a fenced-in area blocked with an orange tarp where construction debris was waiting to be hauled away.

Andrew rounded the corner and stopped in his tracks when he saw Frannie being manhandled by someone dressed in a TSA uniform. The man was leading her to a parking lot at the back of the airport where service and security vehicles were parked. The officer put a hand on the butt of his weapon and the other on the radio but Andrew put a warning hand on his arm and shook his head.

From where they were standing it was hard to tell if the guy had a gun to Frannie's back and Andrew wasn't going to take a chance on her accidentally getting shot if they spooked the guy.

Andrew pointed to the garage-like area beneath the airport and whispered, "Get a team to come in from behind, I'm going to see if I can get him backed into that corner."

"That's against procedure." The officer shook his head. "And I'm the only one who can approach."

Andrew didn't have time to argue. "Fine. Call it in, tell your guys to go around back but I'm going with you."

Andrew took a second to read the officer's name. Denison. He didn't look much older than Andrew and he could feel the nervous energy radiating from him. Andrew took a breath, remembering all of the rookie hockey players before their first game. It was up to the veterans to keep them calm and remind them they wouldn't be on the ice if they hadn't already proven they were capable.

"I'll hang back and come up from the side but I won't make any moves unless there's a reason. I trust *you* but I don't trust him and if he runs, I'm going after him."

Officer Denison nodded and then stepped back around the corner so he could call in their location. Andrew kept his eyes on Frannie. She was poised, her shoulders back, chin lifted. He smiled. She was formidable and capable and he'd make sure Ryan understood that the first chance he got.

"We're good," Officer Denison said when he returned. "Captain says a team will be here in one minute."

One minute.

Officer Denison began a slow approach, using a luggage trolley to block himself from view until—"Stop. NYPD. Put your hands up."

The man holding Frannie twisted around, dragging her with him so that her body shielded him. *Jerk*. Andrew kept to the shadows of an airline catering truck as he moved in closer. He had no intention of not keeping his word to Officer Denison but he wanted to be close enough in case things went south.

"I said put your hands—"

The sound of bones crunching wasn't easy to forget and while playing hockey Andrew had heard his fair share of the cringy noise. He edged out of the shadows and saw Officer Denison on the ground at the feet of a man who was reaching for Denison's weapon.

Andrew charged him, tucking his shoulder as his body collided into the man, throwing them both to the asphalt.

"Andrew!"

Frannie's cry distracted him long enough for the man to get a nice kidney punch in that nearly doubled Andrew over. He fought through the pain, elbowing the man in the solar plexus so that his breath whooshed out of him.

Taking advantage of the slight upper hand, Andrew landed another two hits to the guy's chin. The fight seemed to drain out of him and Andrew took the chance to glance up at Frannie.

She was in her own fight, wriggling to free herself from the grip of the man trying to drag her away.

Andrew flipped the guy onto his stomach and pulled the guy's arms behind him but he was still struggling. He couldn't let him go to reach for the gun. He looked over at Frannie, who had freed one arm and was digging her heels into the ground.

This was the longest minute of his life and that included when he was face down on the ice watching his teammate get taken out.

He wasn't going to let that happen to Frannie. "Pepper ..." Andrew grunted as the guy beneath him began to writhe with more strength. "Pepper spray!"

Using the whole of his body weight, Andrew flattened himself against the guy and glanced up in time to see Frannie drop to her knees next to Officer Denison. With her free hand, she yanked the canister of pepper spray from the police officer's belt and wielded it like a sword, showering the TSA agent's face with it. He let go of her and covered his face, choking.

Behind him, Andrew heard the NYPD shouting as they spilled around him, their weapons drawn. Two officers helped him while several more attended to Officer Denison and Frannie. When they had the men handcuffed, Andrew ran to Frannie and wrapped her in his arms, his lips grazing her forehead before he met her blue eyes.

"Are you okay?"

She nodded but he felt her body shuddering against his. He tightened his hold on her, never wanting to let her go, and vowing to wait as long as necessary until she was ready for that.

He brushed a lock of hair away from her eyes and was surprised to find the spark still there. "Nice aim, by the way."

Frannie gave a little shrug, threading her arms around his waist. "I've had a little practice."

Her lips tipped up and it was all Andrew could do not to kiss her silly, but his integrity told him to wait. It wasn't the right time now but when that day came ... A flush warmed his cheeks. He turned. "Come on, Frankie, let's get you on your flight."

Chapter Twenty-Nine

Fifty minutes was not enough time. Andrew gazed out of the window of the Citation Mustang as the private jet pitched right over Washington, D.C., giving him a bird's-eye view of the National Mall.

Frannie's hand found his as the aircraft's landing gears hummed to life. He glanced over. "Thanks for coming with me."

His fingers laced with hers, giving them a gentle squeeze. "I made a promise to your brother."

She looked disappointed with his answer. "To get me to the airport." She glanced around the small but luxurious aircraft, compliments of Mr. Malone to get Frannie to D.C. after she missed her flight. "I don't think this was what he had in mind."

"Mr. Malone insisted." After Andrew filled Frannie in on why she had been targeted, he had insisted the plane be inspected twice and the pilots be vetted with a background check Agent Simpkins was more than happy to provide. Andrew rubbed a slow circle with his thumb across the top of her hand. "And I wasn't quite ready to say good-bye yet."

Her blue eyes sparkled. "Thank you." She settled back in the soft leather chair. "Do you think anyone will believe what happened?"

After the police took the fake TSA agents into custody, their confession led to the location of Gerald Kline where he was being held until he made good on the contract he put on his niece. It didn't take the FBI long to get Mr. Kline to confess his involvement in the investment scheme. It turned out there were several threats against his and Michael Tanner's life. The plan was to use the money Simon Malone invested in Hope Village charity to pay back who they could but when Simon backed out of the deal, Gerald Kline became desperate just like Valentina said. Thankfully, the Godfather Frannie had run into at the restaurant was an undercover NYPD officer who Doug had sent to the airport as a backup security measure just in case anything went sideways.

In Dallas, Agent Martin interviewed Gerry's secretary, Barbara Thompson, and she admitted to sending the ransomware threat after she discovered the fraud within the charity. She was also the one who sent the roses with the warning after overhearing Gerald Kline talking about hurting Valentina. Afraid for herself and her family, she hoped the ransomware threat would keep Mr. Malone from going through with the investment into Hope Village and keep Valentina safe as well.

Andrew thought what he'd lived through was unbelievable but listening to Simpkins and the NYPD describe the details of Mr. Kline's "rob Peter to pay Paul" plot, he knew today could've been so much worse. The entire Ponzi scheme had played out like an action movie starring Riggs Atwood, but Andrew wasn't sure Frannie talking about it was a smart or safe idea.

"You planning on telling everyone what happened?"

"No." She laughed. "But I was thinking ..." Her eyes met his. "What about a book?"

"You want to write a book about this?" Frannie bit her lower lip and he could see the hesitation. She was looking for his approval and more than anything he didn't want to be the one to hold her back. "What kind of book?"

"Fiction—inspired by true events." She pulled her hand free, sitting forward. "See, what if there's this girl and she's a travel journalist and she goes on these adventures but everywhere she goes there's some kind of mishap?" Frannie gestured with her hands, her voice rising with excitement. "And my heroine is just trying to write her travel story—you know, visiting landmarks and tourist destinations—"

"She has a bucket list."

"Yes." Frannie grabbed his forearm. "And she accidentally gets caught up in the whole big mess and of course, she has to use her skills to help local law enforcement figure everything out just in the nick of time so she can finish her trip, write her story, and plan her next adventure."

Andrew smiled, watching her watch him with wide eyes, waiting for his response. He tipped his chin, narrowing his eyes. "I didn't hear you mention the part about the hunky hero who fights the bad guys and protects the girl."

"Oh, she'll have a sidekick. He tries to help but accidentally finds himself getting pepper-sprayed or being chased by a good Samaritan. Every story needs some comic relief."

Andrew grabbed her hand and quickly pulled her toward him. He wrapped an arm around her shoulder and tucked his lips close to her ear. "He sounds like a great hero but does he get the girl?"

Frannie shivered, nestling her head into his shoulder as she looked up beneath long lashes. A coy smile played on her lips. "You'll have to read it to find out."

The silent seconds slipping between them simmered and once more Andrew's eyes moved to her lips. They were kissably close, just a slight dip of his chin and his lips would find the soft edges of hers. His pulse pounded beneath his skin as he met the intensity in her blue eyes that made him believe she wanted the same thing.

The jerk of the jet's tires hitting the tarmac caused her forehead to smack into his chin, killing the mood immediately as Frannie laughed, clutching her head.

"Are you okay?"

"Yes." She giggled, straightening in her chair. "I might have to make my hero a bit more suave in the romance department."

Andrew eyed her teasingly before leaning across the armrest. He brushed the hair from her forehead and leaned closer, pretending to inspect a non-existent bump. Frannie's breath sharpened as he brought his lips to her skin, brushing her forehead ever so softly. He felt her body lean in and he smiled, pulling back slowly. "Maybe your hero *is* suave but wants to take his time, build up the desire for the perfect moment."

She swallowed. "That could work." Her voice was soft and breathless. "But I'll make sure the hero doesn't wait too long."

Andrew didn't think they were talking about fictional characters anymore. He cupped her cheek, letting his thumb brush against her smooth skin. "I don't think your hero will wait a second longer than he has to."

❄

FRANNIE HAD NEVER HATED a person in her life, not even her ex, Calvin, but she came pretty darn close to thinking hateful thoughts about their pilot when he swung the cockpit door open, interrupting Andrew from *finally* kissing her.

She'd lost count of the opportunities—*the perfect moments*—and would've started worrying her feelings for Andrew were stronger than his were for her but she'd felt the current of attraction sizzling between them. He *liked* her. And she liked him. A lot.

Enough to be annoyed by another missed moment. *Thanks, Pilot Phil.* But how could she complain when Andrew's reason for waiting was so ... chivalrous?

Andrew wheeled her carry-on to a pair of leather armchairs inside the private lounge on the third floor of Reagan National. Floor-to-ceiling windows gave the privileged passengers a panoramic view of Washington, D.C., from Crystal City all the way to the dome of the Capitol in the distance. There were a trio of decorated Christmas trees near the window, and soft Christmas jazz playing from the speakers overhead gave the space a festive but soothing atmosphere the rest of the harried travelers in the airport were missing out on.

"I'm sorry to have to make you wait." Vivian had texted Frannie while they were flying to let her know she was stuck in traffic after picking Jisoo up from her dance class. "I told Vivian I could take an Uber but she insisted I wait for her to come get me."

"I agree with her."

Frannie stopped Andrew with a hand to his bicep. His very strong bicep that she was increasingly enjoying feeling wrapped around her. She used to laugh at the unrealistic moments in movies where the hero and heroine were fighting the bad guy but still falling in love in the middle of bullets flying at them, but maybe there was something to danger amping up attraction. She'd definitely use that in her story.

"Frannie?"

She put a pin in her future story ideas and refocused on why she'd stopped Andrew in the first place. "I know what happened today was serious. I recognize things could've gone really badly for me." Distress filled his eyes and it was endearing but also made her worry Andrew would go the way of her brother and treat her like she couldn't take care of herself. That's the last thing she wanted from him, especially when his confidence in her these last few days made her feel like she was strong and capable. "I don't plan on engaging in nefarious activity in the future but the next man in my life, the one I want to give my heart to, needs to be someone who will have my back and support my decisions without worrying I'm naïve to the world. Despite everything that happened, my trip to New York was one of the best experiences of my life, and I wouldn't change any of it."

Andrew's brow spiked. "Everything?"

She tilted her head. "Okay, so maybe the whole nearly being kidnapped was a bit much but think about how I can use that in my travel suspense story."

"It'll definitely be accurate." His tone held the subtlest hint of humor.

The air between them began to spark. "Readers appreciate accuracy." Her eyes drifted to his lips for a second. "Especially when it comes to the romance."

Andrew dipped his chin, gaze serious. "And this man you want to give your heart to ... would he be required not to worry at all about the woman *his* heart belongs to?"

His low voice was rumbly, causing her breath to turn shallow. "I think a little worry is good for the relationship." Those baby blues of his darkened with intensity. "Shows her how much he cares."

Andrew sidled closer to her, his hand resting on her hip. "So, he needs to encourage her to pursue her dreams to travel and write but needs to remember she's fully and completely capable of taking out the bad guy with pepper spray if necessary."

Frannie's cheeks pinched, her face splitting into a smile. Inching closer, she pressed her hands against his chest and felt the heavy beat of his heart beneath her fingers. "She's very capable but behind every strong woman is a man who believes in her."

Lifting her left hand from his chest, he drew her toward a Christmas tree just as a familiar Ella Fitzgerald song filled the air around them. Andrew spun her around in a slow circle before pulling her close to his chest.

They swayed to the music, his hands slipping around her waist and finding their spot along her back like they were always supposed to be there. There were other passengers in the lounge but their presence seemed to drift away, leaving only her and Andrew in this moment.

This perfect moment.

Andrew studied her, the look in his eyes tantalizing as he tipped his chin, moving closer, his mouth hovering near hers. "I'd like to be that man."

His breath was minty and warm against her skin and her body lit up. "I'd like that too."

Andrew cradled the back of her neck gently, his lips finding hers with tenderness, almost as if he still wasn't certain she was okay with this. She slid her hands up his arms and over his shoulders and deepened the kiss, hoping it communicated that she was more than okay with this.

He got the message as he pressed her closer, his kiss exploring and hungry. Her lips tingled with the pressure and nothing had felt more perfect. A second later, and much to her disappointment, Andrew's lips slipped away, not far, but just enough she could see his smoldering smile.

"Number ten." His lips brushed against hers again.

"What?"

Andrew glanced up at the beautiful Christmas tree. "The last item on your bucket list." He kissed a tender trail down her cheek to her lips. "Kiss in front of a Christmas tree."

Frannie's heart puddled. This man had given her so much

more than a completed bucket list and it truly felt like a Christmas miracle but she knew it was more than that. *Her* life plan had been upended, forcing her to confront the insecurities she'd wrestled with for so long and accept that the unexpected moments in life might lead to something better than she could've ever planned.

Staring up at Andrew, she didn't know what their future held but hope flickered brightly, and she couldn't wait for the adventure.

"So, Miss Francis, what are you doing for New Year's Eve?"

Ella Fitzgerald's smooth voice sang out the same lyrics and Frannie's heart danced to the slow melody of the song. "I don't have any plans. What about you?"

"I kind of have Georgia on my mind." His lips teased a kiss over her lips. "And a bucket list of my own."

The End

Acknowledgements and Author's Note

In the words of Frannie, *Oh my jingle jangle stars!!* I was so excited to write this Christmas story and I couldn't think of a better character to experience the holiday fun in New York City than Frannie. And introducing a team of former NHL players as personal protection agents just lends itself to the kind of romantic adventure perfect for the suspense fans. Balancing the jingle jangle fun with criminal activity was a bit more challenging than I expected but I love the story and I hope you did too!

Fun facts about the story:

Johnny Castillo: Yes, Johnny Castillo (he has the kind of first and last name that MUST be spoken together at all times—lol) was my real life second-grade crush but I NEVER tried to kiss him therefore saving myself from any Grinch cooties!

Macy's Santa: GIJOE took me to New York City to see the Macy's Thanksgiving Day Parade—a bucket list item of my own—and seeing the Macy's Santa was a must! It was one of my favorite experiences.

Bryant Park Ice Tubing: This is real!! If you've read or watched any Christmas story they always have ice skating and when we took our kids there, we did ice skate at Rockefeller Center but I wanted to do something different. A little digging and I discovered that there are bumper cars on ice at Bryant Park! I took some liberties with the dates but if we ever make it back to NYC you better believe I'm doing this!

Vintage Train and lights at Dyker Heights are all true experiences!

The Godfather: Years ago, my family and I visited NYC and we were walking through Little Italy and there were some Italian men who asked my mom if she was single (my dad and siblings were a few feet behind us) and she said, "No, I'm married." To which they responded, "We can take care of that."

In case you couldn't tell, I had SO much fun writing this story and incorporating some real-life experiences throughout. Frannie and Andrew's story couldn't have happened without a few very important people.

I wouldn't be able to write this story without my amazing agent, Tamela Hancock-Murray and my editor Charlene Patterson who helped me make this the best story it could be. A HUGE thanks to extremely talented Emilie Haney for the beautiful cover design—it's magical and perfect. There's no way this story would've made it past the first draft without the encouragement, support, and technical edits from Joy Tiffany and Rachel McDaniel. There aren't enough words to express how grateful I am to you both. Be sure to ask Santa for something special because y'all are on the NICE list for life!!

It takes a tribe of friends and family to support the angsty nerves of a writer and I literally have the best tribe! Joy Tiffany, Crissy Loughridge, Emilie Haney, Christen Krumm, Steffani Webb, Rachel McDaniel, Becky Wade, and Ashley Johnson, y'all walked me through this book and publishing process, and I am forever grateful for your friendship, prayers, and encouragement.

GIJOE, thank you for always supporting my dreams and living the adventures of life with me. Kiddos, you've all flown the nest so writing stories like this allow me to relive and share the beautiful memories we made together.

To my Lord, thank you for giving me a love of story and surrounding me with friends, family, and professionals who pour into me on the hard days and cheer with me on the good days. My heart overflows with gratitude and love for your blessings on my life and my writing.

Bonus Scene

When Frannie and Andrew meet Santa at Macy's they end up in the middle of a radio competition the likes of which Buddy the Elf would enthusiastically cross "the seven levels of candy cane forest" to participate in—Andrew, not so much!

Unfortunately, this scene would've slowed the plot and had to be cut. So, as a special bonus for my newsletter subscribers, you can snag the extra scene here:

https://BookHip.com/NTFFBPN

About the Author

Natalie Walters is the author of Carol Award finalist *Living Lies*, as well as *Deadly Deceit* and *Silent Shadows*. A military wife, she currently resides in Texas with her soldier husband and is a proud mom of three adult kiddos. She has been published in *Proverbs 31* magazine and has blogged for *Guideposts* online. She loves connecting on social media, sharing her love of books, cooking, and traveling. Natalie comes from a long line of military and law enforcement veterans and is passionate about supporting them through volunteer work, races, and writing stories that affirm no one is defined by their past.

Learn more at www.nataliewalterswriter.com

Want to connect? I'd love for you to join my Facebook Reader Group: Natalie Walters Battalion

NATALIE WALTERS NAILS IT WITH LIGHTS OUT—HEART-POUNDING SUSPENSE AND DETAILS SO REAL YOU HAVE TO WONDER WHO SHE'S REALLY WORKING FOR.

—JAMES R. HANNIBALL,
award-winning, bestselling author of ***The Paris Betrayal***

FROM LIGHTS OUT:

To fight the global war on terroism, CIA Analyst Brynn Taylor invited foreign spies into America. Now one of them is missing. To track him down and stop a cyber blackout, she must work with an elite security team--and the ex-boyfriend she betrayed.

GET THE SNAP AGENCY SECRETS SERIES TODAY!

Available wherever books and eBooks are sold.

NATALIE WALTERS HAS MASTERFULLY WOVEN AN EMOTINALLY CHARGED SUSPENSE AND LOVE STORY.

—DIANN MILLS,
author of ***Burden of Proof***

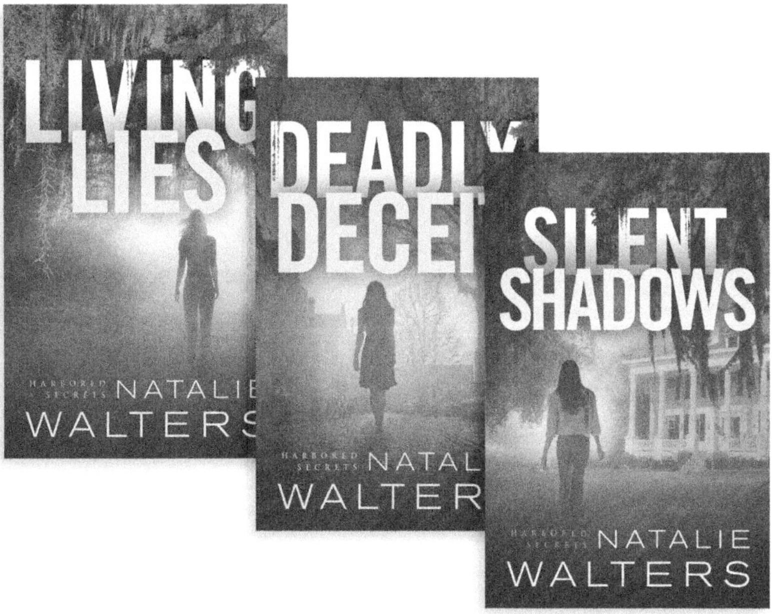

FROM LIVING LIES:

When Lane Kent stumbles across a body in the Georgia woods, she must team up with the town's newest deputy and decide if saving the life of another is worth her darkest secret.

GET THE HARBORED SECRETS SERIES TODAY!

Available wherever books and eBooks are sold.

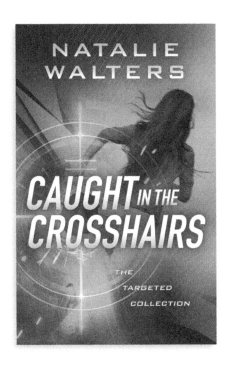

Made in the USA
Las Vegas, NV
09 December 2024

13639436R00166